TI
BUTCHERBIRD
TREE

By
Steven Richard
Harris

First Edition: September 2021
ISBN: 9798548289575

For Natalia

18ᵗʰ January 1994

"I hate myself and want to die."

He hung his head, biting his lower lip, and stared at the floor.

"I hate myself and want to die. It's … it's like some kind of voice inside my mind that's not me. Someone I don't recognise. It's a voice that just keeps repeating and repeating itself over and over again."

He stopped speaking for some seconds, fixing his eyes firmly on the light-brown carpet tiles beneath his feet.

"But, but I know it's me – at least I *think* it's me – and I'm conscious of what I'm saying, but it's like my whole world's just crumbling around me and I start blaming myself for everything and I can't stop saying and thinking that I want to die. That it would be better for me to just … just disappear."

He lowered his head further still, slumped deeper into his chair, and then stopped speaking altogether.

"It's OK, Simon. I think you're being very brave telling me this today. And you should feel extremely proud of yourself admitting to these thoughts and sharing them with me here right now. I know it's not easy to tell another person these kinds of things – especially someone you've just met – so, really, well done."

Frank Newman pushed his glasses up towards the bridge of his nose and scribbled something indecipherable on the page of the large, faintly-lined notebook on his desk.

"Thank you again for opening up like this with me at such an early stage. I know it must be very hard for you to do so."

He smiled warmly, sincerely. "It really is a great start to our time together."

Simon raised his head slowly and made tentative eye contact with his psychologist, before quickly looking away again.

"Could you tell me how long you've been feeling like this? If that's OK with you."

Silence filled the room for several tense seconds before the young man's reply.

"I … I don't know." Simon shook his head. "Not sure. I remember, remember feeling this for some time. I don't know. A year. Maybe two? Sorry, I can't remember these things very well."

"That's absolutely fine. No problem." Frank continued looking directly at his patient, ready to provide encouragement should any visual contact between them resume. "And can you tell me exactly when you feel like this? I mean, what are you normally doing just before you find yourself in these stressful situations you're telling me about?"

With his face twitching as he chewed on the tender flesh inside his mouth, Simon answered hesitantly, "I'm not sure. Maybe, maybe when I've had a bad day, done something wrong – something stupid – or, or *said* something stupid. Something like that." His breathing had become more rapid and shallow. "Or, or I can't remember something simple. So simple it's unreal, and, and I end up getting confused and start thinking I'm, I'm *stupid*, worthless, and then everything I do is bad and I'm some kind of disaster and then I start thinking that I hate myself and want to die."

Frank was nodding his head slowly, listening intently to every word that Simon was saying to him from the other side of the desk, while at the same time carefully planning his own subsequent discourse.

"The psychiatrist here – Doctor Rossouw – told me that you've been hurting yourself. Is this normally when you do these kinds of things? When you start thinking negatively about everything, especially about yourself?"

Simon drew a short, sharp breath but the question remained unanswered.

"If you don't want to tell me now it's absolutely fine."

Simon breathed in deeply this time in an attempt to control the nerves that were threatening to overcome him. "No, no, it's OK. I'm here so … so I might as well." He studied the palms of his clammy hands before wiping them dry on the lap of his black jeans as he steadied himself to continue. "When I feel I've done something wrong, I, I start hating myself and lose control. I get, kind of, dark thoughts and, and it's like my vision goes black. I don't really know what I'm doing, but I start to hurt myself. I'm not in control sometimes." He was now staring blankly in the direction of the wall behind the psychologist.

"Does this normally happen in one place in particular? Somewhere specific in your house maybe?"

"No, not really. It, it could be anywhere, depending on what I'm doing. If I get these thoughts in the kitchen, I use a … I use a knife … to cut myself. Or in the bathroom … some scissors. It depends. Most of the time I hit myself in the face or the leg – my thigh mostly – over and over again. I can't control it. It's chaos in my head." Tears welled up in his eyes as he fought desperately to restrain his emotions. On his face and neck red blotches had started to appear.

"I think you're doing *really* well saying all this to me Simon," added Frank when his patient had fallen silent. "Could you tell me how long these thoughts or acts of hurting yourself last?"

"I'm not, not sure. I don't know about the time. It could be a few minutes, I guess, or, or maybe an hour. I don't know."

"And how do you try to manage these feelings when you feel

3

angry with yourself?"

Simon was visibly struggling to choose the right words among the cascade of thoughts in his mind. He hung his head again and focussed his eyes back on the floor. "I … I don´t. I just, just go to my room and stay in bed until it goes away."

"What do you do when it does go away? How do you feel?" Frank asked, gently coaxing out the information he was looking for in order to better understand Simon´s condition.

"Terrible. Down … depressed. I don´t know. A mix. But really depressed, like I don´t want to move for days. Or forever. I feel like a lead weight, a useless lump, and I really don´t want to do anything or see anybody."

"Do you tell anyone else in your family this? Your mother or father? Do they try to help you?"

"There´s … there´s nothing they can do." The resentment was clear in Simon´s voice. "When I feel like this I don´t want anybody´s help."

Frank smiled encouragingly. "But you´re here today, aren´t you? That´s a great start and it shows that you want to get better and stop feeling the way you do sometimes."

"I´m only here because my mum insisted. If it were up to me, I wouldn´t be here at all. I almost left earlier, you know, when I was sitting outside waiting."

"But you didn´t. You´re here. You´re over eighteen – an adult – and you make your own decisions, and what´s more, you´re here in front of me now telling me about your problems, which is brilliant. It´s a long road, yes, and we´ve got some work to do, but you´ll get there in the end."

Frank added something else to his notebook. The low hum of the strip light on the ceiling the only noise filling the room. Simon moved his head slowly and looked around, seemingly only noticing his surroundings for the first time since entering a little over twenty minutes before.

A yucca plant stood in a plastic pot on an old dinner plate in the right-hand corner opposite him, its dark-green leaves thick with dust. A faded plastic label indicating its Latin name and care instructions was stuck into the soil at the base of its round trunk. Next to the yucca was the only window in the room, through which the half-empty car park could be seen. There was an unusually high percentage of red cars parked there on this chilly winter afternoon. Behind the car park, bare trees were silhouetted against a grey, overcast sky and the rolling hills of the South Downs were just visible in the distance.

"Does your mother help you a lot when you feel bad?"

Simon was brought back to the session by the psychologist´s question. He hesitated before answering.

"Yes, I suppose she does. But I end up feeling guilty as she doesn´t need all these problems that I bring. She´s got her own. But, I suppose she tries to help me out more or less … in her own way."

"And how exactly does she do this, if you don´t mind me asking?"

"She, she tells me it´s all going to be OK, and that there´s nothing wrong – nothing wrong with me – that it´s all fine and it´ll pass. I can hear what she´s saying, but I want to push her away and be alone. I don´t want help then. Sometimes, sometimes I´m worried that when I lose control, I´ll … I´ll hurt her."

"Have you hurt her before?" Frank asked quickly.

"No, I haven´t. But … it´s a possibility."

"Why do you think it´s a possibility if it´s never happened? You´ve never done it before when you´ve felt bad, have you?"

"No, I suppose not. But, I don´t know. I could. Bad things could happen."

Frank inhaled slowly and smiled his sympathetic smile once more. "You know thoughts aren´t facts, don´t you? Just because you think you´re going to do something, it doesn´t mean that it´s going to happen, does it?" He paused to give Simon the time to process what he was saying. "I have to tell you – to share with you – one of the prominent characteristics that came out strongly in the tests that you did for us before you came here to see me. In quite a lot of the situations where some kind of positive or negative outcome is expected you scored extremely highly in something called *catastrophic thinking*. Do you, do you know what that is?"

"I guess so. By the name," Simon answered sounding a little sarcastic.

Frank pressed on, unaware or unconcerned by his patient´s tone of voice. "This anxiety you have about the future can lead to distorted, often inaccurate thoughts about what could happen or what you think is going to happen. Don´t worry, Simon," Frank said compassionately, "this is very normal when you feel under stress, and you are at the moment. What is important is that we – *you* – identify these intrusive thoughts and try to counteract them with positive ones. I know it´s difficult to change what you think when you believe the worst is going to happen, but we´ll work on it and practise it. Don´t worry."

"That would be good. Thank you," Simon replied politely, looking shamefully away towards the floor again.

Frank´s questions kept coming, although it was clear Simon was finding talking with a psychologist for the first time quite a challenge in his current state of mind.

"Does anyone else in your family help you?"

Simon´s eyes momentarily darted from side to side before he answered. "Not really." His right leg was bobbing up and down nervously now. "My dad travels a lot on business and isn´t at home

6

most of the time … and, and my sister is working abroad right now," he added, measuring his words carefully, seemingly reticent to give too much away at the present time.

"Would you prefer to speak about your family another time, or would you like to talk about this now?" Frank asked, noticing Simon's obvious reluctance to elaborate on the subject.

"Better another time, please," Simon replied, without giving the question even a second of thought.

"Sure, no problem." Glancing down at his notes, Frank moved on seamlessly with his pre-set list of questions. "Would you mind telling me about some of the things you like to do? Maybe some hobbies or activities you enjoy?" He was trying hard to hide the fact that his biro was ready to add more to the growing tally on the page in his notebook.

"I, I don't really enjoy doing anything at the moment. I can't. I can't do anything or feel anything. I kind of have … nothing."

"That's OK. It's OK to feel like that sometimes. It's perfectly normal. What about some things you did *before* that you enjoyed? Or maybe places you liked to go to?"

Simon's eyes narrowed as he thought hard for answers. "Well, I haven't done anything enjoyable for a while now. Not since, probably, last year. But, but I suppose I used to play the guitar. The classical guitar. If that's the kind of thing you mean." He was nodding silently to himself as he remembered this long-forgotten facet of his life.

"And you enjoyed it?"

"I think so. Maybe. But, but I'm not good. I'm not good at it, so I don't play it anymore. I can't."

"Well, I think it's quite an achievement to be able to play an instrument in the first place, or even attempt to play one." Frank was smiling again. "So, you must like music then?"

7

Without any sign of emotion on his face, Simon looked straight at his therapist and replied, "Yes."

"That´s great." Frank´s voice wavered slightly. "What kind of music do you like listening to?"

"Umm, guitar stuff. Rock. More or less," Simon responded monotonously.

"Really? Me too. Although not too heavy or anything. There´s actually a new radio station from the university that plays some good, new music. I often put it on here if I have a moment, you know, between sessions."

Relief flooded through Frank, smiling now at the perceived connection he had just made with his new patient.

"Anything else? A place you like to go to? Something you did with friends that maybe you could start doing again, little by little?"

Simon went back to biting his lip, uncomfortable now with the questions that were being directed at him.

"I didn´t … I don´t have a lot of friends. Never have done. I like being on my own –doing things on my own. I can´t be with people. Or, or too many people. I can´t."

Frank looked thoughtful for a few seconds, clearly searching for a way to collect the details he needed, while at the same time trying to empathise as best he could. "OK, and could you tell me what you like to do when you´re on your own, maybe?"

"Not much."

Frank waited patiently for a more detailed response.

"I don´t know. Maybe, maybe running? It´s something that I used to like doing. Alone. I …" Simon´s voice tailed off, a confused look came to his face as he spoke, appearing suddenly to become unsure of what he was saying. "And reading. I think."

"Reading? That´s great. What kinds of books do you enjoy?"

Simon was frowning now, as if listening to the sound of his own distant words was something alien to him. "Umm … authors? Umm, García Márquez, Bulgakov … Huxley."

"Fantastic. You´ve got good taste, I have to say." Frank was grinning broadly now. "Do you think these are things – activities – that you could try to do now if you feel a little stressed?"

"No," Simon said at once, almost shouting in response. "Definitely not. I don´t want to do anything. I don't want to go out, or leave the house. I can´t go to school most days. I, I can´t see people, I can´t do anything. I, I just want to sleep and be on my own." He bowed his head once again; his hands were trembling.

"That´s really no problem. Everything takes its time. There´s no rush," Frank, who had been taken a little aback by the outburst, said soothingly. He reclined an inch or two in his chair and wove the fingers of his left and right hands together, assessing the situation and allowing Simon all the time he needed to compose himself.

"It is quite important though to do a bit of work outside our time in session here to help you get better," Frank said eventually. "If you could just do a couple of things for me before we see each other again next week, that would be great."

A worried look had started to appear in Simon´s eyes. The fragile confidence that he had drawn from somewhere deep inside was fast disappearing. "OK," he uttered.

"First, I´d like you to try to make a few notes after you find yourself in a situation when you hurt or want to hurt yourself, OK?" He placed a sheet of paper in front of Simon on the desk. "If you could write down anything you were doing when you started to feel bad; how you felt at the time and how intense those feelings were on a scale of one to ten; what you did as a result of your feelings; and then what happened afterwards, it would be great. Something we could work with. It´s all here for you to fill in if you want to use this."

Simon took the paper automatically without looking at what was written on either of its printed sides.

"I´d also like you to try to create a kind of safe zone somewhere in your house, if you can. Somewhere you can go to if you start to feel stressed or anxious about something. It could be your bedroom, or a quiet place somewhere else at home. Just a place where you can go, maybe listen to some music you like on the hi-fi with headphones or do something else there that relaxes you, OK?"

Simon nodded silently.

"And just one more thing. I´d like us now to establish our objectives. What we´re going to get out of our sessions together. We´ll start just with the short term for now." He paused for a second to make sure Simon was following. "*My* objectives are to help you stop hurting yourself and try to control those situations in which you feel the anxiety and stress are too much for you. What about your short-term objectives?"

Simon rubbed a hand up and down between the crown of his head and the nape of his neck repeatedly, disturbing further his already unkempt, dark-brown hair. His hazelnut-coloured eyes, framed with deep black circles, danced around looking for the right response in order to leave the consulting room as quickly as possible.

"I guess the same. To try to stop hurting myself and having bad thoughts."

"Anything else?" Frank enquired, his tone indicating that he sensed there was something deep down that was troubling his patient.

The seconds passed as Simon sat in silence.

"Yes," he said finally. "To stop the nightmares."

2.

Frank Newman sat at his desk studying the various sheets of paper that were fanned out in front of him as he prepared diligently for his next appointment. In his late thirties he was still a relatively young man, but had an appearance that added ten years to his real age. His mousy brown hair – although thick and curly at the sides and back – had already receded to the extent that he could be described as balding. He was clean-shaven, but the combination of the broken blood vessels on his cheeks and nose, along with his receding hairline, made him look at least a decade older or like someone whose drinking habits had already started to take their toll.

He wore wide-rimmed glasses with grey frames that covered up a large part of his face, and lenses with faintly-visible finger marks left there from something greasy he had eaten earlier in the day. He was breathing through his mouth between barely-parted lips, every now and then mouthing a silent word to himself as he read the material on his desk. An expression somewhere between deep concentration and serenity marked his face, occasionally interrupted by a frown as he brusquely underlined random parts of sentences and circled boxes that his next patient had ticked over the course of the preceding weeks.

His clothes were nondescript. His trousers – synthetic, charcoal-grey with a faint crease line left from when they were originally bought – ended at a pair of worn, brown leather shoes, splashed with specks of dry mud; the result of the recent winter rains. The collar of a white polo shirt poked out from the neckline of a navy-blue, woollen jumper with a small, yellow logo of a bird sewn onto the left side of the chest.

To Frank´s right, on top of a dark-grey filing cabinet with two large drawers, the high-pitched, psychedelic whine of Shannon Hoon, wringing out every last drop of his self-confessed insanity, could be heard seeping through the speaker of a small transistor radio.

The song was interrupted by a long, flat ringtone coming from the telephone on the desk. Frank turned off the radio, picked up the receiver, and answered, "Yes?"

A muffled female voice could be heard on the other end of the line.

"Thanks, Fiona. Can you send him in please?"

Frank placed the phone back in its cradle, quickly rearranged the papers, and then slotted them into a cardboard A4 file. Seconds later there was a quiet knock on the door.

"Come in", Frank said cheerfully.

Simon opened the door slowly and entered the room. He wore an expression on his face as if already embarrassed about what he was going to have to say in the day´s session. Frank gestured to him to take a seat in the grand, old, leather chair in front of his desk.

"Good afternoon, Simon. How are you today?" Frank asked with a genuinely friendly smile.

"I´m … OK. Thank you." He tried to raise the corners of his mouth, more out of habit than actual happiness to see his psychologist. "You?" he added, without giving his automatic response much in the way of thought.

"I´m very well. Thanks for asking. And how was your week?"

Surprised by Frank´s enthusiasm, Simon replied instinctively, "Fine. Umm … OK." He dropped his head as he had done several times during their first meeting, shame already washing over him.

"Are you sure you´re OK, Simon?"

He hesitated for a second. "I … I didn´t have a very good week. I´ve been feeling pretty, pretty bad to be honest."

"Could you tell me what's happened this last week?"

He shook his head from side to side, appearing to be trying to work up the courage to confess his feelings. "I've, I've been angry. Really angry with myself and I don't know why. I'm tired. I can't sleep. I ... I can't think."

Frank still had the remains of a grin on his face but this time his expression had started to turn more serious. "Have you hurt yourself this week?" he asked directly.

Simon again held back, thinking hard about how to answer. "Yes," he replied.

"Would you mind telling me what happened? What you did."

"I ... I hit myself a lot. In, in the leg. I could hardly walk afterwards. Just hitting myself again and again. I hated myself at that time. Just wanted to attack myself."

"Why did you get angry? Is there something specific that made you feel like this?" Frank's queries were greeted with silence. "What were you doing before you got stressed?" he added soon after.

"I don't know," Simon finally responded. "I, I was just trying to remember something. I don't know what is was. I don't even remember what I was thinking. Maybe something I'd done, or said ... I don't know what I'm saying or doing most of the time." He started rubbing his temples furiously using the thumb and fingers of his right hand. "My head starting hurting. Spinning. And I was thinking you, you *idiot*. You can't do anything well. Anything correct. You're useless. And then I started hitting myself. I didn't know what I was doing, I just kept going and going ... wanting more and more pain."

Looking concerned at Simon's admission, Frank thought carefully before he spoke. "It's OK, Simon. I really appreciate what you're sharing with me," he said eventually, buying himself some time with words cherry-picked from his stockpile of empathetic phrases. "Now, could you tell me where you were? Were you at home?"

"Yes, I´d just got back from school. I was in my room trying to organise my, my things. My work. But I just … couldn´t. I couldn´t remember anything, what I was doing or what I´d done. It was like something was stopping me. My head – my *brain*. It´s not working correctly. Something´s wrong."

He put his right hand to his face, rubbing it around his temples again and then along his jawline towards his chin, which he started to scratch roughly.

Although the worst years of suffering were now behind him, Simon´s cheeks bore the scars of deep pock-marks from an adolescence marred by fierce outbreaks of acne. His journey towards adulthood had also sown the scruffy beginnings of a dark beard, which made him look much older than the eighteen years he actually possessed.

"Did something happen at school this week? Something that made you stressed or was hard for you to handle?" Frank enquired.

"No. Nothing. Nothing there. I don´t like it much. Most of the time I feel bad and don´t like being there. Nothing´s interesting there. I always feel, I don´t know, kind of … uninspired."

"Motivation is something that needs to be worked on," Frank explained, in a way that made him sound like he was reading a famous quote from the back of a small sachet of sugar. "Even if you don´t feel like doing something, force yourself and don´t wait for things to happen. Maybe you don´t want to go to school but perhaps there could be something interesting that sparks your imagination. Work on it. Actively doing something can trigger creativity, and in turn, your motivation."

Simon looked distinctly indifferent at Frank´s advice. The therapist looked a little abashed with himself and at his coldly-received spiel. "Do you have any problems at school?" he quickly asked.

"Not really. Not real problems, I guess. I don't speak to many people. I just go there … when I can. It's difficult to go sometimes for me, but, but our classes are small. Not many people opted for my subjects so I don't have to speak to people too much and … and I don't have to have them looking at me. But I know the teachers don't like me." He stopped abruptly, not wanting or knowing how to elaborate, seeming to take himself by surprise by what he had just revealed.

"Why do you think that?" Frank asked, feeling obliged to follow this line of enquiry.

"I, I get in trouble for not listening. But I *can't*. I can't concentrate or follow instructions or things like that most of the time."

"If you're tired or stressed that's normal. It can sometimes be difficult to have a clear head if you feel like that." An exaggerated frown suddenly appeared on Frank's brow. "But, I'd just like you to think about something for a second. What *real* evidence do you have that they – the teachers – don't like you?"

Simon clearly wasn't comfortable with this line of questioning and responded annoyed at what had been asked. "They just get angry with me, alright?"

"Oh, I believe you, Simon, I really do. But I'd like you to try to observe the situation the next time this happens. Try to assess your interpretation of their reaction and see if you're one hundred percent sure that they're actually angry with you, OK? Just to check if the perception of the situation is completely correct. You can do it later when you get home, or when you're on your own again. Just try to think back and put it on a scale of how sure you are that they were angry with you – ten being the most sure. Do you think you would

15

be able to do that for me?"

"OK," Simon responded quietly, looking a little less irritated and more embarrassed at his previous, rather short response.

"Great. Thank you … OK." Frank collected his thoughts for a second before smiling encouragingly. "Going back to what you were telling me before. After you felt bad and had the negative thoughts about yourself, what did you do? Were you on your own?"

Simon paused as he played back his recent episode of self-harm to himself. "Yes, I was. Mum was out. After I hit myself, I just lay on the bed. I didn´t want to move or do anything. I couldn´t think about anything at all. I just wanted to be there, and do nothing. Be nothing. I feel at these times … I don´t know. Like I know I believe in nothing, but it´s *my* nothing."

Frank wrote something down quickly in his notebook. "How long did that feeling last?"

Simon suddenly looked worried about what to say and started rocking gently backwards and forwards in his chair, the tension consuming his nerves. "I … I really don´t know. I don´t remember. It could have been ten, twenty minutes … or, or longer. I really, I really don´t know."

"That´s OK, it´s not important," said Frank supportively. "The important thing is that you managed to calm down in the end. Were you able to make a note about your feelings? Write anything down?"

Again, Simon hesitated. His face was flushed and his hand was drawn back to scratching his chin and jaw, his torso still swaying a little. "No, no I didn´t. I´m sorry. I, I couldn´t find the papers and I´d forgotten what I had to do. Sorry."

"Hey, that´s OK. We can talk about these things now, if you like." Frank gave Simon a moment to try to regain his composure. "How did you feel before you started to hurt yourself?"

Simon was sitting still and looking at the floor, but now slowly

16

raised his head to look directly at his therapist, his twisted facial expression impossible to read.

"Confused. Sad. Anger and fury … and hatred."

Frank sat in silence for a moment. Despite his experience, he appeared ruffled by these last words as they were spat out. He thought momentarily before responding.

"We´re going to do some exercises in our sessions, OK? To give you the tools – the skills if you like – to be able to deal with these moments of anger and stress, and to help you realise that it´s not what happens to you but how you react to it that matters. I know everything seems very hard for you at the moment but we´ll get there eventually and we´ll work together to make sure you can lead a normal life in the future and get you back feeling well again, OK?"

"OK." Somewhere behind the desperation, irritation and confusion there was a flicker of hope in Simon´s eyes.

Frank shifted his position slightly in his chair and sat up a little straighter than before. He smiled at his patient as he reached across his desk and took the file containing the documents that had been spread out before the session commenced.

"I´d like to talk about something else with you now, if I may?" Frank asked, arranging a selection of documents in front of him like a croupier at a blackjack table.

Simon silently gave his assent with several small nods of his head.

"I´d like to talk about something that came up in the tests that you´ve done for me and Doctor Rossouw over the last week."

Simon looked at the inverted papers from the other side of the desk, as if trying to find a clue as to what subject was about to be broached.

"In two of the questionnaires, you´ve answered that you have often contemplated taking your own life."

Simon´s chest heaved with a deep intake of breath.

"I know that this may be very difficult for you to talk about, but I´d like to you take your time and tell me about these moments. Do you think you can?"

Time appeared to stand still. The sound of both patient and psychologist breathing in and out suddenly became unbearably loud. The cars on the newly-built by-pass over a mile away could be heard through the closed window. The ticking of the clock on the wall – until now unnoticed – rudely announced the passing of each second. Simon finally shattered the silence.

"I´ve thought about … about killing myself before. Lots of times."

Frank nodded slowly, listening intently. He rested the fingertips of each hand together, forming a pyramid as he did so. "And how often do you have these thoughts? Is this something you think about all the time, or just at specific moments? Please, there´s no rush to answer this."

Simon spoke with surprisingly little hesitation this time. "Specific moments, I guess. I just get to a point when I think that I don´t want to be here anymore. What´s the use? I keep doing things wrong and everything´s my fault. Sometimes, sometimes, I don´t even think anything is real. I mean, I don´t know who I am or what I´m doing, or even how I get to places most of the time. I just kind of find myself there."

He breathed in deeply again, staring blankly at the tests in front of him.

"If I look at a knife in the kitchen, I imagine it piercing my skin. Imagine the blood and the pain. It´s like I need the pain – *deserve* the pain. I want to suffer. To bleed … to die. If, if I´m in the bathroom and I pick up a razor, I imagine cutting my throat in front of the mirror, seeing the blood run down my body. I see scissors in my neck, pulling out my tendons and veins. I watch myself dying in front of me, but it´s like, it´s *not* me. It´s something evil instead. Someone else smiling back at me. Someone that hates me."

This was the first time that Simon had spoken so quickly in front of Frank. He became more animated, enthusiastic almost.

"If I see a bottle or a broken glass, I want to cut myself with it. It´s like an obsession that I can´t stop thinking about. If I cross a road, I want to throw myself in front of a car or a lorry. If I´m in a high place, I want to jump. I imagine my body falling on the ground. I, I imagine the pain for a second. My bones breaking. My back breaking. My, my bones bursting through my skin. I see what´s left of me lying there on the ground like an old sack."

He stopped speaking, suddenly becoming more aware of his own voice and clearly ashamed of what he had just shared with the person sitting passively in front of him.

"That´s really, very, very brave of you to tell me these things and I feel privileged that you have," Frank said with deep sincerity. "You´ve done really well and I think it´s a huge step to take to say such things out loud – especially to someone you don´t know very well." He hesitated for a brief moment, seemingly unsure whether to say the next sentence. "Look, I want you to imagine that when you come here – with me – this is like a safe haven, where you can share anything in the strictest of confidence. What you say here will not be repeated outside these four walls."

Frank smiled at Simon, whose head was bowed again now, looking somewhere between his lap and the floor.

"Can I ask you if you´ve ever actually tried to do any of the things you´ve just told me? The things you imagine doing to yourself?"

"I´ve …" Simon took a deep breath mid-sentence, overwhelmed by the situation but apparently willing to divulge his thoughts. "I´ve cut myself a lot," he finally managed to say, "but nothing serious.

I wasn´t trying to kill myself those times. I just wanted to hurt myself. I felt like I needed to punish myself … see blood. To have the marks and scars of what I did to remind me of what I´ve done. I … I touch them again afterwards to feel the pain as a reminder over the next few days and weeks. If I have a bruise, I press it. A scab or a cut, I make it bleed again. I need to see it. To feel what I´ve done. But … but those times and those feelings are different."

"How are they different, Simon?"

"When I hurt or cut myself I´m angry. I lose control. When I think about … about doing something more serious, it´s like I´m calm. Something else is guiding me. I see things more slowly, like I´m looking at myself and observing what I´m doing. It´s like I´m planning what to do. It´s not like, spontaneous, like the hitting or cutting."

"Have you experienced these thoughts recently?

He nodded.

"What happened?"

Simon briefly looked like he was in physical pain, as if the whole experience had flashed through his mind in an instant.

"It was a few weeks ago. A couple of days after New Year."

Simon was no longer animated. He seemed to be in a daze, remembering the events with almost the same calm clarity as the day they happened.

"I was like … like a zombie. I hadn´t slept and had been having terrible dreams." He paused. "I´d had a bad one the night before. It was … just terrible."

"Do you remember what the dream was about?" Frank asked, poised to take notes.

"About dying … about people dying … in some kind of accident. There was fire and dead people – or what was left of people – everywhere. And I think, animals. What looked like cows … dead cows in the snow. There was blood and metal and other objects everywhere on the snow. And fire and smoke. I could smell the smoke and … like diesel or something. I was there. Seeing it all and feeling it all. And I wanted to die.

"When I woke up, I had the feeling that somehow it was my fault. I´d caused this. I know it´s crazy but I felt responsible for all this death and wanted to kill myself and make all the guilt go away … it was horrible, uncontrollable."

He fidgeted in his chair, wringing his hands together, his fingers turning white as his grip tightened.

"So I took a bus and I went over to Beachy."

Frank looked at his patient more seriously than he had done before in their short time together.

"I took the bus there as I knew it was the best place. I´d jump, and that would be it. I´d feel the pain I´d wanted for so long and there would be no more sadness, no more anger, no depression, no more guilt. No one would judge me anymore. I´d be free from my head … and my thoughts.

"I got there and I started to walk from the bus stop. It was windy and really cold but bright, and sunny. I walked to the path, thinking about how everything would be. I was almost happy, I guess. I suddenly felt an energy that I hadn´t felt for a long time. Or ever before. I thought that this would be the best day of my life. And it was at that moment. It really was."

He shuddered as if something had crawled down his spine, but calmly went on speaking all the same.

"I stopped along the path at the top of the cliffs and sat down on a bench for a while. I don´t know how long for. I was enjoying the freezing wind biting into my face. I couldn´t feel my hands, but I didn´t care. It was like this was the moment I was living for – preparing for. All the hate I had for myself would stop soon. I had this time … this was *my* time." A trace of a sad smile came to Simon's lips as he spoke. "I looked out at the sea and got up from the bench. I started walking towards the cliffs. I climbed over the fence and walked into the long grass by the edge. I started to imagine all the other people that had gone off from here before … so many people over hundreds of years." He paused, lost in the memories of that bitterly cold day. "Just three or four more steps would have done it … but, but I couldn't."

A tear rolled down his left cheek and into the corner of his mouth. Absent-mindedly, he wiped it away with his tongue.

"I couldn't even do that. I thought about all the people I know. My family, people that know me. They'd think I was a terrible person … a failure. A failure in life. But I'm more of a failure to myself now … I can't even kill myself. If I kill myself, people will see me as a failure, that I don't know how to live. If I don't do it, I, I suffer with hating myself. I feel trapped."

Frank still held his pen in his left hand, although nothing had been written down on the open page in his notebook.

"You're still here, and you didn't jump and you didn't hurt yourself and that's amazing, it really is. To be in a situation like this and to come out of it is huge. A *huge* success. That's really great, Simon. It can be very hard coping with our thoughts sometimes and I know it may seem impossible to carry on; but you're not a failure, you're here looking for solutions and you've decided you need and *want* help … and we'll do it together."

Simon was listening attentively now.

"The first thing to realise is that you're not alone. Many people feel like this, and a great deal of them overcome these kinds of thoughts very successfully – or at least know how to manage them and keep them under control." Frank held Simon's intense gaze in his own. "You're a very intelligent young man and I know that most of this will seem obvious or even patronising to you – it may even seem impossible at the times when you have these thoughts – but you must know that they *can* be stopped—"

"But at these times it´s not me," interrupted Simon. "It feels like something has taken over my body and mind. I can´t think of anything else apart from the hate, guilt and wanting to end it all."

"Your thoughts lead to emotions, and your emotions then lead you to behave in a certain way. It´s not the situation – in this case your dreams – that´s causing the distress, it´s the way you interpret it. Your guilty emotions are caused by your thoughts – whether subconscious in the dreams or when you´re awake – but your thoughts are not who you are, Simon, so don´t adopt that behaviour because it´s just not you. You can choose the way you behave if you just pause and make a choice. Of course, you may feel guilty when you wake up, but that´s not the essence of who you are. *Recognise* the emotion and use it as a resource – don´t block it off completely – and you´ll come to realise that these emotions and feelings are just passing by, like on a conveyor belt." Frank´s voice was soft and smooth. "Let them flow by you, replace them with other thoughts and think of times when you felt good and try to replay those moments back in your mind and let the negative ones just pass on by. Let´s try – together – to tackle these things one part at a time, individually. Break them down and take ownership of the guilt and its symptoms and learn how to control them, not the other way round."

Simon was still looking at Frank, but a sceptical expression had crept onto his face.

"But for now, if you do need help urgently, just call me. I´ll give you my home number as well as the clinic here and also another number to call if you´re near a phone. You can ring any time. Someone will always be there on the other end."

"That´s the point," Simon said desperately, "I don´t know when these things happen. If it´s only after the dreams or not? I don´t know. And, and if I´m not at home or somewhere with no phone or don´t have any money, what should I do? Anyway, I don´t think I could phone when, you know, I feel that bad."

Frank looked across his desk at Simon, studying his features. The intense orange of the setting sun now flooded the room and shone into the young man´s face, forcing him to squint. Behind the sunken eyes, the drooping shoulders, and the defeated appearance, Simon´s handsomeness was still present; even more so as the last weak rays of the January afternoon lit up the room.

"Then you need to take flight, Simon. Abandon the place in which you feel bad. Get away from any danger that is around you. If you´re in the kitchen, go to another room away from any potential hazards. The same for the bathroom. You need to try to stop yourself. You could maybe use some kind of key word that can help bring you back into the present when you start to get angry. Something like shouting 'STOP!' or 'ENOUGH!' to yourself. Block out the negative thoughts and emotions. Also, if you need to run, then run. As fast and hard as you can. Get the negative energy out. This is what you need to do in an emergency when you can´t speak to someone."

Simon was listening keenly again to the advice.

"But, if you can speak to someone first – before you feel like this – then that would be the best thing to do if you think you won´t be able to control what you´re thinking or feeling. You can call one of the numbers here," he hastily wrote various names and numbers on a page and then ripped it out of his notebook and handed it to Simon, "or try to talk to someone in your family or some friends. If not about how you feel, then just by talking about something else to someone can help distract you from your thoughts. Or, maybe – if you can – write your thoughts down. Just spill out everything on paper, no matter what it is."

Despite the distant voice of Frank´s next patient talking to Fiona in the reception area, waiting for their now overdue appointment, the psychologist continued.

"Our aim – *your* aim – is to become responsible for your own life. To pre-empt these moments of hopelessness. To give yourself a source of strength and emotional refuge in times of crisis. There are many ways we can try to help ourselves to feel better, you just need to find the ones that work for you best." He flicked through his file and pulled out a handful of photocopied sheets of paper. "What we have here, are some techniques to try to stop the anger and despair when it starts to build up. Before you begin to feel like you´re starting to lose control of what you´re thinking, OK?" He handed Simon the pages. "They´re breathing exercises and some self-instruction sentences to repeat to yourself if you start to feel anxious or nervous. Something to help bring our level of anger down. There are also some suggestions to try to distract you from what you´re thinking about. I know you´ve probably always been told to think more … well, this time we don´t want you to think so much about things – at least not to dwell on troubling thoughts. Try to distract your mind. You´re probably not going to believe this but I had a client who used to eat chilli peppers every time that he felt like he couldn´t cope and had the urge to do something to himself. He was so preoccupied about putting out the fire in his mouth, he used to forget about how he was feeling before."

Simon looked unimpressed with the untimely anecdote.

"Anyway, just find something that works for you. Exercise – both physical and mental – can help. You know, to get you to stop thinking about what´s happening to you at that time. I know I said these ideas sound obvious, but they´re important things to try to do."

Unlike at the end of the last session, Simon skimmed what was written on the first sheet of paper that Frank had just handed him. He made to get up out of his chair.

"Just one more thing," Frank added, "I´d like you to make an appointment to see the psychiatrist again."

Simon was clearly disturbed by this request. "Why?"

"Because, sometimes when things get a little out of our hands – and maybe just to get us on the right track at first – it might be a good idea to consider taking some medication; something to help a bit with your mood. He´ll of course have the final say about what he thinks would be good for you, but it´s something I´d like you to consider."

Simon, with an expression close to panic now on his face, rose from his chair suddenly, indicating that he´d heard enough. "I´ll think about it," he replied abruptly, heading quickly over to the exit and leaving the room without so much as a goodbye to his surprised therapist.

Frank sat at his desk, looking at the door that his troubled patient had just disappeared through, plunged deep into thought and a hitherto unrecognisable expression dominating his features.

With papers still strewn on his desk and the late-afternoon orange light now fading in the room, he was jolted out of his trance by the long, electronic buzz of the telephone announcing the imminent arrival of his delayed, half past four appointment.

3.

Simon took off his large, black overcoat and hung it up on one of the metal hooks on the back of the consulting room door. Droplets of water slithered down the impermeable surface of the jacket forming thin, snaking streams down its arms and back before merging together and dripping their contents onto the carpeted floor below.

"My coat´s wet," said Simon, waving an arm in the general direction of the entrance as he sat down heavily.

"That´s OK, no problem. What can we do at this time of year?" Frank asked rhetorically. He opened up his notebook to a fresh page, ready to continue adding to his patient´s profile. On the point of making the first marks on the unspoilt sheet of paper, he brought his pen to a halt mid-air and flared his nostrils, seeming to detect something that drew his attention away from his task. Looking at Simon a little more intensely than he normally would at the start of a session, he asked, "So, how was the last week? Have you had a good one?"

"More or less. Less or more," was the strange reply.

"OK … that´s fine." Frank continued with his cheerful demeanour, but was clearly perturbed about both Simon´s response, and his unusual manner. "How have things been? Have you had any difficult moments this week you´d like to tell me about?"

There was a sharp smacking sound as Simon moistened his lips loudly with his tongue before answering. "Nope. It´s OK."

Frank studied Simon´s face, trying unsuccessfully to make eye contact with his patient.

"Is everything OK? You seem a little, umm, different today. Has anything happened? Anything you´d like to tell me about?"

Simon gazed with reddened eyes towards his psychologist, appearing to look somehow through, and at Frank at the same time. He made no reply.

"Have you been drinking?"

There was a fleeting pause, in which a flash of a smile came across Simon´s face, before vanishing as quickly as it had appeared.

"A little. But … I´m alright. I´m not drunk or anything."

"Would you like to come back and do the session another day?" Frank offered.

"Nah, it´s OK. Let´s do it … I´m alright," he repeated. "But my week´s been pretty, well, shit to be honest."

With his professional composure fully restored after being caught off-guard moments earlier, Frank was now prepared with biro in hand.

"Why? What happened this week? Did you, did you hurt yourself again?"

"Yes," Simon said loudly – almost confidently – swinging a clenched fist across his body in time with his monosyllabic reply. He shook his head and laughed quietly before he spoke. "It´s ridiculous. I, I was in the kitchen, making something to eat. I was boiling an egg and it cracked in the water. All the white stuff came out. I ruined it. I ruined it all. I was angry … *so* angry. It was a fucking egg for fuck´s sake and I was angry. Can you *believe* it?" he asked, vehemently.

Simon stopped speaking and looked a little embarrassed at what he had just said. "Sorry for swearing, Frank."

"That´s OK," the therapist replied, trying his best not only to hide his surprise at hearing Simon address him by his Christian name, but also to carry on and make the most of what could potentially be a very useful session from a diagnostic point of view. "Did you try to use any of the techniques we talked about? Any of the things that I gave you to look at to try to deal with your anger?"

Simon suddenly looked apologetic. "No, sorry. I didn´t. I do know what to do – the theory and all – and I looked at the stuff this week and wanted to do it. Honestly. And, and I *know* how to do these things and that they can help me, but when I lose it I can´t do anything. I just lose it. Lose control."

"I understand. What did you do after you got angry?"

"I carried on cooking." He laughed inwardly to himself. "I know now it´s stupid. I don´t know why I did it. But I got another egg and tried to cook that … but I fucked that one up too and then … and then went crazy."

He carefully rolled up the left sleeve of his black and white striped top to proudly reveal the two words he had carved into the inside of his forearm. *BURN OUT*, although written haphazardly as if by someone´s weaker hand, was clearly legible. Each letter raised and painful-looking with the final three a darker shade of reddish-brown as Simon had become accustomed to the pain and dug further into his own flesh. He lowered his head and stared at his psychologist as if looking up from a book over a pair of imaginary reading glasses. There was an unsettling smile on his face.

"When I cut myself I feel so much better. All the little things that might have been annoying me seem so trivial because then I'm concentrating on the pain."

Frank looked briefly down at Simon´s arm, pretending to pay little attention to the wound, though it was clear that his patient´s injury had left a lasting impression on him. "What do the words mean?"

Simon´s grin was now replaced with a puzzled look. "I, I don´t know. They just came to me. Somehow. Maybe in a dream. I don´t remember."

"I know it must be hard sometimes," Frank said sympathetically.

"So thank you for telling me this. By, by speaking about these things, we can help you, OK? What we really need to do now is look—"

"I just don´t understand why I feel like this," Simon continued loudly, interrupting Frank, "Why I feel so bad." He clenched his fists angrily, his sleeve still pulled up and the mysterious inscription on his arm in plain view. "Why do I do this? I want to know *why* I´ve got to this point!"

Frank breathed in deeply before speaking, keenly aware of the importance of the session and the delicate state of the young man´s mind.

"Try to remember for us, at this stage, it´s not about the *why*, but about the *what I can do.* We shouldn´t look for answers that simply won´t help us with our current behaviour. Our time will be better spent, right now, not looking for the origin and explanations that are of no use to us when we feel desperate and angry, OK? We should focus more on how we can deal with what´s in front of us at this moment and how you can prevent yourself from ending up in a stressful situation when you want to hurt yourself, as well as reducing the anxiety if it becomes too much for you."

Although clearly tired and still under the effects of the alcohol he had drunk earlier in the day, Simon was trying to pay close attention to the advice that he was being given.

"Unless there is something important that you haven´t told me yet, it seems that there are a series of lots of experiences and external factors that are having a big impact on your behaviour at present and they are becoming increasingly difficult for you to deal with."

Frank paused – and as his patient had done several times during their first two meetings – he chewed on his own lower lip while thinking about how to continue.

"Just while we´re on the subject of the past, Simon, has there been anything that happened to you when you were younger – in your childhood – something important that you would like to share with me? Or maybe something else more recent that has affected you? Perhaps you´d like to talk about it now?" Frank asked in the kindest tone he could possibly manage.

Simon looked unsure about what to say. "It´s, it´s not that I don´t want to talk about it, it´s just … I can´t remember. I suppose that something must´ve happened to make me feel how I do, but it´s like things are a blur. There´s nothing huge that I can think of … no real, how do you say, umm, abuse or anything. I had a normal childhood. Nothing special … or bad either."

He thought for a few seconds before adding, "Is there any way that I might be able to remember something more if we do something like, I don´t know, hypnosis?"

"That´s an interesting idea." Frank was trying to disguise the growing admiration that he had started to feel for Simon by maintaining his scholarly veneer. "The problem with hypnosis – or hypnotherapy – is that it´s very much about suggestion. If we try to remember using these techniques, then our brains tend to create false memories. Even when we´re not using hypnotherapy we often elaborate on a memory, sometimes to the extent that we believe that some things that didn´t even happen to us to actually be true and a real part of our lives."

"Then if there´s nothing in the past that´s caused me to be like this then … then, could it be something like a mental problem I have? Something wrong with my body or my brain? Something I can´t control? Maybe there´s something out of sync with me and the rest of the world … something wrong with, with my energy field or something like that. I know I´m different." The disquieting smile was back on his face. "I hate this world – the world we live in. I hate the people in it … all the superficial people. People with mobile phones making money from the rest. I hate the corruption, the greed, the poverty, people, people that only care about themselves and how they look and what character they're like from a fucking sitcom." The smile had disappeared, replaced now with a worried expression. "Or, or maybe they're all right and *I'm* the wrong one – the crazy one. I don't know … I must be mad. Am I suffering from some kind of madness?" he asked desperately.

"I think there are quite a lot of things that have influenced you throughout your life, Simon; events and other stimuli that have conditioned your responses and reactions. But no, you are not mad." Frank stopped speaking and looked at his notes. "You saw the psychiatrist earlier this week, didn't you?"

"Yes."

"And how did you get on with him? With the session."

"Not great to be honest."

"Why not?"

Simon was frowning. He had become uneasy with the conversation and was now sitting with his arms crossed like a sulking child, looking at the clock on the wall, clearly wanting to escape the discomfort he was feeling as soon as he could.

"He wants me to take drugs too. Like you. To drug myself. I'm not doing that, and, and to be honest, I really don't want to see him again. It's too difficult to speak about anything with him. I … it's hard enough to speak to you. To make the effort. I … I only want to do it with you, alright?"

Frank observed, biro motionless in his hand but mentally making as many notes as he could, how Simon's mood swung back and forth.

"Look, I cannot comment on the medication he wants to give you, but if he suggested that something may be of use, then my advice is to listen to him and try it for a few weeks to see how you feel. It´s his field, and he knows best in these circumstances." Frank thought harder for a second before he continued. "It may even help you with the nightmares you mentioned, so why not give it a go?"

Simon´s bloodshot eyes widened and tiny – almost imperceptible – beads of sweat were suddenly visible on his forehead. "I … I don´t know," he said quickly with a hint of panic in his voice.

"As for just seeing me, if you´re comfortable with this situation, it´s absolutely fine. We won´t try to do things you don´t want to do. Everything´s up to you."

Simon forced a half-smile, more out of acceptance than any kind of happiness at what he was hearing. He followed the psychologist´s hands with his stare as Frank wrote down something in his notebook. Hands that could be described as chubby, with short, stubby, ringless fingers with a thin dark-brown line of dirt under several of the well-manicured nails.

Simon now looked around the room during the short break in the conversation and let his eyes rest for a moment on the four diplomas neatly presented in pairs on the wall to his left. The walls of the consulting room were duck-egg green and bare apart from the evidence of the many years of Frank Newman´s studies, the large round clock with Roman numerals, and a small calendar with a photo of a grey kitten – its head tilted cutely to one side – with bright-yellow eyes staring out for one last day before being replaced by another young cat that would get its four weeks in the spotlight.

Frank shifted his gaze from his notes back to Simon, who for some reason was still looking intently at the photo on the calendar.

"It´s actually quite a coincidence today that you mentioned hypnotherapy. In fact, I think it´s something that might be of some assistance to you. It may be a good tool for you to help control your anxiety, and therefore your anger."

Simon turned his head slowly back to face his interlocutor.

"Have you ever been hypnotised before?"

"No, I haven´t," replied Simon, attempting unsuccessfully to control a slight slur in his truncated speech.

"What about anyone you know that´s used hypnotherapy? For something like giving up smoking or fear or flying – things like that?"

Simon snorted through his nose in genuine amusement at something that he allowed to filter into his mind.

"No. But my father was hypnotised when we were on holiday once, at a holiday club as part of the entertainment. It was really funny." He continued smiling as he started to recount the experience from his early preteen years.

"They made him put his hands together. Put his fingers together. And when the hypnotist asked him to try to pull them apart, he couldn´t. They were like glue!" Simon said loudly, his usual inhibitions vanquished by his intoxicated condition. "I knew he wasn´t faking it as he gets really embarrassed easily and would *never* normally do something like that." He sat grinning to himself as Frank waited, without hurry, for him to continue. "So, anyway, the hypnotist made him believe he was riding a horse in the Grand National. Even when he fell off his chair he was still riding his imaginary horse. He fell off his plastic chair, then and there, and was writhing around on the floor for ages with all the people watching and laughing at him. He even tried to whip the horse to make it go faster. It was really funny." Simon let out an airy, voiceless laugh. "So, so I know it works on people. Well … I don´t know about hypnotherapy, but this was pretty real."

Frank was beaming at Simon now, clearly revelling in seeing his patient speaking freely about these memories, and enjoying the way that his cheekbones became more prominent when he smiled.

"Would you be willing to try some hypnotherapy with me here

in one of our sessions? We'll just try a little light hypnosis to see if we think you're susceptible to it, and then go from there. It could really help in the moments when you think you might be in danger of losing control of your emotions."

It may have been the alcohol in Simon's veins, or the effect of remembering something positive among the usual despair of his current life, but he answered cheerily, "Sure, we can give it go," before adding in a comically menacing voice, "but don't do anything strange to me when I'm under, alright?"

Frank blushed, his face appearing redder than it should have been owing to the rosacea that spread across a large part of his face.

"Of, of course not. You'll be in control the whole time, OK?" He jotted something down quickly at the bottom of the page in his notebook, which was now full of scrawled words and sentences. "If you feel uncomfortable or don't want to answer anything, or if you want to stop the therapy at any stage, you can. It's quite straightforward and at no time will you be unaware of what you're doing."

Still slightly red in the face, and avoiding looking across the desk at his young charge, Frank focused on the archipelago of small, dark puddles that had formed by the consulting room door under Simon's winter coat.

"I promise," he said in a voice strangely higher than normal, before adding even more uncomfortably, "You can trust me."

4

"That was of course the unmistakably awesome sound of Nirvana with Rape Me. It´s coming up to four o´clock on Pure FM, so it´s time to hand over to—"

Frank flicked a switch on his radio, cutting off the young presenter and the fading background of guitar feedback before it could be interrupted by the phone on his desk. He sat waiting for the sound of the long buzz that would announce that his next client had arrived and was ready to enter.

Several minutes passed before the unpleasant electronic noise finally broke the silence and Simon was directed to Frank´s consulting room.

"Sorry I´m a bit late today." Simon smiled a self-effacing smile and, like a cat that doesn´t want to be noticed, sat down delicately without a making a sound.

"That´s no problem – it really isn´t," replied Frank kindly.

"And I´m sorry I missed last week. I wasn´t feeling very well and couldn´t … and couldn´t face anything or … or see anyone. I couldn´t leave the house and be near other people. I couldn´t do anything. I was really exhausted and didn´t even have the energy to, or … or didn´t want to be in any kind of place." He then added even more apologetically, "And sorry for the last time, you know, drinking and everything."

"That´s really not a problem at all. We´ve all done it sometimes." Frank tilted his head to one side and asked matter-of-factly, "Do you drink much alcohol, Simon?"

Still looking disturbed from the outpouring of his previous comments, he answered, "Umm, more or less … yes. If I go out. Or, or before I go out. Sometimes, sometimes it´s the only way that I can be out with some people and go to places."

"What kind of places do you go to when you drink?"

"I don't go out a lot. I don't like it too much. But if I do, like, to a pub or somewhere. Sometimes to see a band ... although I haven't done that for a while. But if I go out, I, I usually get a bit, you know, drunk."

"And do you think the drinking helps you to do something?"

Simon blushed at the question. "I feel ... I feel, it's the only way I can speak to someone if I need to. The only way to try to enjoy where I am. To feel numb, I guess. To stop feeling that people are looking at me all the time. I just want to get drunk, so I don't feel anything, or see anything. Or be seen."

"Would you say that it's a way for you to escape?"

"Yes ... I suppose so."

"And if you don't drink, do you go out socially?"

"No, normally I don't. I avoid people and places."

"How does that make you feel when you avoid these situations?"

Simon thought about the question before answering, unaccustomed to analysing himself. "Umm ... relief, I guess."

"OK." Frank wrote down his first quick note of the session. "What do you think is the overall impact of avoiding things in the long-term?"

Again the question was considered at length; the session suddenly becoming more of a challenge than Simon had expected. "I guess it makes me want to go out less and less ... and makes me feel I can't do it. It's too difficult for me."

"That's it, Simon. It decreases your confidence over time. Alcohol will of course make you feel more confident when you're actually drinking, but you can't keep using it as a crutch to get you through. You need to find the confidence in yourself."

Simon was staring down at his lap, clearly full of shame at the talk of his alcohol use and the effect his habits were having on his life.

"And what about other drugs? Have you taken anything else before?"

Simon closed his eyes as he spoke, appearing to feel safer without having to look into those of his inquisitive therapist. "Yes. Cannabis mostly. I've smoked … a bit, for a while now. It helps me relax when I feel bad. I just want to lie down and smoke and see the room – the ceiling above me – move and feel like I'm floating or something. I want to just lie there and do nothing. Think nothing … and this helps."

"Are you smoking much at the moment? These last few weeks, I mean?" Frank asked as unobtrusively as he could, seeming to sense that he was putting Simon under pressure with his questions.

"Not as much. I feel so bad right now. I feel terrible and tired and can't sleep and if I smoke too much I kind of, kind of get scared of things – scared there are things around me. I know people are watching me and know that weed makes you paranoid. But, I do. I smoke sometimes … I do."

"What about other drugs? Do you use anything else? Don't worry, this information goes no further than this room," Frank promised, noticing how tense Simon had become.

Simon appeared reluctant to continue giving too much information away on the subject of his drug use, but heeding Frank's promise, in the end relented. "I've, I've tried a few things … ecstasy once, some acid – just once too. But mainly cannabis. No speed or anything like that. And no cocaine either, it's a dirty drug. It makes people aggressive. I don't like it and how people are when they take it."

"OK, thank you for your honesty." Frank was nodding his head as he expressed his gratitude at Simon's forthright answers. "Could you tell me how you feel when you´re drunk or if you´ve smoked something?"

Simon paused for a moment, thinking about his response. "Well … umm, obviously relaxed when I smoke … and, umm, more confident when I drink." He looked a little worried about where the conversation was heading.

"OK," said Frank. "And what about after getting drunk or smoking something? I mean, not when you´re actually under the influence. I mean, the next day or days afterwards?"

Simon was still frowning when he responded. "Umm … bad I guess. It depends how much I´ve drunk or if I have a hangover. But normally pretty down, I guess. Like most people." He paused again for a second or two. "And with the weed. I feel … fine? I guess. But also, I feel kind of … slow. I can´t do things very well afterwards and kind of forget a lot of things too."

"That´s quite normal, of course. Alcohol and marijuana are depressants, which will – as the name of course suggests – bring you down. You may feel good in the short-term, you know, when you´re under the influence, but in the long-run they´ll just increase any self-depreciating thoughts you have. I´ve seen with many clients before that alcohol and substance abuse can accentuate their self-harm episodes too."

Frank left a gap in the conversation for Simon to contribute if he wished; before finally speaking again himself after a long, unused pause.

"So, Simon. What we need to do, is find some kind of substitutes for these things so you can cope with situations without having to resort to using them. Things to make you feel better and – as you said – the important aspects of making you more confident and more relaxed." Frank was looking like he was somehow enjoying the ebb and flow of the day´s session with his patient. "Any ideas?"

Simon was understandably edgy about being put on the spot in such a way. "Umm, I don´t know. I guess meditation could help a bit to be more relaxed, I suppose," he said unconvincingly. Frank remained silent, waiting for Simon to take the initiative and move the conversation forward himself.

"And, umm … walking in the countryside? Something like that." Simon´s tone indicated that his brief attempt at brainstorming had come to an abrupt end.

"Definitely good ideas to help you unwind and relax, sure." Frank´s own intonation implied that his next sentence would counterpose Simon´s rather limited suggestions. "Nevertheless, I think that maybe for you personally, it would be a good idea to find something to try to occupy your mind more. Something productive, so as not to think so much and worry about things. Often, our brains tend to wander if we´re doing something like walking or running, and even surprisingly when people meditate they can end up with their minds going round in circles, dwelling on things so much so that their anxiety levels can actually go up." Realising that he may be moving a little too fast for the tired-looking Simon, Frank paused to allow some time for him to catch up with the conversation. "Is there anything you could do that you think might be useful for you?"

"I, I don´t know. I need to think about it. It´s … it´s difficult today to do that," Simon said, obviously in no condition at present to come up with any suggestions that might be able to complement his treatment outside of the consulting room. He looked earnestly at his therapist. "I´m sorry again about the last session."

"Oh, really Simon, don´t worry about it. It´s perfectly fine. You really didn´t do anything wrong, believe me," Frank explained sincerely. "It´s good to see you here this week. You´re doing really well today." He studied Simon´s features and the strained expression on his face. "Are you OK now?" he asked, starting to look concerned.

Simon's lips thinned as if trying to blot out a bitter memory.

"Not really." He paused, knowing that after uttering these last words, he wouldn't be able to escape Frank's silent insistence for him to elaborate. "I haven't slept much at all, to be honest. I've, I've had loads of bad dreams … nightmares again. More than normal. I don't know … maybe it's the medicine making them worse." He stopped for a moment, shaking his head.

"And how have you been getting on with the medication?"

"Not good. I've, I've been more anxious if anything, I think. And have hardly slept. My mind is racing, chaotic, full of noise and thoughts I can't block out."

The lack of sleep was clearly evident on Simon's face, which was much paler than usual. His eyes – although having been encircled by dark rings for some time now – were today an even deeper shade and excessively swollen, as if he had been rubbing them hard before entering the room. His unwashed hair shone with grease and he had come out in more spots than usual, including one particularly large, white-headed blemish that had appeared to the left of centre on his forehead.

Frank was trying hard not to draw his eyes towards Simon's latest outbreak of acne. "These types of medicines need a bit of time to take their full effect – as you know. More than a fortnight and sometimes up to a month before you feel the real benefit of them in some cases."

"I'm not taking it again. I didn't want to in the first place. I feel terrible. Much worse. And I don't want to feel like this anymore."

"Simon. You know how I feel. Look, I'm not a doctor – well, a medical doctor anyway – but I think this form of treatment can help you. That way, you'll start to look at things a little more calmly, with a different perspective, and be more likely to use the techniques we've looked at in order to get your anxiety levels down. We can

41

start from a more level playing field, if you were."

"I know … I know. But I don´t want to take anything. I want to try without anything. Or anything chemical anyway. Without the drugs. They´re poisoning me. Poisoning my mind."

Frank´s calm expression couldn´t disguise his thinly-veiled disappointment at the thought that he would be unable to convince his patient to change his mind. With a now familiar, predictable movement indicating that he was going to ask another question, he picked up his biro with his left hand, its nib poised to transcribe his patient´s confessions.

"How long have you been having bad dreams, Simon?" Frank asked, moving the conversation on swiftly.

"For as long as I can remember, really," Simon replied without hesitation, glad to be asked about something less personal. "But they´ve got worse recently. In the last few months."

"Would you mind telling me about some of these dreams? These nightmares?" Frank asked seriously.

Simon answered in a strange, threatening, low tone. "I have lots of bad dreams … terrible dreams."

He was scraping his top teeth against the stubble of his beard just below his bottom lip, making a light brushing sound faintly audible in the silence between sentences. He had inadvertently scratched the head off the spot on his forehead, which left a thin line of blood sweeping out from the centre like the tail of a comet.

"Do your dreams ever repeat themselves?" enquired Frank, poker-faced, yet still looking unsettled by the unusual delivery of the young man´s last sentence.

Simon looked at the therapist with something of a wry smile.

"Recurring dreams, you mean? Yes." He paused for a moment and rolled his eyes upwards in their orbit, as if by looking in the direction of his brain he could access his memory more easily.

"There are a couple of them," he said, now staring glassy-eyed into the distance as he began to speak. "There's one, where everything's black – or a very dark brown. I can't see anything … but I can *hear* something. Like walking. Like someone walking." He shivered unintentionally, despite the warmth that the radiator on the wall in the room was emitting. "Like someone stamping their feet on the ground … a stamping man. Something's getting closer and closer to me in the darkness. Getting louder and louder and I feel like something terrible's going to happen. But, in the end, I wake up just before anything does."

Frank sat listening, waiting patiently for Simon, who was shaking his head, to continue.

"Then there's the man with the knife. He always appears in my doorway wearing some kind of rain coat with a hood. I can't see his face, but he's a big man. I just see his, his silhouette in the door frame and he's holding a knife – a huge knife in his hand. He's coming for me and he's going to kill me … so I scream. Somehow I know I'm asleep and dreaming so I shout and scream to try to wake myself up, but my mouth is closed. It's like it's sewn shut. I think sometimes in the dream I don't even have a mouth. Just smooth skin, and no way to make a noise to wake myself up and all I can do is kind of mumble something trying to form words that I can't. It's awful … it really is."

He broke off his account for a moment, trying to stay calm and keep his insecure poise.

"There's another one too. This one's probably the worst."

Simon stopped and rubbed at his eyes, which looked even more puffy and red than when the session had commenced.

"It's simple. So simple, but so scary. I … I can see what looks like transparent thin wire, like fishing lines or something like that stretched out really tight. There's nothing else around, I think.

Like there´s no background or anything, nothing to see around me. Just these lines. Resting on them are huge boulders – *enormous* boulders – that are just balancing on these lines ... these delicate, thin lines. I wait for these giant rocks to break the lines. Wait for them to snap – I *know* they´re going to break. It´s inevitable. But somehow they don´t. They just keep on balancing there. It´s impossible that they don´t break." He shook his head incredulously. "For me, it´s awful. Horrible. I normally wake up really, really sweaty and breathing hard. Panting. I know it´s a bit crazy to dream these things, and I don´t know why. But these dreams are always there with me ... all the time, more or less."

Frank, who had been making notes while Simon was disclosing the details of the dreams that often accompanied him throughout his fitful sleep, raised his eyebrows.

"I´m afraid that I´m no dream expert, but we can certainly look to see if there´s any relation between when you dream these things and what´s happening in your life at the time. Have you noticed any kind of pattern to when these dreams occur, or repeat themselves?"

"I´ve thought about this before, yes. I used to think that I dreamt these things when I was sick – you know, with a fever or the like – or when I was worried about something like an exam. But I´m having them nearly all the time now. So no, I can´t see any pattern at all."

"Well, I know I´m asking you to do a lot of things, but I´d like you to try to make a note of when you have these dreams and tell me about what you were doing before. How you were feeling, etcetera, OK?"

"I´ll try," Simon replied tiredly.

"I think it might also be a good idea to try to keep some kind of journal or log too and write down how you feel in general on a daily basis. Not just at the times when you have some problems. Do you think you might be able to do that as well?"

"I'll, umm … give it a go, OK," responded Simon, looking a little anxious about being given this extra responsibility.

"Thank you," Frank said, as he jotted down yet another note on the lined page in front of him. "So … what can you tell me about the dreams you've been having over these last two weeks? Have they been similar to the ones you've just told me about?"

"No. These ones were different. They've been different … much worse." He started to wring his hands together aggressively. "These dreams are terrible. And so real. I normally remember most of what happens in them too. I don't even remember what I'm doing half the time in my life, or what's happened to me in my past before … but *these* dreams stay with me. I have to live with them and they're so vivid. So lifelike." He sighed before continuing and a sadness appeared in his eyes, which then gave way to a sudden storm of panic and fear. "People die in my dreams. People die in terrible ways. All the time … dying …"

The last word of the sentence was almost whispered as his speech tailed off.

"Do *you* ever die in the dreams, Simon?"

"No." He collected his thoughts before continuing. "I'm there … when these people die, I'm there. Or least I'm there right after something terrible's happened. I'm seeing everything – observing everything. I hear people screaming … crying in pain sometimes. Sometimes, sometimes I can even smell things that are there."

He let his eyes drift off until he was looking somewhere in the corner, behind the dusty yucca.

"Like in the dream you told me about in the other session? When you could smell the, the fuel, wasn't it?"

Simon focused again on Frank. "Yes, that's right," he answered solemnly. "But the last couple of weeks have been different. More numerous. So many more dreams. And so real."

He stared at the palm of his right hand, passively observing the streak of blood that was left there from when he had passed it across his forehead.

"So many people have died. In fires, car accidents, in rivers, in earthquakes. I remember them all. What they were about anyway. But there was one that I had maybe a week or two ago that's just stuck with me. Even if, or when, I lose my mind and go crazy, it'll probably stay with me forever."

The tip of his tongue was poking out and pressing against the middle of his top lip and his eyes were unfocussed on anything present in the room as he recalled the horrors of his troubled sleep. Although unprompted by his psychologist, Simon began to methodically describe what he had dreamt several days before.

"I was somewhere. I don't know where. There was a lot of smoke – grey smoke. It was hard to breathe as the air was thick with it, almost choking me. Then I noticed the noise. Voices shouting, people screaming in pain in a language I couldn't understand. The air was filled with their screams and the sound of cars beeping their horns somewhere close by. Then the smoke started to clear and I saw what was around me." He sighed sadly again. "There were wooden benches, or tables, everywhere. Shattered and splintered into pieces many of them. Lots were overturned and there was food on the floor and all around me ... damaged food. Fruits and, and vegetables on the ground, and, and people ... parts of people ... parts of people's bodies lying everywhere. There were people on the ground. Many dead. Their clothes torn off in places ... arms and legs torn off too. A woman, wearing black boots, her legs twisted and bent underneath her. An old man was dragging himself along the ground ... dragging what was left of his legs behind him, asking, *begging*, in my direction for help. An arm stretching out towards

46

me. Or past me.

"There was panic and noise everywhere and people running around trying to help the people who were crying out, carrying others away from the scene, throwing them in the open boots of cars to take them somewhere. I … I didn´t know if they were alive or dead. Another woman wearing a denim jacket was being pulled along on a piece of corrugated iron, like a stretcher. I, I don´t know … I don´t know if her head was missing or, or if her jacket was pulled up over her shoulders. I couldn´t tell. A trail of blood was left behind on the concrete floor as they moved her.

"I looked around and saw other people lying on the ground too. A man, I think, was in the middle of the road just outside this place. His legs still wrapped around the motorbike he´d been riding as he died. Another man, in a white t-shirt, was draped over a railing, almost like … like a coat someone had left over a bannister. He had a hole in the side of his body and I could see part of his spine and his shattered ribs, the white of the bones standing out against the dark-red backdrop of what was left of his flesh. Everywhere, the screams and the noise.

"But … but the worst thing of all was the blood. So much blood. The ground was red. There was nothing else I saw then … just the ground and the deep, red blood running into the gutters as death surrounded me and the screams of the dying faded away into echoes in my mind. And then … nothing."

5

Upon walking into Frank Newman´s consulting room, Simon heard immediately the resonating sound of a powerful, yet relaxed voice, sorrowfully intertwining their lyrics with the acoustic guitar and harmonica that were accompanying the singer on the track. Frank deliberately allowed the blues harp a few more seconds to continue its haunting melody before silencing the radio.

"Hi there, Simon. Please, take a seat."

"Alice in Chains," Simon said, standing in the middle of the room.

"Sorry?"

"The group. The music." He pointed at the radio. "It´s Alice in Chains. I´ve got the CD. It´s got a jar on the cover. A picture of a jar," Simon explained.

"Oh really?" Frank looked surprised at Simon´s comments, unaccustomed to his out-of-character conversation starter. "I´ll have to give them a listen sometime. They sound quite interesting. Thanks for that."

Simon nodded his head, silently acknowledging the gratitude.

"Is everything OK with you today?" Frank asked as Simon took a seat.

"Fine. Thank you," he replied, looking at the edge of the desk in front of him. "Just fine. Umm, nothing else to say really."

"OK. Anything you´d like to tell me about today? Anything you´d like to share with me about the last week?" Frank readied his notebook.

"To be honest, no. Sorry," was the curt reply.

"That´s not a problem at all. I just want you to feel comfortable here, OK? There´s no pressure to say things you don´t want to and plenty of time for everything else when you´re ready." Frank resisted writing anything down, despite his pen hovering just millimetres over the page. "What I thought we´d do today – if it´s OK with you – are a couple of activities in order to try to make us think a little about how we feel and maybe how we can manage these feelings, emotions and reactions when they come up, OK?"

"OK," Simon replied after a short silence

"So, what we´ll start with today is an activity in which I´d like you to just say what pops into your head while we´re speaking." Frank cleared his throat. "Here´s the situation. I´d like you to imagine that I´m a friend of yours. A good friend. A close friend. I´m going to tell you something about my life at the moment and I´d like you to try to give me some kind of advice if you can, OK? Just anything that comes into your mind that you think might help me – help your friend, I mean."

Despite his usual encouraging manner, there was something about the disjointed way Frank delivered the last few words that hinted at an underlying lack of confidence in what he was saying to his patient.

"A role-play," Simon muttered, more to himself than in the form of a question.

"That´s it. Exactly. I´d like you to try to imagine my situation and see if you can give me some good advice." Frank paused for a moment and cleared his throat again with another quiet cough. "OK?"

"I suppose. I´ll try," was the unenthusiastic response.

"Hey, Simon. I´m having some difficulties at the moment with a few things. You know, I´ve been thinking a lot of negative thoughts about myself and getting quite depressed and I just don´t know what I can do right now. Everything I do, I feel like I´m doing it badly and it´s really getting me down. I´m more and more depressed all the time. Is there anything you can recommend that I can do to try to make me feel a bit better?"

Simon was looking at the wooden edge of the desk again, trying hard to think of something to say. "Umm … umm … Sorry, I can´t think of anything. Maybe, maybe you could go out? See something, someone … friends. I don´t know … like …" He dried up and sat there in silence, the blood rushing into his cheeks and neck. The familiar red rash had appeared and was uncontrollably spreading down his chest.

"Oh, OK. It could be good to go out and see some friends, yes." Frank persevered energetically with the conversation, although he looked more unconvinced by the exercise as every second passed. "What would be a good thing to go and do with them? Do you think you could you recommend some kind of activity for us to do together?"

Simon sat in complete silence with his head bowed. He was motionless, as if by remaining still he wouldn´t be asked anything else. Frank nudged his glasses up his nose towards his eyebrows and sat and thought for a second.

"Shall we try another situation, Simon? Do you think you´d be able to do that?"

"Don´t ask me anything. Please don´t ask me to do anything," Simon replied quietly, without moving a muscle. "I … I can´t do anything. I can´t answer these things. I can´t give advice about anything. What do *I* know?"

Frank tried hard not to look a little flustered at his patient´s reaction. "It´s OK. You don´t have to do anything you don´t want to here. We can try something like this again another time when you feel you might be able to, OK?"

Simon´s face had started to return to its normal pale colour, although the marks on his neck and the top of his chest had yet to begin to fade away. He looked up in the general direction of his psychologist, waiting apprehensively to see what daunting task would be suggested next.

"OK. Don´t worry about that, it´s not a problem. We´ll move on to another activity." An embarrassed-looking Frank avoided returning Simon´s stare by taking off his glasses to examine the lenses, as if something there had been bothering him and disturbing his vision. After a few seconds of inspection, he put them back on, without so much as a cursory wipe with the small, square cloth he normally used to clean them. "Let´s try to do something else today. Something that may be able to help you with your anxiety levels at the times when you start feeling stressed. OK?"

Looking more like he was back in his comfort zone, Frank swiftly added something to the page in his notebook.

"I´ve already given you some information, including various breathing exercises that can help you relax, and I know you´ve got quite a bit of material that you can use to help yourself when you need to, but I´m going to give you something else before you leave here today to take home with you that I believe might be of assistance to you."

Frank´s eyes momentarily flicked to his left at what had been – up until now – the elephant in the room.

Unlike the rest of the vintage-looking furniture present, the psychologist´s couch more closely resembled a masseur´s table – albeit without the hole for the face – with its adjustable back already propped up at a forty-five-degree angle ready for use. The mix of shiny metal supports and black leather made it look out of place among the more traditional surroundings of the consulting room. It also seemed nearly brand new, as if only a handful of troubled souls had poured out their deepest worries to their therapist lying on its comfortable, padded upholstery.

Frank leaned across to his right, opened one of the desk's three drawers, and placed a small, rectangular tape recorder, completely black apart from the red record button, in front of him.

"We're going to do a guided relaxation for you today, if you're OK with that?"

Simon had followed Frank's previous line of vision and was himself now staring at the couch. He nodded.

"I'd like to record the relaxation today so you can take it home with you, and when you start to feel anxious or stressed about something, you can play the tape back and use it to try to reduce your anxiety levels. If you're not in a position to play it, then at least you'll hopefully be able to remember most of the techniques and what was said, and then use something from them when you need to, OK?"

Simon nodded again. "That would be good. I don't know what to do. Sometimes … sometimes I just curl up in a ball on the floor and … and don't know what to do. Even when I'm out on the street, sometimes it happens. I just fall on the floor and cover my head with my hands. I don't know why. So I need something, anything, that may help with the stress … and the fear. Thank you."

"That's quite alright, Simon. No need to thank me." Frank got up from his chair, walked around his desk and patted the couch softly with the palm of his hand. "If you'd just like to pop up here and make yourself comfortable."

Simon got up slowly from the relative sanctuary of his own chair and sighed heavily, clearly nervous at this big step in his therapy.

"My shoes." He pointed to his black boots, which were a little muddy despite the last few days having been dry.

"That's OK. No problem," replied Frank, who had taken a new cassette from another one of the three drawers in his desk.

Simon lay down on the couch with his upper torso raised to the furniture´s pre-set angle, hands clasped together with interlocked fingers resting just above his waist. He stared at the back of the consulting room door, listening to the crinkle of plastic as Frank found with his thumb the end of the thin, red thread that allowed him to peel open the wrapping of the blank tape.

"Are you comfortable there?" Frank asked.

Simon shifted slightly, adjusting his position. "Yes, I´m fine … thank you."

"If you could just put your arms next to your body there, it would be great."

Simon unlocked his fingers and duly followed the instructions. Frank slipped the cassette into the mouth of the black recorder and closed it with a click.

"OK, let´s begin." He pressed the red button on the machine, walked to the centre of the room, folded his arms, and frowning, looked at the floor as he began to speak in a soft, calming tone.

"Close your eyes … I want you to imagine that you´re in front of a white wall. It´s completely white. There´s nothing else in front of you. Only this white wall. Imagine now, that in the centre of this wall is a black dot the size of a pin. Focus on this black dot and concentrate all your attention on it."

A vertical line was visible above the space between Simon´s eyebrows and his jaw twitched as he ground his teeth together. Still focussing on the vicinity of the area around his own feet, Frank continued.

"Now, you´re going to move your concentration to each and every part of your body that I´m going say. Let´s start with your face … try to concentrate all your attention there … more specifically your eyes. All around your eyes are small muscles. Try to relax them. Your eyes should neither be open, nor too tightly shut. Just close your eyelids softly, without using any unnecessary muscular force.

"Now, concentrate on your forehead. We're going to take away all the tension there. To do this, your eyebrows will help. Raise your eyebrows slowly and steadily, and then let them fall gradually down again. Notice that by doing this a few times, little by little, the tension in your forehead is beginning to disappear."

The line above Simon's eyebrows started to become just marginally less pronounced as the muscles in the upper part of his face slowly loosened his knotted brow. Frank looked down at his patient lying there on the black leather couch before him. He moistened his lips with his tongue before he resumed.

"Concentrate now on your mouth … it's another muscle and can neither stay open, nor closed all the time. To relax it, your lips should be slightly parted and not forced in any way. Very good … Notice that when we relax the mouth and the eyes, we also relax the whole face and this, in turn, is making your cheeks and jaw also feel relaxed."

The movement in Simon's jaw had ceased and the faint grinding sound that he had been producing with his teeth could no longer be heard.

"Now, we're going to concentrate all our attention on the next point on your body … the shoulders. Pay attention to your shoulders and start getting rid of all the tension from them. Take away the tension slowly. Relax them a little more … Very good. Now, feel how your shoulders don't have any tension left in them."

The psychologist's voice continued, calm and soft, and even started to become more melodic as he grew into his role.

"Notice that by relaxing your face and shoulders, your neck is now free of tension too. And if you focus on your neck, you'll be able to notice a slight warm sensation – a pleasant sensation. This is due to the blood flowing much more freely towards the brain when we're more relaxed. What's more, this warm, comfortable sensation helps us relax even more overall and helps us feel much better in ourselves."

As he spoke, Frank's eyes followed the path of his instructions as he observed the different parts of Simon's body.

"Now, we're going to focus all our attention on our arms … Concentrate on both your arms and start eliminating all the tension from the top, and then go further down along them. Starting with your upper arm … then your forearm … to your wrists, and then your hands. Eliminate all the tension from your fingers too. Pay attention to the way that they are resting, the separation between each one of them and how the fingers are relaxed and slightly curled … and get rid of all the tension … That's it. Very good.

"Little by little, you're feeling more relaxed, more comfortable. You're very well. Repeat this mentally to yourself: I'm calm and perfectly relaxed … I'm calm and perfectly relaxed."

As his patient lay repeating the mantra internally to himself, Frank turned his attention to Simon's lower body. He swallowed hard.

"We're going to focus our attention now on your legs. Little by little, you're going to get rid of all the tension that's in them. Let's start at the top with your gluteal muscles – your buttocks … and relax them."

Frank gazed at the faded black jeans Simon was wearing. He touched his chin, and began stroking it gently with his fingers; pensive as he continued.

"Passing along your thighs … your knees, and continuing down to your calf muscles, and then your ankles. Finally, we're going to arrive at your feet. Little by little eliminating all the tension throughout the whole of your leg. You're going to feel much more relaxed, more comfortable … It's a really pleasant sensation feeling so relaxed.

"Focus your attention now on your back and start eliminating all the tension from it. Now, it´s easier to relax the back when the shoulders, arms and gluteals are already relaxed as they are now … Very good."

Speaking a little more hurriedly than before, Frank went on with the relaxation instructions; instructions that had been given countless times to his patients over the years as they lay, vulnerable but trusting, before their psychologist.

"To finish, we´re going to focus on two points of the body where a large amount of tension accumulates. One of them is the stomach. Concentrate on your stomach and notice the amount of tension that is there. But you, Simon, are going to eliminate it all. Now, breathe in from your abdomen, *very* slowly. Breathe in very deeply and when you breathe the air out, little by little, you´ll notice how the tension is disappearing … Very good. Repeat this breathing several more times and eliminate all the tension from your stomach."

As Simon lay face-up before him, Frank observed how his chest rose and fell each time he took a deep breath, inhaling noisily through his aquiline nose, and exhaling through a thin gap between his lips. The tips of his perfectly aligned, marginally off-white teeth were just visible as they guarded the entrance to the dark cavity of his mouth. Frank turned away quickly and looked out of the window.

"Very good … now concentrate on your chest. Notice that your chest too has a great deal of tension. But you, are going to eliminate that as well. Breathe in now very deeply … and when breathing out very slowly, you´ll see how all the tension starts to disappear. Repeat to yourself in your head: I´m very calm and relaxed. I feel really good."

There was a pause as Simon presumably interiorised what he was hearing and repeated it to himself in his own inner speech. Frank –

who was still looking through the glass out towards the car park –
continued his soliloquy.

"Let´s go through this exercise from the beginning, and as we do,
if you notice that any one of these points of your body still has any
kind of stress, you can eliminate it.

"Remember that we started with your face – specifically, your
eyes – eliminating the tension. Afterwards, we went to your
forehead, eliminating the tension using your eyebrows … Next we
went to your mouth …"

Frank turned for a moment, observing his patient, before
returning his gaze to the semi-vacant parking area. With more haste
now, Frank re-visited each part of Simon´s young body in his
tranquil tone – almost automatically – as he reached the final stages
of the activity.

"… breathe in deeply through your nose, and as you breathe out
again very slowly through your mouth, notice how it´s relaxing you
even more. It´s a very pleasant feeling. You´re perfectly relaxed and
calm … Very good."

The sound of Simon´s deep breathing filled the room again and
he clearly appeared more relaxed than ever; the vertical wrinkle of
his forehead now just a faint, red line.

"We´ve finished at your chest … Notice now that it doesn´t have
any tension. This point, where anxiety normally builds up, is now
relaxed because *you* have eliminated all the tension from it. Breathe
in normally as many times as you wish, and leave your chest
completely relaxed. Enjoy for a few seconds your state of
relaxation."

Silence reined for a few precious moments as Simon lay deep in
relaxation, disconnected from the horrors of his sleep and the
anxieties of his waking hours. He lay there, undisturbed by the
ticking of the clock and the occasional click of the thermostat

controlling the radiator on the wall.

"Now, we´re going to leave this state of relaxation ... To do so, we have to do it slowly and gradually, the same way we entered, because if you try to get up suddenly, you could get dizzy as your body now doesn´t have enough tension in it to support you. To start to recover, breathe in deeply ... and out ... breathe in again, and start to move your hands. Exhale. Now you can start stretching as you would if you were waking up in the morning after a good night´s sleep."

Simon started to move as he regained awareness of his surroundings. His forehead – just moments before smooth without the preoccupations that haunt him daily – was now starting to crumple again with the worrisome reality that the brief respite that Frank´s words had given him was coming to an end.

"Breathe in again ... and out. Now you can open your eyes, because the relaxation has finished."

Seconds later, Simon´s fearful eyes sprang open, not in reaction to Frank´s final command, but at the sound of a loud click as the red record button noisily jumped back level with its neighbouring keys on the cassette recorder. Back to its original position flush with the others, identical in size, shape and design, but destined by its colour to stand out and never fit in. To be the most important component, vital for the correct functioning of the machine; but to always be – for better or for worse – different from the rest.

6

The rain lashed against the glass of the consulting room, driven by the blustery late winter winds blowing in from the Downs to the north. The steady patter of water gave way occasionally to loud, crackling bursts – like fistfuls of arbitrarily-thrown gravel – as strong gusts whipped the precipitation against the window pane.

Simon sat squarely in front of Frank, still wearing his black overcoat, unaware that he was dripping water onto the floor around him.

"How´s your week been, Simon?" Frank asked, persevering with his habitual opening gambit.

Simon let out a long breath, seemingly resigned to unloading his burden once again this damp, dark afternoon.

"Not really that well. I, I haven´t done anything. Well, I´ve been to school a couple of days, but … but that´s it, nothing else."

"Thanks … OK. Umm, how´s school been then?" The question stumbled awkwardly out of Frank´s mouth.

"Fine. I go, I keep my head down, do some work, and get out. Nothing else … I can´t do anything else. I can´t concentrate. I´m so tired … and angry. Nearly all the time."

"How have the techniques been? You know, to help you manage the anger and anxiety."

Stuttering, Simon responded, "I, I … I couldn´t do them. I just, just don´t remember to do them when I feel bad. I remember afterwards and feel that I could´ve done things differently … better maybe. But at the time, I just, just lose control and can´t do anything else." He paused for a moment, shaking his head at his own ruminations.

"Can you tell me what you´ve been angry about this time?"

Simon looked forlorn. "Most of the usual things, you know. Feeling useless. Not feeling like I can do anything. Thinking that I´ve messed up really badly and, and everything´s my fault."

"And did you hurt yourself again?" asked Frank, in what was now becoming a familiar question.

Simon hesitated for a moment, the corners of his mouth downturned and the bruised bags beneath his eyes more prominent than they had been at any other time recently. Unseen by Frank, he squeezed the inside of his left forearm tightly through his coat.

"Yes … but nothing bad. Nothing serious. I did … I did manage to stop myself once. So …" He didn´t finish his sentence, losing his train of thought somewhere in the entanglement of his mind.

"That´s great, Simon." A flash of fatherly pride had appeared on Frank´s face. "It really is. It takes strength to do that. Did you use anything from the relaxation we did together?"

"No. I … I went to the bathroom and looked in the mirror. I started counting backwards, nothing else. I don´t know why. I´ve never done that before or even heard of it. Doing that … counting. And looking at myself while counting … and the anger went away, you know, bit by bit. At first, at first I swore at myself – well, the reflexion that was looking at me. Abusing myself in the mirror and wanting pain. But, but the numbers just came into my head and … and they helped me. Thinking about something helped me. The numbers, backwards."

"Well, whatever technique you use, it´s good to see you´re getting somewhere by taking a moment – a time out, if you were – and occupying your mind with something else when this happens. That´s one of the things you need to do." Frank said, clutching at any straw of positivity while trying his best to encourage Simon without sounding patronising. He underlined something he had written earlier in his notebook, paused, and then underlined it again for a second time, leaving the words boldly underscored and Simon craning his neck curiously to see if he could read from his angle what Frank had found so necessary to highlight.

"It´s also important that you occupy your mind, not only at these times, but also on a day to day basis. Have you been able to get out and do something this last week?"

Simon shook his head.

"If you could try, little by little, to incorporate an activity you like to do into your daily routine, that would be a great way to get you to start thinking about something else. You like reading, don´t you? That could be something to do when you´re alone at home. What about that?"

Simon snorted through his nose as if finding the suggestion amusing.

"I … can´t. I´m just too tired. I can´t concentrate. Words keep swimming in front of my eyes. Blurry. I´m not sure if … if …" He began to knead the muscles in the back of his neck with the knuckles of his right fist, grimacing as he did so.

"OK. How about doing some kind of regular exercise? That will make you feel better and improve your mood, for sure. I know it´s difficult for you to go out and face people sometimes, so what about – for the time being anyway – something at home. Something to get you started. A lot of sports people are doing yoga or Pilates these days. It´s something you can do on your own until you´re ready to confront doing things easily outdoors again, and to be honest, the weather we´ve been having doesn´t really inspire anyone to go out much at the moment anyway. So, that could be a good way to kick-start your exercising again. What do you think?"

Simon shook his head once more and started now to massage his forehead with the same hand that was clenched tight moments before.

"I'm just so tired. I can't do anything. I can't sleep well. I've … I've been having more terrible nightmares. I … I don't know …"

He trailed off yet again, as he struggled to find the words to describe what he was feeling and unscramble the disorder in his head.

"It's OK," Frank said sympathetically, realising that his patient was unwilling, or incapable of responding to any of his suggestions in their current session. He changed tack and followed one of the only lines of questioning that he knew would provoke a more fluid response from his patient. "OK. Could you tell me about any dreams you've been having recently? If you'd like to, of course."

Simon looked up at Frank, a sudden clarity in his eyes.

"I had one of the vivid ones a few days ago. I can remember it all … I think. Most of it at least anyway. Like it was real. Again, like I was there."

Frank subtly gestured with a nod for Simon to continue.

"I was in a room. A large room with a high ceiling with sort of stone arches here and there in some places. There were kind of … umm, stripes on the wall. Red, black, and white stripes. I don't know how I got there … I don't remember going through a door or anything like that. There was screaming and shouting all around. Male voices I couldn't understand. There were men everywhere. Well, mostly men but some boys of different ages too. Crying and shouting in anger and pain. There were people lying on the floor, bleeding … screaming out in, in agony."

Simon stared through Frank to a place somewhere on the wall under the window behind the therapist. The familiar vacant look on his face appeared as he described his latest nightmare.

"There were bodies on the ground … and people running around carrying other people with their clothes soaked in blood … carrying them in blankets – colourful blankets. Carrying them away from this place to what they thought was … was safety. But, it wasn´t safe where they were going. I could hear loud bangs outside … the sound of guns, I think, in the direction where the people were escaping to. They were carrying the dead outside, away from this terrible place, but, but going to somewhere else bad … somewhere just as dangerous. Or worse."

There was a pause as he tried to make sense of the events in his dream.

"There were other blankets – or rugs – on the floor, everywhere, among the bodies and the blood. People were barefoot … I was barefoot, walking on the rugs. I felt the soft texture of the material and … and the warmth of the thick, dark-red blood on the soles of my feet."

He stopped for a moment, completely still and silent in thought, although his pupils moved crazily around in their sockets like someone dreaming with their eyes wide open.

"There was a boy. A young boy … maybe eight or nine years old, I think. He was missing part of … part of his face. The left side of his face and head were … missing. He was being carried by a man … he was screaming, crying, running with the boy, his head lolling around, bouncing up and down as the man ran with him in his arms. His shirt completely red. Other people were running too. Some carrying others in the coloured rugs … the blood-soaked rugs … running for the doors, but there were so many people trying to get out of this room and the others pushing to come back in, trying to hide from the shooting outside."

He sighed heavily, the weight of the suffering bearing down on him, but carried on recounting his nightmare in as much detail as he could nonetheless.

"I was looking around, but it was like I was there but not there. I couldn´t do anything to help these people. I was like … an observer.

Just watching. I saw the walls inside the building. The walls with the stripes. The white ones were splashed with the blood of the men and boys who were injured, dying, and dead. There were a lot of men screaming. Angry. Furious ... Surrounding someone on the ground. Someone dressed in what looked like a uniform of some kind ... a green uniform. Police or army, maybe. His face ... his face was unrecognisable. It had been completely smashed in. You couldn't make out his features ... just a mess of bone, blood and flesh. Next to him, there was something red, like a fire extinguisher, I think, discarded on the ground. I don't know ... Men were screaming at him, and at each other ... and crying. Were they screaming at *me*? Somehow ... somehow I thought *I* had caused this. It was *my* fault and I needed to pay for what I'd done."

He closed his eyes, put his head in his hands and then fell silent.

"Simon? Simon?" Frank spoke to his patient softy, trying as gently as possible to bring him back into a conversation between the two of them. Eventually, Simon left the refuge of his self-imposed darkness and looked back at Frank.

"These are just dreams – bad dreams of course – but just dreams. Probably caused by the worries that you have right now. They will stop as you get better, believe me."

As if not hearing what he was being told, Simon continued.

"It was my fault somehow. When I woke up, I didn't know what to do. I *hated* myself and wanted to do something about it ... to hurt myself, again. I, I must've got dressed. I ... I don't remember. But, but I went out of the house. It was like a dream. My reality was like a dream that I couldn't wake up from."

"Can you remember where you went?" a worried-looking Frank asked.

"I was on the street. Like I was trying to escape something. But I was the one I was trying to escape from. My thoughts or ... or my actions, or something, are causing these people to die in my dreams. But they're like my reality. I think … I think I could remember you telling me to escape – to run – to get away from the place that I felt bad in. But it was *me* that was causing me to feel bad and I couldn't escape from myself."

As Simon closed his eyes again, Frank took advantage and quickly scribbled something surreptitiously in his notebook without disturbing his patient.

"I was on the street. I don't know how I got there. Next to a road with a lot of traffic. A lot of cars. I … I shut my eyes. I didn't want to see all the people looking at me … and, and then I stepped out. I didn't really know for sure what I was doing, but I felt I had no choice. I wanted to feel something hit me. I wanted to be struck down, there and then, onto the cold, hard ground. I …"

Simon abandoned his sentence and stared at the wooden edge of the desk in front of him, finding comfort in its familiar, non-judgmental presence. With his thumbnail, he picked at a tiny piece of wood that had started to splinter off, before absent-mindedly flicking it onto the floor at his feet.

"Could you tell me what happened then please, Simon?"

After a pause of thirty-seconds or thereabouts, he answered, "Someone pulled me back. A man. An Indian man, or maybe from Bangladesh … I don't know. He grabbed my coat and pulled me back. I think he shouted at me. I don't know … he said something maybe. I think he could've asked me something. I can't remember well, but someone walked me back home. Maybe it was the man that pulled me back? My *saviour*. I was looking at the floor moving under my feet, at the lines between the paving stones, like I was floating. I don't know how he knew where I live … maybe …"

His words again were left hanging in the air. Frank tried his best to stifle the sigh that was heaving in his own chest. The emotion of hearing how desperate Simon had become had – unlike any time before with a patient – struck the rawest of nerves with him.

"You´re really very fortunate that someone was there to help you. You do realise that there are people here for you, don´t you? I can help you, your mother can help you, many other people can too. You need to help yourself as well though, OK?"

"I know," Simon responded, like a small child who had just been scolded. He picked something out from under his thumb nail and stared at it distractedly.

"It´s really promising that you´ve been remembering some of our techniques and trying to use them when you need to—"

"But they don´t work," Simon interrupted. His deadpan manner did little to disguise the misery behind his words.

"It takes time. You´re making progress but … but I really need you to consider taking your medication again. It will make you feel more at ease, and we can definitely work better from there."

Simon glared angrily across the desk. "Definitely not. I´m definitely not taking anything again … ever. I´m not putting those things in my body … or my mind."

Frank met Simon´s stare with a challenging look of his own.

"Things are quite serious now, Simon. It´s clear that you have some issues that we need to deal with quickly, so we shouldn´t rule anything out that might be of assistance to us, should we?"

Simon impassively held his psychologist´s gaze for various seconds.

"Can I use the toilet, please?" he asked eventually.

***

Returning to the room, Simon glanced down at the papers on the desk before him; his distrustful expression showing at once that he recognised his own answers to the many questions in the tests he had completed over the last few weeks.

He sat down and this time slipped off his coat, which draped inside-out over the back of the chair behind him, revealing the red and black chequered lining inside. His face was a little flushed and still damp from the water he had splashed on it in the restroom. A tiny piece of toilet paper was stuck amongst the hairs on his chin; a result of his futile attempt to pat his face dry before recommencing the session.

"So, what´s the diagnosis? Am I officially mad then?" Simon asked without any emotion.

Frank smiled and expelled a small amount of air through his nostrils, although it was unclear whether he was genuinely amused by Simon´s comment.

"We are under strict instructions not to use that kind of terminology in front of our clients," he answered, in perhaps his first attempt at any kind of humour with his patient, before returning to his habitual, serious default setting. "You do, however, have quite a lot of different things going on from what I´ve seen with you here and also from the information we have – the answers you´ve been giving us in the diagnostic tests." He looked down at the papers in front of him as if to back up what he was saying. "You´re obviously very anxious and depressed about things and feel very negatively about yourself. You have very low self-esteem too. Would you go along with that?"

Moving his head up and down affirmatively, Simon mumbled, "Um-hmm."

"But your tests," he waved a hand over the results on the desk, "your tests, are a little, how can I put it? Unreliable. I mean, they score high in unreliability for some reason."

Simon's worried frown spurred Frank on to explain himself further.

"What this basically means is that some of the things you've answered, in a way, contradict other responses you've given. This, in turn, makes it a little harder for us to be able to – for want of a better expression – pigeon-hole you as having characteristics of a specific condition, and therefore give you the exact treatment that you need."

Simon appeared more awake all of a sudden, more upright in his posture, listening raptly to what Frank was telling him.

"But we can see some patterns in the results all the same," added the psychologist.

"I had some problems answering the questions, to be honest," Simon offered in way of an explanation.

"Why was that?"

"I don't know. I answered some questions, and then other ones which were really similar, I … I just thought differently and gave an answer that wasn't the same." He paused, thinking back over the previous weeks' tasks. "I just didn't know what to put in some places. It's like, like I was afraid of writing the wrong answer, so … I lied, I guess. I don't know why."

"OK … Would you say that you lie much? About other things?"

Simon hesitated, uncomfortable with the question, but willing and trusting enough in Frank to give as much true information as he could.

"Yes, I do. I lie to try to make my life easier … to avoid things. But … but then sometimes the lie gets out of hand. It spirals out of control and I'm left with a mess … a chaos … and, and I can't remember what I said, or even if what I said was true in the first place … or in the end, or not. I end up believing my lies. In the end."

Simon looked like he was confusing himself with his own scrambled rhetoric.

"It´s good to see that you´re trying to understand why you´re doing some things – in this case the lying. You say that you use it as a way of avoiding things … What kind of things exactly?"

"As many things as I can," he answered honestly. "People, things I have to do, going to places … having to speak to someone, even if I know them well. You know, I normally avoid people I know if I bump into them somewhere, like on the street. I hide. Even in my own house if my parents have friends round, I hide away and don´t see them. Other times I pretend to be ill to avoid school or something I have to do."

"Thanks for telling me all this. Recognising these things is a big step and it shows you´re analysing more and more how you behave." He smiled at Simon. "Avoidance is a normal consequence of your anxiety, especially in social situations, but staying at home will end up just maintaining your negative mood. So, let´s try to look at the situations – the triggers of your anxiety if you were – and try to accept them and our part in them. Accept the situation as it is, neither good nor bad, as these are just labels we put on things. Most of the time we can´t change what´s happening, but of course, if there is any way you can improve the situation, that´s great, do it. Otherwise, just try to accept it. Of course you don´t have to like it, but accept it as it is and, if you can, at the same time try to look at the situation and observe it objectively. See if you can observe yourself and your thoughts in the situation, your role there, and how you react to it. Little by little become part of the scene that is playing out around you and don´t try to avoid it."

Simon was still trying to listen as well as he could, but was obviously suffering the ill effects of the sleep deprivation he had been experiencing over recent weeks.

"You – and everyone else, in fact – need to learn how to accept time as well. Accept the present reality, and deal with it. Be effective at the moment you find yourself in and live in that moment. Cope with present difficulties, but also try to enjoy the time you´re living in now if possible too. Try to find your inner peace in the present, and not in the past or the future. If you ruminate about the past, this will only lead you to feeling remorse and shame. Of course, we need to learn from what we´ve experienced and be accountable for our actions, and even analyse them to make sure that we don´t repeat certain behaviour, but we can´t live thinking and speaking in the third conditional and in *if onlys* and *what ifs* about things we just can´t change.

"The same applies to the future. Worrying about it will only augment your anxiety further still. If you have to plan something, of course do so; sort out the practicalities about what you have to do, but don´t let fear of rejection or an unfounded anticipated future failure take over your life."

Frank had started to lose himself in his own sermon, before noticing that Simon – plagued by fatigue and with eyelids heavier as each second went by – was finding it increasingly difficult to follow his preaching.

"OK," Frank said, loudly enough to have the desired effect of jolting his patient back to somewhere resembling near full awareness. "There are some things you can do to try to help yourself deal with your anxiety of certain situations and to learn to live with it better. You can set small challenges that will make you come face to face with specific things that make you anxious and these, in turn, will help you overcome greater fears later on. We could do some kind of homework for this week, if you wish to put something like this into practice. Do you think you could give it a try?"

Simon nodded, slowly.

"OK, I'd like you to think about something you can do over the next week. A situation in which you can expose yourself to something that you might feel a little bit uncomfortable, and possibly anxious about. Nothing that will cause too much stress at first, mind. Something low risk and not a big problem if you struggle with it, but challenging enough to make you feel like you've accomplished something afterwards if you succeed. Maybe something connected to school?"

Simon thought for a moment. His lips thinned and the vertical line appeared more deeply engraved again on his forehead.

"I ... I've only been one or two days recently. It's hard being there – really hard. But, I don't have to speak if I don't want to. But, but I'm not sure if I can do anything there. It's too stressful. It's enough if I actually go, isn't it?" He looked towards Frank for reassurance.

"Building up the courage to attend when you can is an achievement in itself, of course. But I think you could try – and are capable of – doing a little more; something else more challenging for you. What about meeting someone for a coffee or a spot of lunch? A friend or someone in your family perhaps? Do you think you could do that?"

"Going out? No. Somewhere like a café is too difficult for me. There are too many people there. I don't want them to look at me. To listen to me."

"OK ... how about phoning someone for a chat?" Frank suggested. "You don't have to speak about anything special, but it could be quite good for you to do that. At the moment, it wouldn't mean going out anywhere, so you'd feel more comfortable, wouldn't you?"

Simon sat and considered this for a few seconds, staring in the direction of his therapist with glazed eyes that made it difficult for

Frank to judge exactly how he was feeling or how he would respond.

Eventually, Simon said, "I think … I could try. I´ve, I´ve got a cousin that I used to see a lot … when I was younger that is. I could give him a ring, I suppose."

Frank smiled, seemingly pleased with even the smallest hint of progress in what were becoming increasingly difficult sessions for him, even with the experience that his framed certificates on the wall alluded to.

Closing his notebook, appearing to accept that any other tasks or conversations would be too much of a challenge for his exhausted patient this afternoon, Frank wrapped up the remainder of the afternoon´s session as quickly as possible.

Simon left the room with all the pleasantries that he could muster and closed the door silently behind him. Frank rose from his chair soon afterwards and stood facing the window, contemplating what was left of the squally showers which had now died down into a light drizzle that drifted in waves as it was picked up on the erratic northerly breeze.

Despite the gloominess outside, he pulled down the venetian blind and twisted the clear plastic pole anti-clockwise to block out the remaining daylight. He then flicked on the transistor radio on top of the filing cabinet. Staring into the darkness of the room, his ears were suddenly met with a cascade of drums, soon overlapped by a warm, metallic, baritone belting out its apocalyptic message.

"*Black hole sun …*" the voice prophesised, as it wound its way through the chorus of the song. A song which would leave its mark on young minds around the world as they questioned their own existence and struggled to find a place among the madness of the society into which they had been so unwittingly, and forcibly, thrust.

7

"So, how did you get on with calling your cousin this week?" Frank asked, pushing his glasses up his nose as he usually did – among other things – when shifting his focus from his notes to his patients.

"Actually, OK," Simon replied after a moment's hesitation. "We spoke, or he spoke mostly, for a while. Not for long really, but he told me about what he'd been up to and things like that."

"And how did you feel about speaking to him?"

Silence for a few seconds. "Actually, to be honest, like I was completing a task. Something I felt I had to do."

"Well, in a way it was. This was something that we spoke about doing that would be beneficial for you. And you did it; you managed to have a conversation with someone and you achieved what you'd set out to do. So, well done." Frank smiled and nodded his head in approval. "There's no rush in building up to these social situations so quickly, but they're important things to start doing again and little by little, week by week, you'll be able to do more, I assure you."

"I don't know. I'm not so sure about that," Simon said pessimistically.

"I have to say, Simon, you've kind of adopted the role of someone who is always negative when there really is no need to be," Frank said, in a gentle manner with a tinge of mock desperation designed to lighten the mood. "I know you're feeling bad, and yes, you do have some problems that need to be – and will be – resolved, but you must stop always assuming that there is nothing positive about the things you do or try to do. Really, was there anything negative about speaking with someone over the phone? Even if you didn't do a great deal of the talking?"

Simon was looking slightly annoyed with his psychologist now. "No, I guess you´re right. There was nothing really negative about the conversation. I was nervous and found it difficult to get my words together ... but I suppose it was OK, in the end."

There was something different about Simon today. Something barely noticeable but there all the same. The bags were still visible under his eyes, his complexion was still pale, and his hair – if anything – was even messier than ever. However, there was something in the way he held himself a little more upright. Something in his gait as he took the four or five steps from the doorway to his chair; an air of alleviation about him.

Seizing on a possible window of opportunity that had been thrown open for him, Frank pressed his patient for more information.

"What about the relationships you have with other people in your family? Could you tell me a little about how you get on with some of them?"

"OK," Simon replied.

Frank´s eyebrows rose in a gesture of surprise he found impossible to conceal on hearing Simon´s lack of resistance and swift response to this potentially delicate question.

"So, can you tell me about someone in your family – when you´re ready of course – and the kind of relationship you have with them?"

"Umm ... my mum, I suppose. We, we get on quite well. She´s around more than my dad as she has to do quite a lot of things at home, you know, cooking, cleaning, house stuff, things like that. If I need a lift somewhere, she takes me. We don´t really speak about anything important or deep. Just kind of logistical stuff."

"She tries to help you when you´re anxious sometimes, doesn´t she?" Frank queried.

Simon started to look a little uneasy. "Yes ... when I let her.

74

She's worried about me, I know. But … but I don't think she knows how to handle the situation when I lose control, or when I'm feeling bad. It's not really fair of me to put so much pressure on her. I … I feel like a burden sometimes. She has to do a lot alone."

Frank's normally encouraging smile when Simon was talking about subjects that were difficult for him to share, was strangely absent. Instead, he wore a sad expression that suggested there was a deep sorrow lying dormant inside, awoken by the current topic of conversation. He considered something for a moment before speaking. "What would you think about doing a session here together with her?"

"No." Simon shook his head from side to side quickly. "Sorry, I don't think I can. I, I can't speak about things in front of her … in front of my parents."

"Your father neither?"

"Especially not with him." Simon's own expression now changed, as his mind was pulled away to another time and place. "I … I don't speak to them about anything. I'm too embarrassed to say anything to them."

"Do you have a good relationship with your father?"

Simon paused, thinking about his answer, doubt etched on his face. "More or less, yes."

"You mentioned that he's not at home much, didn't you?" Frank asked, encouraging Simon to elaborate.

"He goes away for work quite a lot, yes. When he's home we don't spend a lot of time together. He plays golf with a work colleague … or snooker sometimes in the evenings."

Simon's body was rigid with tension as he waited apprehensively for Frank's next query, keenly aware of the dramatic pause followed by a deep intake of breath that preceded his therapist's more meaningful questions.

"Do you think that your father's absence has shaped you in any way?" Frank probed.

Simon had anticipated this line of questioning and answered quickly. "I guess it must have done. Don't all our relationships affect us in some way?" There was a sarcastic tone to his voice, although straight afterwards he looked repentant for the way his words had slipped from his mouth.

"How do you think you've been affected by your relationship with him, Simon?" Frank asked, unperturbed by his patient's attitude.

"I … I guess I've disappointed him," Simon said after a long pause.

"How?"

"He's always criticising me for everything I do."

"Such as?"

"I don't know. I guess that he wants me to be something … someone I'm not." Simon paused again. "He wants me to take over his business, but I don't want to work in that world … I want to do something else. I'm not sure what, but I don't just want to buy and sell things to make money."

Frank wrote something down in his notebook. "Do you feel like you haven't lived up to his expectations?" he asked, keeping his eyes fixed on what he had just added to the page.

Simon nodded. "Yes. In many ways."

"And how does that make you feel?"

"Angry, I guess." An aggressive expression appeared on Simon's face. "And frustrated. But then that makes me feel guilty too … so, so I try to make it up to him when I see him and to try to prove, to show him I'm not useless." Simon's passion subsided and he sank back into his chair, appearing even more torn with guilt about how he was feeling and what he was saying about his father.

"Do you wish he was around more? To spend more time with you?" Frank divined for hidden clues to Simon´s true feelings with a penetrating stare into his patient´s eyes.

"I don´t know." Simon sounded despondent. "We´re all kind of used to it now. He´s working hard to build up a business and make sure we all live well. I suppose he´s a good father … if that´s what you want to know."

"The definition of a good father is very subjective, Simon," Frank said, looking away from his patient as if trying to conceal the feelings that had suddenly gate-crashed the conversation. He added quickly afterwards, "Do you do anything together? Spend time doing something with one another?"

Simon was now looking studiously at Frank, as if trying to gauge what emotions were running through his psychologist´s mind. Eventually he answered, "Sometimes. Sometimes we watch a bit of sport or something like that, although I´m not too keen on it. I just do it to please him most of the time. To try to have something in common. When he´s watching the news, we talk a bit about what´s going on. Things like that. We go to restaurants from time to time. With my mum too … and my sister when she lived at home."

Frank consulted his notes.

"How´s your relationship with her? With Sarah?"

Simon again paused to collect his thoughts, looking like he hadn´t given much importance to this aspect of his life before.

"We, we don´t really have much of a relationship. She left home a few years ago and we haven´t seen each other much since then. There´s a bit of an age gap between us – four years, more or less. We´ve never really spoken or done anything together since we were kids. I think she still sees me as some kind of annoying baby brother and gets jealous. You know, of my parents´ attention. But I don´t want any attention from anyone. I just want to stay out of things. Be alone."

77

"Do you ever speak to your sister?"

"No, hardly ever. She speaks to mum on the phone, but I guess she doesn´t really get on with dad much. They used to shout and argue a fair bit."

"Can you remember about what?"

Simon thought long and hard for some time. He looked up at the calendar on the wall, now displaying a photo of a Siamese cat sitting in a plant pot, its intense, blue eyes staring coldly at the photographer who had rudely disturbed its privacy.

"No. Really I can´t," Simon said, still observing the photo. "About her going out a lot or something like that, if I have to say something. I don´t know. Protective parent stuff, towards teenage daughters, I guess." He turned back to face the general direction of the desk in front of him.

"And do you ever argue with your parents?"

Simon stared into space before speaking. "I don´t think so … no."

"OK. That´s great, Simon. Thank you." Frank made yet another note in his increasingly growing compendium of Simon´s life. "What about other relationships? Friends?"

"One or two. Again nothing deep … just people to go out and get drunk or have a smoke with sometimes. Things like that. Not in groups or anything. I guess we just get together … well, *used* to get together, to get, umm, a bit messed up." He snorted through his nose as he realised how foolish this sounded in the cold light of the consulting room.

"OK. Talking about friends, I´d like you to think about something for a moment please. I´d like you to try to imagine how your friends would describe you. Just in a few words. You can take your time, no problem." Frank smiled, and then immediately averted his gaze by looking down at his hands resting on the desk, trying to make his questions less intimidating for his shy patient.

Simon was taken by surprise by Frank´s request, but sat there all the same, racking his brains for something to say. Anything.

"Umm … solitary. That´s one. Umm … quiet, and … umm, I don´t know, maybe … arrogant and aloof." Knowing full well that Frank was going to delve deeper into the source of these adjectives, he headed off the next question. "Because I don´t talk much and keep myself to myself, I guess."

Frank looked strangely satisfied with Simon´s self-deprecating response. With his patient firmly in his sights, he fired another question. "Girlfriends? Or any similar relationships, if you don´t mind me asking?"

Simon blushed. "Umm, two in the last couple of years."

"How was your relationship with them?"

"Brief."

The colour continued to pulse in Simon´s face, but something in Frank´s silent encouragement and simple way of eliciting information seemed to make him more comfortable, in spite of his embarrassment.

"They finished it in the end. Left me." The bitterness was noticeable in his voice, although it was not so clear at whom it was aimed. "I guess when they realised who I really am, they just wanted to get away as quickly as possible."

"Well, it´s their loss, I guess." Silence fell. Frank blinked several times in quick succession and avoided eye contact once more, although this time the motive was distinctly different. "Did you ever talk about your feelings with them?" he asked after stalling for several seconds.

Simon laughed out loud uninhibitedly for the first time during his therapy. "I´m a teenager with mental problems. Do you really think I´d share how I feel with these people?"

Frank remained serious, thoughtful – serene almost – well-used to these kinds of outbursts.

"Have you ever shared your feelings with anyone else before? With your family or friends? Told them what you're feeling?"

The smile had now disappeared from Simon's face. "No. I've never shared anything with anyone before. Just … just with you. Only you. I, I only feel comfortable doing these things with you."

It was Frank's turn to blush now. Only fleetingly, but it was evident that he had felt somewhat uncomfortable – albeit honoured – by Simon's words.

"Well … it's great that you're doing that now. I know it can be difficult, especially for young people – and men in particular – to do this in the society and culture that we live in, what with the British stiff upper lip and everything. It's very often seen as a weakness to share your true feelings and swim against the tide of expectations of such a sexist mind-set." Frank searched for the right smile to add but ended up with an uncomfortable, strained expression on his face. "OK, umm … So … what about school? In class? How do you get on with people there?"

"It's difficult," Simon struggled on with his explanations, "but I've, umm, adapted … *accepted*, as you'd say, I guess."

"How so?"

"I told you before. I go, I get on with work – if I can – and I get out. I don't speak to anyone if I can help it. I avoid it. A lot of days, I don't … *can't* go … like recently. I just end up staying at home. I can't get out of bed."

"It's really important that we work on this *I can't* belief you have – this core belief that you can't do something – and try to change it to something else such as *OK, it's tricky and it will cause anxiety, I know, but I'll try*. You've got to start trying to shift your perspective about things."

Simon had his arms folded and was shaking his head, completely

80

unreceptive to the advice that was being given to him.

"What about relationships with your teachers?" Frank persisted.

Again, Simon found this question somehow amusing, his top lip curling into something between and snarl and a strange grin. "I know they don´t like me … most of them. And you know they don´t like me too. I´ve been checking and I know it´s true. The history teacher, Swann, for example, keeps asking me things – kept asking me things anyway – knowing how bad I felt in class when I had to do that. I don´t know why he did it. It´s like some kind of petty revenge for something I´ve done to him or how he feels in his sad little life. I, I don´t go to that class anymore. I can´t. I … I don´t know what I would do if I had to go again. Then in geography, my report said I needed to stop acting like a moody rock star. They don´t *know* me … how can they say that?" he asked, giving the impression that this seemingly innocuous episode in his school life had affected him more than he was letting on.

Frank glimpsed Simon´s hands resting on the edge of the desk. Despite being clasped firmly together, they were shaking as anger boiled inside him. Frank stared at the scars that were evident on practically every knuckle on Simon´s hands, including the freshly scabbed wounds that ran across his right fist from index to little finger.

"Well, I think it´s clear to say that they don´t really know you, so try not to worry about them too much. They´ve obviously made an error of judgement when it comes to your personality and feelings and who you really are." He smiled his familiar empathic smile again. "Is there anyone you do speak to at school?"

"Yes," Simon replied after a while. "The English literature teacher, Mr Spencer."

"OK. Can you tell me about him?" Frank said brightly.

"Yeah … OK. He´s a little guy. An old-fashioned man. He

81

normally wears tweed suits with patches on the elbows and really looks like a cross between Dickens and Shakespeare ... believe it or not."

"Very appropriate," Frank interjected.

"Yeah. He´s a nice man. I feel a bit sorry for him, actually."

"Why?"

"I don´t know. I have the feeling that he doesn´t fit in at the school. I mean, he´s a great teacher, a passionate teacher about his subject. But he seems alone, sad even. I don´t know. It´s like he´s from another time and doesn´t belong here. In this world."

Simon looked upset, his forehead wrinkled and he was suddenly deep in thought.

"One morning, there was graffiti on the school building. Huge letters abusing him. He´s Jewish, and it said that he should be gassed – or something like that – and swastikas. They´d painted giant swastikas and a picture of him hanging on a rope on the wall. He was really affected by it. It´s incredible why someone would do that. I mean ... here and now. But thinking about it again, I´m not that surprised really."

Frank was shaking his head in disbelief. "That´s terrible for someone to do that. He must have been really shocked." He paused, long enough to be able to move the conversation on without seeming disrespectful and callous towards Simon´s teacher´s feelings.

"And you had a good relationship with him?"

Simon´s face brightened. "I did, yes. I mean ... I do. He´s very motivating, he tries his best and I just feel that I should do what I can to make sure he feels OK, and umm, comfortable with us in the class. I don´t know why, but I feel kind of ... protective towards him somehow." Simon was smiling now, enjoying the rare, pleasant thoughts that had found a temporary foothold among the relentless maelstrom in his head.

"There are only six of us in the class. It´s a small group and the other students are nice people. Quiet and polite. Good people – not like a lot of the others at school. We read a lot in the class … out loud."

"How do you feel when you do that?"

"I feel … OK. I don´t know, it´s like it´s not me speaking. It´s my character or whatever I´m reading that takes control. I know the other students are nervous too, so it makes me feel better. Sorry, I know it´s a bit bad to say that."

"Not at all. It´s actually quite positive to share experiences with other people and to see and sense how they´re feeling too. It´s a way of seeing how *you* feel to some extent. To almost see a reflection of you and your behaviour, and realise that there´s nothing wrong with it."

"Maybe," Simon said doubtfully.

"Do you speak to Mr Spencer about anything else apart from what you do in class?" Frank dared to ask, taking advantage of the fact that Simon appeared less tense and more open to revealing information than before.

"No, not really … well, he encouraged me to be in the drama group a couple of times. To do some plays."

"That´s … really impressive, Simon. It really is. How did you feel when you were acting?" enquired Frank, eager to explore this unforeseen dimension of his patient´s life.

Simon shrugged his shoulders. "I don´t know … I can´t remember. It all seems like a blur. Like it wasn´t me. I got so nervous before we used to start that everything seemed like a dream, like it wasn´t real." His brow furrowed. "But, it felt like no one was looking at me for once. They were looking at my character, listening to my character. It´s like I could … I could *hide* behind this person I was being at that time. No one could see me … the real me."

"But it *was* you. You did that. You stood up there and acted and the people in the audience were watching you – listening to *you*, Simon. You´ve done something quite special considering you have so much trouble with people looking at you. This is something we can definitely work on as part of your therapy at a later stage. In fact, drama and acting – and improvisation too come to think of it – are quite commonly used to deal with social anxiety and to help people with their communication skills in their normal day-to-day lives. Is this something you think we can use together to help with your improvement?"

Simon´s lips vibrated as he let out a long puff of air. "I don´t know … maybe?"

"OK, OK, good," Frank added as he happily went about noting down what he obviously considered a breakthrough moment for them both. Not wanting any lull in the proceedings, he quickly shot his next question at Simon in an attempt to garner a more in-depth understanding of his – until now – rather deficient picture of Simon´s family background.

"So, thinking again about your relationships with the people that are important to you in your life, can you think about any experiences you may have had with anyone in your family, or people close to you, that have left a strong impression on you? Arguments, drastic changes, something that was very difficult for you? Grief, maybe?"

Simon again seemed prepared for the question, answering immediately.

"Really nothing. I, I really think my problems don´t come from my family or … or my relationships with them. I really think I´ve had … I had, a good childhood. Nothing out of the ordinary´s happened. I was quite a happy child too, according to my dad. A smiley boy, joking all the time. In photos I looked happy too –.at

84

least when I was younger. My grandparents are all still alive and we see them from time to time, well until recently anyway. We had good holidays, a nice house, pets. Everything was fine, but … almost too fine."

Frank peered over the top of his glasses and frowned. "What do you mean by that?"

"I … I … I …" Simon stuttered. He closed his eyes, took a deep breath and regained his composure.

"I almost wished that some bad things would happen," he said finally. The calm delivery of the sentence made Frank inadvertently sit up a little straighter in his chair and narrow his eyes in anticipation of what he was about to hear.

"What do you mean?"

"I mean … I mean, that I wanted something to happen. Something *terrible* to happen. To feel some grief or pain or whatever … just to feel something. I wanted bad things to happen. I tried to *make* them happen by thinking them, wishing them. I wanted … I wanted people to die. People in my family to die … just, just to feel something different. To feel … I don´t know. Special in some way."

He held his head in his hands, the fragile confidence that had been growing throughout the session now a distant memory. He spoke, head bowed, but his quiet, unnerving voice could easily be heard.

"It … it was like my life was a dream … but, but I needed a nightmare … I needed it all to end. I needed darkness."

8.

Alone sat Simon, waiting for his psychologist to finish speaking to an unknown somebody in the clinic´s reception area. Waiting, in theory, for the next rung on the ladder of his recovery to be stepped upon.

From the comfort of the old leather chair in which he sat, Simon could hear indistinct voices coming in faint waves down the corridor behind him as Frank presumably sorted out something connected to another one of his patients; although through the closed door of the consulting room it was impossible to tell with any degree of certainty.

Simon looked ill at ease, randomly popping the joints of his fingers and repeatedly touching the area under his left pectoral as though checking that something he had in his shirt pocket was still safely tucked away there. He sat on his hands, trying to control his involuntary fidgeting, as Frank entered the room.

"Sorry about that." A soft hiss of air being pushed out of the leather padding on his chair accompanied Frank as he sat down. He looked carefully at Simon, attempting to ascertain his patient´s current mood.

Having become accustomed to the reluctance he faced when talking with Simon about the events of the seven days between one meeting to the next, Frank now relied on the young man´s body language and hard to read facial expressions to decide whether this opening avenue of questioning was worth exploring further at the start of each session. Noticing today how Simon was hunched forward, eyes lowered, and with his palms sandwiched between the back of his thighs and the seat of the chair, he decided to pursue an alternative course of interrogation to commence the day´s dialogue.

"So, Simon, you told me before that your life doesn't feel real sometimes, didn't you?" More of an affirmation than a question, to which Simon made no reply.

"And that ..." he glanced down at one of the many pages of completed diagnostic tests on the desk, complete with pencilled notes in the margins, "it all feels like a dream or a film sometimes." He looked at Simon questioningly. "Do you often feel that unusual things happen to you and that you have strange experiences that can't be explained?"

"I remember the questions in the tests, so you know strange things happen to me, don't you."

Spoken in another tone, Simon's response would have sounded impertinent; but his robotic delivery demonstrated nothing more than a plain statement of facts.

"Do you think you'd be able to tell me about some of these strange experiences?"

Simon took his hands out from under him and folded his arms across his chest.

"Well, I told you. My life often doesn't feel real. It's like living in a dream or ... déjà vu, or something like that. A blur, or, or a mix of all these feelings. I don't know. I kind of feel like a character in a film or a play ... or something like that. Like I'm not real, or like I don't really belong here. I don't know. It sounds stupid, I know."

"It's not stupid, Simon. These are your feelings and perceptions. It's how you feel at a specific moment, caused by whatever you're thinking about or whatever you're suffering from at that particular point in time. It's OK to feel like this sometimes, and excellent that you can recognise and admit to someone else to having these feelings." Another glance down at the notes and a short moment of hesitancy preceded the next question. "Do you, do you feel sometimes that you hear voices? Voices that are not your own?"

Simon smiled, seeming to find the question amusing, although there was a glint of fear in his eyes.

"No. Well … yes. Sometimes." He shook his head at what he regarded as his own craziness. "Sometimes … sometimes I think I can hear people calling me. Calling my name. I … I´ve thought that sometimes I can hear people calling me through the radio. Through the speakers. I, I know it´s stupid." Simon looked overwhelmed with embarrassment.

"Do the voices ever tell you to do things?" The question somehow sounded sinister, in spite of Frank´s warm and calming voice.

"No, no, no. I think … that they don´t say much apart from my name, like they´re trying to catch my attention … it´s weird. But the *other* voices, I hear all the time. But I think that these are *my* voices. So they must be just my thoughts. They … or I, keep calling myself useless, stupid, a disaster. Things like that. Sometimes … sometimes my head is so full of my thoughts … too many thoughts. I can´t control them, it´s chaotic, so noisy in there." He jabbed his index finger several times into the side of his head much harder than was really necessary to illustrate his point.

Frank winced at the force with which Simon had thrust his finger into his temple. "It´s quite important that you become aware of this self-talk and recognise the unhelpful thoughts that you have and try your best to turn them around into positive ones. It *is* possible to change what you say to yourself, and if you do, this will in turn change your automatic thoughts – that is to say, the thoughts that instantly pop into your head and make you behave and react the way you do."

Frank paused, noticing that although Simon appeared to be following his explanation, he was fighting something in his mind that was distracting him from paying complete attention. Frank began to speak more slowly and clearly.

"For example, if you find yourself saying that you´re an idiot, try saying over and over again in your mind that you´re smart, intelligent, witty – something like that. Even if you don´t believe it at first, you´ll hear yourself say it – like a mantra – and get used to hearing it. This, in turn, will create more diversity in how you think and foster a more positive environment in which your self-talk won´t just be negative and destructive all the time."

Simon was nervously biting his already overly-chewed nails, a look of strained concentration on his face as he listened to what Frank was suggesting to him.

"I´d also like you to try to think about where this talk may have come from, if you can. Maybe it hasn´t come only from you and your thoughts. Maybe it´s a repetition of something you´ve heard coming from someone close to you – a family member maybe – and you´ve assimilated these as your own thoughts which you´re now repeating to yourself. I mean, someone could have mocked or belittled you for something, and that event may have severely affected you. If this has been the case, make every effort to ignore these people and what they´ve said and put your energy into other more positive ways of thinking." Frank paused before he continued. "Does this make sense to you?"

"It seems logical, I suppose," answered Simon unconvincingly.

Frank nodded and rearranged some of the papers that were placed on his desk, distracting them both briefly. "Do you ever feel that your mind plays tricks on you?" Frank asked suddenly.

"All the time," Simon replied, as quickly as the question that had just been directed at him; although offering little in the way of an explanation.

"Are there any times that you don´t feel safe?" Frank added immediately, maintaining the quick-fire exchanges.

The look of fear returned to Simon's eyes, which told the psychologist all he needed to know. The combination of the young man's body language and facial expression led Frank to carefully steer the conversation away from his previous question.

"You, you sometimes see things, don't you, Simon? You mentioned that too."

Simon scanned the room – almost theatrically – like he was making sure that there were no eavesdroppers present.

"I see people … and other stuff. And feel things sometimes too."

"What kind of things?"

Simon looked around the room again with exaggerated, almost pantomimic movements; however, there was nothing humorous about his startled manner. He leaned forward, his voice hushed like he was letting someone in on a well-kept secret.

"Ghosts."

On proclaiming the word, Simon sat back as if owning up to some illicit act worthy of punishment. Frank sat unmoved – either expecting Simon's answer or sheltering behind his professional façade.

"I know that most people don't believe in these things, but I know what I've experienced. I know what I've seen."

"How often do you see or feel these things?"

"I don't know. My concept of time is, is messed up. Once or twice a month maybe … more sometimes. I don't know. It depends where I am too."

"And when was the last time you had an experience like this?"

Simon thought for a second or two. "I'm not sure. I don't remember. It could've been last month, I guess. I was at home, in the kitchen, washing something up, I think, and I felt someone touch me … somebody kind of, pinch me. I turned around but no one was there. I usually feel like someone is behind me or walks past me, and I sometimes see, I don´t know … shapes, something like that passing by. Dark shapes. On the landing outside my room. I feel it a lot."

"OK. And have you actually seen anyone, rather than just feeling like something´s there?"

"Yes. A few times."

Simon gathered his thoughts before he began to reveal one of his more seminal childhood experiences.

"When I was a kid, I saw a ghost of an old man. Both me and my sister saw him, not just me. He was an old man that´d died in the house that we moved into a little while afterwards. I know it sounds strange, but he looked kind of yellow and glowing and he was wearing a waistcoat – I think a spotted waistcoat – and he always had quite a neat and tidy look to him, although for some reason I thought he looked a bit dusty too. Not dirty, but delicate, fine dust like on the wings of a butterfly or moth. He also had a beard. A white one. He used to come and sit on the end of our beds at night sometimes and read us a story, but no sound ever came from his mouth … just his lips moving. We had an orange light in our room. Ghosts are attracted to orange lights … apparently." Simon looked a little repentant at sharing this last piece of information, as if unsure about whether what he was saying was true, or if it had somehow become ingrained into him as a false memory.

"How old were you when you saw this?"

"Umm … one or two … I think." He blushed, realising only now that what he was saying didn´t seem to make much sense.

"And can you remember this? Seeing the man?" a surprised Frank asked.

"Well … not exactly. But my sister saw it and told me … I think. I, I used to point to spaces as well … to nothing, empty spaces in the room and shout *man, man*. My mum told me I used to do this."

"OK." There was a touch of scepticism in Frank's voice that he carelessly failed to hide. "Any other experiences of seeing people you can tell me about?"

Simon looked a little more reticent to carry on with his commentary after appearing to doubt the reliability of what he, himself, was saying.

"Umm … yes." The look on Simon's face indicated that he felt there was no going back now and it really didn't matter what else he told his therapist. "I was out walking in the hills, well, in the forest not too far from here, and saw a man sitting on something like a rock or a trump stump, I think. I remember him … he was quite a young man and was wearing what looked like kind of blue overalls, like a mechanic's. He was just sitting there and I must've looked away for a second and then back again because he was gone. Just like that. Disappeared. So I ran … it was ridiculous, but I ran all the way back into town. It was a long way to run back down the hill … but I didn't stop."

He sat thinking for a moment, weighing up in his mind whether to continue sharing these types of incriminating thoughts with his psychologist.

"There's an old prison in the town," he continued eventually. "It's supposed to be haunted. Maybe … maybe he was wearing an old prison uniform? I don't know."

"That's very interesting. Fascinating, really. Are there any—"

"Sorry, there was another time that I saw someone, well … not clearly, but it was definitely a person … on a school trip. We were staying in a hotel and I thought I saw somebody fall from the balcony of our room. Straight down, over the railing. Pretty much all the time I was there, I felt a … a kind of presence, like someone was there in the room with me … but they were suffering." Simon suddenly looked on the verge of tears, surprisingly struck by this particular memory. "I found out later that someone had died in that room trying to jump from one balcony to another." He shivered.

"How did you find that out?" asked Frank. The scepticism now replaced with obvious interest in the practicalities of the story.

Simon seemed perplexed at the question and overcome by self-doubt once more. "I … I don´t know. I can´t remember who told me." He looked at Frank directly, meeting the psychologist´s challenge. "Look, I know what you think. That I didn´t see these things, or that I´m making them up … or, or that my mind is just suggesting things to me, that it´s influenced by something that I know or that I´ve already heard before, so then I imagine these things … but they´re real. I know they are. I see them, hear them, *feel* them."

"Of course you believe they´re real, Simon. I´m not saying that you´re not telling me the truth."

"Seriously," Simon added quickly, "I don´t believe it myself when I hear people tell me that they´ve seen things like this. I have to have evidence. But so many other people claim to see things too, don´t they? Does that make all of us mad? Does that make *me* mad? That I´ve seen these things?" He raised his voice more than normal; not in anger but with a seldom seem passion. "What about Jehovah's Witnesses? Don´t *they* claim that they´ve seen a holy ghost or something like that? People pray to a spirit, for fuck´s sake," he said, making inverted commas in the air with his fingers at the word *spirit*. "When someone says they´ve seen a ghost, people think they´re crazy. When someone prays to a god, they have faith. It´s completely contradictory."

"I know, Simon. I agree with you. Religious visions, for example, despite fitting the description perfectly of a psychotic experience, are more commonly considered as something of a gift. It really does sound contradictory I know, but in the society we live in – and our culture here in what are, to some, incorrectly described as developed countries – some things are widely accepted, while others are not. Take the parameters we use in psychology, for instance. In the western world, if you believe you see things or experience things out of the ordinary, it can indicate that you may have some kind of personality disorder."

"Like what?" All of a sudden, Simon was gripped by what Frank was saying.

"Like schizophrenia, for instance."

Simon shifted uncomfortably in his chair. Although he didn´t verbally express his surprise and resulting unrest at the words of his psychologist, it was clearly written all over his face.

"Look, I´m not saying that it´s true in your case, but if we analyse some of the answers to the questions in your tests – like the unusual experiences that you sometimes have, or some of the things you believe in – there may be a link to schizophrenia-like tendencies; for example, when it´s sometimes difficult to separate reality from what we perceive as reality."

"Churches must be full of schizos, then," Simon said in a low, serious tone.

Frank chuckled – albeit a little nervously – at this observation. "They may well be." He looked down at the page in front of him. "Look, these type of questions are just a handful in a few hundred – which along with our observations here in the sessions – help give us a better picture of you as a whole. However, nothing´s set in stone and we need to be flexible with our diagnoses." He looked up again, hoping Simon wouldn´t question him further. "Can you think of any other strange experiences that you may have had?" he asked, in effort to move on as briskly as possible.

Simon chewed on his bottom lip, clearly fighting an interior battle with himself as to whether he wanted to give any more information away on the subject. After a few seconds he stopped biting his lip and replied, "I´ve seen UFOs. Well, one … once."

"Really? That´s great." Frank replied, let off the hook by Simon´s answer, "I mean, that´s very interesting. Could you tell me what happened?"

"I was on holiday with my family … in Menorca. They´ve got loads of kind of Stone Henge-type circles and monuments all over the island. One night I was with my family in a hire-car driving back from somewhere, probably a restaurant knowing them, and I was looking out of the window when I saw something in the sky. My mum saw it too, so I know it was real … or at least she said that she did …" Simon´s sentence tailed off, and not for the first time during the session he was lost in the whirlpool of his own, doubtful thoughts.

"What did you see?"

Coming back round to the conversation in hand, he answered slowly but clearly.

"It was a shape. There was a shape in the sky like a … a rugby ball, I guess. It was glowing, but not shining. It didn´t have any lights or anything like that, like some people describe when they say they´ve seen a UFO. Not like a flying saucer or anything either, but you could see it clearly. It was there in the night sky, high up above one of these sites with the stones. Then suddenly it kind of … flipped around and shot away at a speed that´s impossible for something man-made. We both saw it, my mum and me. We asked my dad and sister but they hadn´t seen anything. It wasn´t a light or a reflection on the window or anything. It was real."

"Wow, that´s an incredible experience," said Frank, seemingly enjoying listening to the tale. "So, do you believe that there are other forms of extra-terrestrial life out there?"

"Why not?" replied Simon instantly. "*We* saw something. Other

95

people say they've seen things too." Simon paused, accessing some long-forgotten memory from somewhere deep within his hippocampus. "I was watching a documentary about things like this one day and someone described something really similar. The same shaped object and the way it disappeared. I think it was even at a site of some old stones … I think. I'm not sure, but there's definitely something alive other than us … somewhere."

"Simon," just for a split second, Frank held the end of his pen between his teeth, until quickly removing it before he spoke. "I was just wondering; do you think there is something more after we die?"

"An after-life, you mean? Why not? But probably not in the sense that many people believe. I think it could be more like a … a kind of energy that we leave behind … an echo of us. I don't know. Maybe we're just energy ourselves now, and nothing, none of this," he waved an arm around gesturing at the room, "none of this is real. Maybe *we're* not real … in this form, I mean."

"These are quite existential questions, Simon. And really something that we could debate for a huge amount of time together. It's very interesting to—"

"I know you think I'm strange … people think I'm strange."

Frank was surprised by this sudden accusation. "Why do you say that?"

"People look at me and think I'm weird. They see me as different. But they're right though, I *am* different. I … I … I don't know how to explain, but I don't know who I am."

"Most people don't know who they are exactly, believe me. That's why it's a good idea to try to analyse our behaviour and that's why people come to talk to people like me to try to help them do that."

Simon wasn't listening to what Frank was saying and continued in the same vein as before.

"I don't know who I am … or even if I exist. I feel … I feel like I'm not real, or at least like the rest of the people. I sometimes feel like I'm the only one of my kind … my species. I'm alone. Like I don't belong on this planet. Like a god or an alien or something … I don't know. I look at myself in the mirror and try to communicate with the person there … but, but I don't know who I'm looking at. I'm just … an observer."

"It's very normal that you feel like this from time to time, given that you have some specific challenges to overcome; stress, anxiety … depression. These all affect your behaviour and your feelings. Look, you're now starting to identify your emotions and the moments when you have the most difficulties, and also your behaviour at these times – which is great." He smiled affectionately at Simon. "Apart from the dreams you've been having – which I have to admit are still something of an enigma at present – I think both of us are getting to understand more about who you are and the course of action that we need to take to get you better again." He frowned and let out an inadvertent *tut* sound before continuing. "You're still not keen on taking any medication, are you?"

Simon's eyes narrowed. "No, I'm not."

"OK. Would you be willing to come in and do a few more tests – physical tests? A scan, and a few other things, just to check that everything is working as it should be?" Frank asked tentatively.

"I don't want anything done to me. Nothing else," Simon replied firmly, but not angrily as he had done on the other occasions when the subject of medication had been brought up. "I'll do what you want to do here, in the sessions – talking and other things – but I don't want to do anything else. It's hard enough for me to come here. Hard enough for me to get out of bed, out of the house, speak to people, be near people. The last thing I want is for someone to start touching me and putting things on my head. Or *in* my head."

"OK. I understand," responded Frank, not wishing to upset Simon any further and undo the slim progress that they had made during the afternoon. "We'll do what we can here, together, you and me, OK?"

After his patient had left the room, Frank Newman sat at his desk, staring into space, wrapped in a blanket of thought. The afternoon sunlight was shining through the window, forming zebra-like stripes on his back as it filtered through the slats in the blind.

The beginning of spring was just a week away and although the afternoons were gradually brighter every time that Simon and Frank met for their time together, the trees on the other side of the car park were still a dull brown as they waited for warmer weather to stimulate their new foliage into action.

Frank studied his notes, every now and then transferring various scruffy sentences written during his conversations with his patient onto cleaner headed paper, which he then archived into Simon's official file. He closed both his notebook and the file and was left with a solitary, lined page in the middle of the desk. He skimmed past various bullet-pointed words and phrases on a list on the left hand side of the sheet, ceasing momentarily to either put a small tick or a cross next to each one as he went further down the items.

At the bottom of the list his pen stopped, pausing for much longer than it had previously done, as he reached the last two words he had written on the page:

Electroconvulsive therapy?

He licked his lips, pushed his glasses back up to their normal resting position and thought long and hard, before finally flicking his wrist swiftly from left to right and eliminating this last remaining, controversial option with one final, decisive swish of his biro.

9

"My god, Simon! What happened to you?"

"I fell." He sat down, head covered by the hood of his black sweatshirt, hands thrust deep into the one large pocket at the front of the garment.

"Down the stairs," he added, before pre-empting Frank´s subsequent inquisitiveness. "I was sleepwalking and fell down the stairs and, umm, got this."

Pulling back his head covering, he revealed the full extent of the injury he had sustained the previous evening.

"That´s some shiner you´ve got there. Ouch. It looks really painful," Frank said, letting out a short whistle, sounding much like a schoolboy admiring his friend´s playground scrapes and bruises. "What happened exactly?"

Simon looked at Frank through the one eye that he could still open properly. The other – now a bright, purplish-black colour – had been forced closed by the swelling around, and especially below the orbit. Weeping unintentionally, the clear, salty liquid was channelled into the inner corner of his eye until the accumulative weight of the droplets sent a tear cascading down over the new orography of his face and then into the ever-growing forest of his beard.

"I don´t really know. I was sleepwalking, apparently, and went into my mum and dad´s bedroom. They told me that I just stood there and said, '*Hello, my name´s Simon*' and then headed back to my room. But then they heard a thud … and then more thuds, as I fell down the stairs. My bedroom door´s next to the top of them, so I must´ve turned a bit too early and, umm, ended up at the bottom."

Frank raised his eyebrows, opening up his face in what came

across as unfeigned surprise at what he'd just heard. "Well, it's really lucky you didn't do yourself any more damage – apart from that." He pointed a finger at Simon's face. "But it looks pretty bad anyway."

Simon shrugged his shoulders as if his black eye and swollen cheekbone were the least of his worries.

"Do you remember any of this? When you were sleepwalking?"

"No, nothing. I just remember waking up at the bottom of the stairs. Someone switched a light on and then mum was screaming, and then I felt the pain start to creep into my face. I, I must've hit my head on the bannister or something on the way down."

Frank squirmed as Simon roughly fingered the fresh injury while he spoke. "I don't remember anything else, but my parents said I'd been yelling in my sleep earlier in the night, but of course I don't remember anything about that either." Anticipating again Frank's next question, he added, "Or even what I was dreaming about."

"Do you often sleepwalk or was this the first time it's happened?" Frank enquired.

Simon looked a little embarrassed. "I've, umm, pissed … you know, urinated in a few places before without knowing or remembering what I was doing. A wardrobe, on a chair … so I guess I must've sleepwalked … sleptwalked before. Yes."

"Well, if you could keep a note of when, or if, you do again – I mean, if you sleepwalk – and write down anything that you remember about the experience; any dreams, any stresses or worries that you have before you go to sleep? That way we could see if anything might be affecting you and your sleeping patterns directly."

"OK … more homework," Simon said humourlessly.

"Yes, kind of. Were you worried about anything before you went to sleep last night? Or during the day?"

"Nothing out of the ordinary … the usual … you know. I don't feel great, and you know the things that I'm feeling and thinking about right now. But no, nothing particularly special."

"Sure." Frank brought the end of his biro up to the corner of his mouth and placed it between his teeth – an unconscious habit that had started to become commonplace during his sessions with Simon – before quickly retracting the pen as he realised what he was doing. "OK. Today, I'd like us to work on something else that I think will help you relax and hopefully let you cope better with your stressful situations when they arise – much in the same way as the relaxation session we did. Funnily enough, it's something that you mentioned to me a few weeks ago. Something that you brought up, actually."

"Hypnosis," said Simon unemotionally.

"Yes, exactly," Frank answered, despite not having been presented with a question of any sorts. "Would you be OK with doing that today?"

"What choice do I have?" Simon responded. It was unclear if this was an attempt at irony, but the result of the combination of his words and flat intonation in which he spoke, in effect, instead left him sounding somewhat defeated.

"Actually, everything we do is up to you. You're in control of your actions and your decisions and, therefore, what we ultimately do here," explained Frank, as though by rote, these words having been repeated a thousand times past.

"OK." Simon got up out of his chair quickly and went over to the couch, as if procrastinating any longer would end up with him changing his mind. "Let's do it."

As Simon lay down, Frank moved himself from behind his old desk to his favoured location in the middle of the room to the right of his patient, as he had done the last time Simon was reclining before him.

"Now, just relax there and make yourself comfortable. Just breathe normally, OK?"

"OK."

"Close your eyes now. We´re just going to see how you react to a bit of gentle hypnosis. I won´t make you ride a horse or anything," Frank joked – rather inappropriately at this present moment – to his impassive patient, before quickly returning to the more serious and calm manner he normally adopted during treatment.

"You won´t be in a very deep state," he continued, looking a shade awkward after his previous comment, "and remember, that at any time in the session you can just tell me if you want to stop, or simply raise a hand … just indicate to me that you don´t want to continue. If you understand, nod your head."

Simon nodded silently.

"OK, we´re going to relax ourselves into a state of calm tranquillity. I´d like you to take two deep breaths. Breathe in … and out … in … out. Good. You´re feeling more relaxed now. Are you in any discomfort or pain? You can speak."

"My back hurts. It always hurts," Simon said sleepily.

"You can move. Change your position and get comfortable if you need to … good. I want you to focus on the pain … the pain in your back. Now, breathe in and out again two or three times … deep breaths, and focus on the pain. Just the pain and where it is in your body."

Frank watched as Simon´s chest inflated and deflated with every breath he took.

"Notice how the pain is disappearing, little by little." Frank observed Simon´s face for some seconds, judging when would be appropriate to continue. "Is it still there?"

"Yes."

"Is it better or worse?"

"It's ... better. Still there ... but better."

"Good. Keep focusing on the pain and your breathing. When it feels even better still – when there's less pain – just nod your head."

Simon breathed in and out several more times before, at last, nodding.

"That's good. Now, concentrate a little on the other parts of your body, like in the relaxation we did, and let everything loosen up a bit more. Let all the stress and tension go from your head ... face ... neck ... shoulders ... stomach ... legs ... feet. Everything is starting to feel more relaxed now."

Another teardrop ran down Simon's right cheek towards his ear before it was halted in the tangle of his thick sideburn. He appeared relaxed. Sleeping.

"Now, I would like you to raise both of your arms up vertically above your chest, palms towards each other. Good. A bit straighter ... OK. Now imagine that there are magnets on both of your palms and that they are slowly, but surely, being pulled together. Good. When they touch each other, you can feel the force of the magnets pulling them closer, even more tightly. Relax your shoulders. It's just your hands being drawn together more and more. Now, relax your arms, and let them fall down next to your body ... that's it. Relax your fingers too."

Simon duly followed the monotonous, dulcet instructions that were given to him as he slipped into the semi-hypnotic state induced by his psychologist.

"Just nod for affirmative when you're ready. Are you feeling well? Feeling relaxed?" Frank asked, almost inaudibly.

His patient moved his head.

"Good. Now, you're going to use the power of your imagination. I'd like you to image that you're in a forest – a huge forest – with nothing else but tall trees all around you and the canopy above your head. You can see yourself and feel yourself walking through the forest."

Frank paused for a moment and looked at Simon´s features. Although barely noticeable, his undamaged eye – albeit closed – appeared to flinch, like someone suffering the short, sharp pain from the needle of a syringe.

"Are you in the forest now, Simon?"

He nodded.

"In front of you are some stairs. They lead downwards. Can you see the stairs?"

Again Simon nodded.

"I´d like you to approach the stairs and stand at the top. There are five steps. Take a step down to the first one, and stop there. Feel the step under your foot … it feels solid. You feel good … relaxed. You can feel all the tension leaving your body. Step down with your other foot and notice how what´s left of the tension is disappearing as you stand on each step. Now … take another step down to the next one. Each time you´re feeling more and more relaxed walking down these stairs and stopping and getting rid of all your stress as you go down."

Frank repeated the process for the remaining steps, all the time using the identical soothing tone he´d been using throughout the hypnosis thus far.

"You´re at the bottom of the steps now, Simon. You feel good … you feel relaxed. Take a couple of deep breaths, and feel yourself standing there. You´re feeling strong, full of positive energy, but relaxed … Good."

Again Frank watched Simon breathe in and out deeply, this time transfixed by the image of the angel in the centre of his sweatshirt. There was something grotesquely beautiful about her skinless, womanly figure as her exposed sinews and muscles moved in time with Simon´s breathing.

"Now, I´d like you to imagine that you´re in a comfortable place – a happy place. Somewhere that you like being. A place, maybe, with pleasant memories for you. It could be outside in the nature, or somewhere indoors. Just a place where you feel very well, happy, and like spending time. Just nod your head when you´ve thought of that place."

Frank stood barely a metre away from Simon, his left arm folded across his diaphragm, and his hand nestling in the crook of the elbow of his opposite arm. The index finger of his right hand diagonally covered half his mouth, forming a V-shape with his thumb, which was gently stroking the junction between chin and jaw as he contemplated his patient and waited for a response. Simon remained silent for more than a minute.

"Have you thought of somewhere?" Frank finally decided to ask, breaking the deadlock.

Simon shook his head drowsily from side to side.

"That´s OK, take your time. Just nod when you are in that happy and comfortable place."

Another pair of minutes passed as Simon lay on Frank´s couch. Two minutes which seemed to encapsulate Simon´s state of mind. Two minutes, which despite being in a condition of relaxation and under the effects of Frank´s hypnotic technique, bore witness to the unhappiness that surrounded the young man´s life as he struggled to find comfort in even the happiest corners of his imagination. Two minutes – that for both patient and therapist alike – stretched eternally onwards in disturbing silence.

Eventually, Simon nodded.

With evident relief washing over Frank´s face, he continued. "OK. Look around and take in the place in which you find yourself; the sights, the sounds – the smells maybe. Enjoy being there. Enjoy your surroundings and the feeling of happiness, joy and safety that you're experiencing by being in this place of yours. You feel comfortable, relaxed and very well here. Take two deep breaths and breathe in the essence of this place and how it makes you feel … Good."

After several minutes of allowing Simon to escape into the inner realms of his mind, Frank commenced his discourse once more.

"OK. You're going to leave this place now – but you won't forget it. You won't forget being in this place and how well you felt while you were standing here. Turn around. You can see the steps again, this time leading upwards … walk towards them. When you reach them, put your foot on the first step. Now, the other foot, and notice how each step you take you're starting to feel more awake, you're getting more feeling back in your legs, and as you climb each step – as you put your feet on each one – you'll notice how you can feel the rest of your body waking up, gaining in energy, little by little … Good."

Frank gave Simon enough time to mentally retrace his route up the steps.

"When you reach the top, you'll find yourself back in the forest again. Start walking through the forest and the trees around you and feel your body start to come back to life. You can move your arms and legs now slightly, if you wish, to get ready to wake up completely. Good. Now, whenever you're ready, you can open your eyes."

Simon – who had been adjusting the position of his legs and moving his hands in small circles, causing faint clicking sounds as his tendons rubbed against the bones in his wrists – slowly opened his eyes. He blinked at the light of the consulting room, the pupil of his left eye contracting, stealing space from his hazelnut iris. To the right of his face, a thin, dark line between pillows of swollen flesh was virtually all that was visible between the puffy, bruised eyelids of his sleepwalking injury.

"You can get up now, carefully. Just sit on the edge for a moment before raising yourself." Frank made his way again around to the other side of his desk, quickly putting the familiar barrier of wood and leather between them. Simon gingerly rose and walked the two steps needed to take his own seat again.

"How was that?" asked Frank.

Simon looked tired but relaxed. Nodding, he replied, "OK … I think."

"And how do you feel now?"

"Fine, I guess. Sleepy … drowsy … but, OK."

"Did you feel that you could stop the activity when you wanted?"

"Yes, I did. I felt, I felt like I could move, move my position if I wanted. I wasn´t completely out of it. I could hear other things, some cars outside … the phone ring there." He waved a hand in the general direction of the door.

"Did they distract you?"

"I don´t know … I don´t think so. I think maybe the only thing that was distracting me really was probably my own mind … things were running through my head and it was really difficult for me to relax. My heart was, was beating quite fast too, at first."

"When that happens, I want you to focus on the heartbeat … *your* heartbeat. Listen to it, notice how strong it is, and then breathe in and out a few times while concentrating on your heart – nothing else. You´ll notice that by isolating and focusing on the sound of it and feeling it beat, it will slow down and you´ll feel more relaxed – as we did with the pain in your back. That was better, wasn´t it?"

"I suppose so … but it was difficult. I feel OK now, but it wasn´t easy to imagine things."

Frank looked enquiringly at Simon, his head angled a fraction of a degree to his left.

"What exactly did you find difficult?"

"The forest. I saw myself in a forest … but, but it was burning … on fire. The trees were diseased and sick there. The stairs too, black and rotting. They were, kind of steps down into hell – or something like that. I don´t know … it´s like everything I imagine. If I try to think of a mountain, it turns into an erupting volcano that wipes out entire villages below … a river becomes dry and polluted with the bones of dead animals in it. If, if I imagine myself on holiday, the plane crashes before I arrive or there´s a tsunami when I´m there. When I see myself walking on a beach, the sand turns into human skulls and bones that I have to step on to escape. It´s, it´s just awful sometimes … my thoughts."

"You´ve got an extremely vivid imagination, indeed. I really think that if you can see these things so clearly in your mind, you should be able to imagine just the opposite, with a little training; a different forest, a different beach. What about the place you imaged being in? The happy place."

Simon frowned and shook his head. "I couldn´t think of anywhere … really I couldn´t imagine or think of anywhere that is happy for me, or has been happy for me. Or at least happy in the true sense of the word. I don´t know why. So … so I kind of invented a place, eventually. More to kind of keep, you know, things moving along. I, I felt pressure to decide … to tell you something. So, I kind of lied to myself … fooled myself that this was my happy place."

"That´s absolutely fine to do that. Using your imagination to help you is a tried and tested technique in fact. How did you feel when you were there?"

Simon thought for a few moments – frowning – a confused look on his face. Before answering, his expression gradually changed and there appeared to be a different hue to his complexion, his remaining fully-functioning eye widened, the convex reflection of the window behind Frank visible in its dark centre.

"I … I suppose, not so sad … I guess."

"Happy?" Frank ventured.

"Umm … I guess."

"That's great, Simon. It really is," said Frank, smiling and wearing a satisfied look on his face, clearly content at how this first session of hypnosis had gone and noticeably relieved that his patient was starting to benefit from the time spent in therapy.

"You see. You have the power to control things. To change your thoughts, feelings and emotions – and in turn – your behaviour."

"I don't know." Simon appeared doubtful – crestfallen even – the momentary relief of the sanctuary of his imaginary safe haven fading away fast. "It's, it's just the pain of living that's the problem. It's, it's like a … a noose around my neck."

As these final words settled upon Frank, burning their acidic etymology into his soul, they seemed to shatter his fragile revelry and plunge him into another place and time far from his consulting room. It was hard to read behind those pale, grey eyes shielded by the thick lenses of his glasses, but there was something there; a shadow of sorrow, diffused with grief, that suddenly changed what should have been the final, congratulatory moments of a landmark session between psychologist and patient, into something more melancholic, sombre and chastening altogether.

10

Despite the cold, wet winter having given way to early spring, little evidence of the change of season could be seen through Frank Newman's consulting room window on another damp, grey afternoon. On the grass verge next to the car park, daffodils strained their necks in search of the sun that would allow them to display their bright-yellow trumpet heads and give visitors to the clinic hope of warmer days ahead. Apart from these narcissistic precursors of the annual bloom of colour that was soon to fill the dull gaps in the landscape as the days lengthened, the flora was otherwise unchanged from previous weeks; the buds of the tall trees still far too small to be seen from Frank's vantage point on the west side of the building.

Simon entered the room on the stroke of his appointment's given hour and quickly strode across the space that separated the door from his chair, without stopping to take his coat off on the way.

Frank met him with a hopeful grin. "Afternoon, Simon. How are things with you today?"

"OK … Good I think," was Simon's breathless response, his face tinged with colour as if he had been walking at pace to be on time for his weekly meeting.

Surprised at hearing this rare slice of positivity from his patient, Frank's smile grew wider and small crow's feet appeared at the corners of his ashen eyes.

"Excellent. That's really good to hear," he said avidly. "Can you tell me about your week? What you've been up to?"

Simon paused for a moment. The expression he wore was something new to these now familiar surroundings. The corners of his normally downturned mouth – although not forming what could be described as a smile – were more horizontal today, creating a look of passive neutrality on his young face; if not in stark contrast to the exhausted, hangdog appearance of recent weeks, it was at least a welcome change for Frank to see all the same. The large bags under his eyes were still very much apparent, but he looked more awake and more confident in himself. His complexion carried its habitual unhealthy aspect, not helped by the colours of the bruising around his eye that had now blended into a mix of shades of purple and yellow. However, there was something to his skin that made it look more supple – younger even – and an aura of supressed vitality inexplicably surrounded him.

"Well, it wasn´t actually what I´d call *good*. I´ve had a few – you know – bad moments, difficult moments, and I´m not sleeping well, of course. But I´ve been trying to use some of the things we´ve been looking at here … things we´ve done together."

Simon reached into the inside pocket of his coat and pulled out a crumpled, but neatly-folded piece of paper. Starting to look a little unsure of himself, he unfolded the sheet and placed it on the central, leather-covered section of the desk.

"I, I wrote down some of the feelings I´ve had when I felt bad … negative things."

"That´s great to hear, well done. Thank you for doing that. Would you like to tell—"

"No, no, no, no, no," Simon interrupted rapidly but softly, "I´d prefer it if you read it, you know, not here with me. It was hard to write them down … and, umm, I don´t really want talk about it now. Sorry."

"That´s quite alright. No problem." Making every effort not to glance at what had been scrawled on the page, Frank clasped the sheet between his thumb and index finger, before placing it carefully to one side of the desk away from temptation along with various other documents that he had been consulting before the session commenced.

"Have you done anything else this week? Anything different from other weeks?" Frank asked, staring fixedly at Simon, ignoring, with some effort, the short list of words he had just been handed.

"I … I haven't been to school. We only have a few classes anyway now, so it's not a big deal. But, but, I've been out a couple of times … walking. Going for a walk."

"That's wonderful," enthused Frank. "And how did you feel?"

"It was a bit hard to be honest. I … I had the impression that people were watching me and saying things about me as they walked past. Talking about me and laughing about me. *Judging* me." There was venom in his voice as he pronounced these final words.

Frank was ready with one of his stock questions. "Can I just ask if you know these people that you think are doing this?" he enquired, trying subtly to guide his patient towards rebutting his own belief.

Simon thought about the question, concentration etched on his face as his mind fought an internal battle between his intrusive thoughts and the logic being presented to him.

"No, I don't," he answered flatly.

"Then, what reason do you have for them to judge you and make fun of you if you have no idea who they are, and vice versa?"

Simon grimaced and answered, "There's no reason why I think this … I just do. I don't know why."

"Then, we need to go back to the question we've asked ourselves before. Is it a *fact* that these people are judging you?" Frank held out his hands, palms facing upwards as he beckoned his patient to search for a response to the question. "We both know the answer to this, don't we?"

Simon let out a stream of air through his nose and made several very small nods with his head as he grudgingly accepted the reasoning presented to him.

"Look, the next time you go out for a walk, when you get to a place with people and you have to pass someone on the street, find somewhere to stop before you continue. Stop and observe the people around you; you´ll see that they don´t care about you – in a good way – and they have their own issues to deal with. Observe and notice how they´re just interested in what they´re doing themselves or who they´re talking to. You´ll see that nobody is watching you or commenting to anyone about you, they´re just going about their own business." Frank now pressed his palms together, his forearms supported by the wooden edge of the desk. "But you stayed out. You carried on walking, didn´t you?"

"Yes. For a bit."

Frank looked pleased at Simon´s achievement. "Well done. It´s very good to hear you´ve been able to do that."

Simon shrugged his shoulders and let out a puff of air from between his lips. "It was OK – the walking. It, it gave me a chance to move around a bit ... to think."

"What did you think about Simon?" Frank asked, a little dubiously.

"I don´t know really. My thoughts all kind of merge into one another and one thought then opens another thought up, like a chain that I can´t stop. It´s, it´s chaos. If I see something, then my thoughts change and something in my mind triggers something else and what I´ve been thinking about before just ... disappears or becomes twisted in my head."

"Well, as far as I´m concerned, it´s extremely positive that you´ve been getting exercise. It really is." Frank´s pause clearly indicated that his next sentence would somehow contrast his previous words. "Just a quick thought though. The walking may be an activity that, although is really good for the body, could lead you to become more introspective due its mechanical nature. It may make you go round in circles in your mind about things." Another pause punctuated the discourse, in which Frank searched for a way to steer the conversation away from ground that had already been covered. "Have you thought about walking with a friend, so maybe you could chat about something while exercising together?" he finally suggested.

Simon shook his head. "I prefer to do these things alone."

"OK ... what about listening to something while you're walking? Some music, or a spoken book cassette or something like that to keep your mind occupied with something else? Have you got one of those, umm, Walkmans?"

"A Discman. I've got a Discman."

"Great. Maybe that's something you could try to do?"

While Simon was nodding his head in response, his eyes were drawn suddenly to something outside the window behind his psychologist. He brought his hand up to his right temple, before quickly withdrawing it from sight, apparently self-conscious about his inadvertent reaction. Frank sat back in his chair, a puzzled look on his face.

"What was that, Simon? What did you just do, if you don't mind me asking?"

Having already shared some of his deepest secrets, thoughts and desires with his weekly confidant, Simon appeared to see no other recourse than give in to the probing nature of his therapist.

"I ... umm, saluted. I saluted a magpie." He looked embarrassed about his admission.

"And why did you do that?"

Looking completely cornered by Frank's unremitting interrogation, Simon responded, "For luck ... to, you know, prevent bad luck."

"Are you very superstitious?"

A deep intake of breath. "Well, I don't know. Maybe in comparison to other people, I guess … I could be."

"Could you tell me what other things you do?"

Simon smiled in self-deprecation but dived into the deep end with his confession just the same.

"I cross my fingers when I go somewhere. Flying … when a plane takes off. I touch wood, or paper if there's no wood around. I, I don't step on cracks on the pavement. I don't walk under ladders. I throw salt over my shoulder if I spill some. I don't know which shoulder is the right one, but I do it anyway. I get nervous if a black cat walks in front of me … things like that. I, I know it's strange."

"And why do you think you do all these things, Simon?"

He looked down diagonally at the floor in front of his right boot and sighed, appearing to realise as he was speaking how illogical all this sounded. "To stop bad things happening to me. Like I said, the bad luck. Bad things."

"Can you remember if anything untoward has happened to you if you didn't do these things?"

Simon spoke in a low, subdued manner, forcing Frank to learn forward so as to hear him properly. "I know, I know it's crazy and, and I don't know why I do these things or where I got them from but … but it's like they're part of me now. Part of who I am."

"There's nothing intrinsically wrong with believing in something like that. The world is full of superstitions; different cultures believe in certain things and they are often part of the general belief of many societies and peoples. What may appear irrational to someone in one part of the world, is a commonplace idea very much within cultural norms in another; mostly it's linked to religion, which I don't think is your case, is it?"

Simon shook his head effusively.

"It's OK to believe in something. Lots of people do and many carry things like lucky charms with them, for instance, to an exam or to a competition for good luck. They're not seen as crazy, are they? The important thing is not to let it take over your life or prevent you from doing something."

Frank broke off from his speech in order to give Simon the opportunity to interject if he so wished. As no comment was forthcoming, he picked up where he had left off.

"Do you really believe with all the safety procedures that modern aviation has these days that you'll prevent a crash because you have your fingers crossed? I'm not making fun of what you believe, Simon, but I'd like you to think things through logically, step by step."

Simon sheepishly looked back at Frank.

"Let's try to do something about this. Let's take one of your superstitions. One of your actions – the saluting, for instance. Try not to do anything when you see a magpie next time. Just let it fly by and don't think about anything other than the fact that it's a bird. That's all. You can make a note of what happens to you afterwards, but don't go looking for consequences of not saluting. If something is going to happen, it will. It's destined to happen, despite what we think, magpie or not. OK?"

"Yeah ... it makes sense, I suppose ... I'll try."

"Good. This is something that may well help you in other situations too. Situations in which you worry that something bad will happen. One thing we – you – can do, is try to predict what's going to happen beforehand and then see if this actually occurs or not. You can use phrases like: *if I do that, then something or other will happen* ... or *what if* questions, and then test the hypotheses in order to see if your thoughts – and your fears – are in line with reality. How about that?"

A look of mistrust had come over Simon´s face. "Again … I´ll try," he said through what appeared to be gritted teeth.

Frank picked up the small pile of papers that was on his desk and slipped the page that Simon had given him earlier into the middle of the stack. He pivoted the sheets so that they were facing his chest, before loosening his grip to allow them to fall neatly into place with the aid of the horizontal surface of his desk. He patted the vertical sides to finish the alignment and then inserted them into the cardboard file that had previously been hidden beneath the documents.

He smiled as he spoke. "Well, I think it would be a good idea to crack on from where we left off last week … with the hypnosis."

"Another one?" Simon asked, looking a little worried by the sudden introduction of the idea, his face at once becoming flushed. He pulled at the neck of his sweatshirt as if the room were rapidly becoming stifling hot, and then fought to take off his coat as quickly as possible, leaving it crumpled on the back of his chair with both arms inside out.

"If we can, yes. I think that it went so well during the last session that we could carry on and complement it with another one this week. Strike while the iron´s hot, if you like."

Simon appeared to have calmed down, his face returning slowly to its normal colour, although his neck still bore the reddened traces of his extreme nervousness. "Umm, OK … I guess."

"So, just pop up onto the couch again as you did last time, and make yourself comfortable."

The same stages as the previous week were repeated; Simon lying down, eyes closed, and Frank standing in the middle of the room instructing his patient using his soft, hypnotic monotone. The same process of relaxation was followed, the same tall trees walked through, and the same stairs descended during this second round of hypnotherapy. When – in his mind's eye – Simon was standing at the bottom of the stairs, the rubric changed.

"Now, I'd like you to think about a place and an experience that was very hard for you to live through. A time when you were feeling anxious, stressed and negative about yourself; a difficult moment in your life. Just nod your head when you've thought of this experience."

Despite a foreseeable pause, Simon nodded in a fraction of the time it took him to mentally recreate a requested scene the last time he was lying on the couch.

"I'd like you to imagine you're there, at that time. At the same moment you felt this stress. Reliving this moment, OK?"

Simon nodded.

"OK, good. I'm going to ask you some questions now, and you can answer me using your voice, OK?"

Simon nodded and replied sluggishly, "OK."

"Can you tell me where you are?"

"I'm at school." Simon spoke very quietly but loud enough for Frank – who was standing less than a metre from him – to hear.

"What's happening around you? Can you describe the situation?"

There was another pause as Simon interiorised the scene before he spoke. "I'm in the school hall … in an exam. At the front of the room, by the stage."

"How do you feel?"

"Really bad. Nervous. It's quiet … too quiet. All the people are behind me … and they're looking at me … at my back. I can't concentrate on the exam. The words are kind of, jumbled, and moving in front of my eyes. I … I can hear my stomach growl … I need to go to the toilet. I know everyone is laughing at me … looking at me and thinking about me."

"Is anything else happening?"

"Yes. I'm hot ... sweating and can't breathe, so ... so I put my hand up and ask to go to the toilet. The whole school's looking at me as I go out. I can hardly walk ... my legs are weak ... like rubber."

Simon paused, his breathing had started to become more shallow as he relived the traumatic experience in the unforgiving school hall.

"Go on," Frank said encouragingly.

"I go to the toilet ... stay there for ages."

"How are you feeling there?"

"Terrible. Like I can't do anything ... can't face the situation. I curl up in a ball on the floor of the cubicle for a few minutes ... it's dirty and wet. Someone comes into the toilet and asks me if I'm OK. I can't remember what I said. I just ... just grunted something ... not words. I feel ... I feel like I want to die ... and I want all the others to die too." A certain degree of hostility had crept into his voice. "I want to ... to shoot them all. I imagine going back into the hall and killing everyone."

"OK. I'd like you to imagine that you're still in the toilet, still there. Take a very deep breath ... good ... and as you let it out, I want you to imagine that you're exhaling something black. A black cloud ... good. This is all your negativity, the fear, and all the bad feelings that you have inside you; all the emotional pain you're feeling. Breathe in again, and as you breathe out, you can see all the black air ... the stress and anxiety and bad thoughts leaving your body ... good ... that's it. Can you see the black air leaving your body, Simon?"

He nodded.

"OK. I want you to leave the toilet and walk calmly back to your chair in the hall, alright?"

More than a minute passed as Simon lay in silence.

"Where are you now?"

"Back in the hall … at my desk."

"How do you feel?"

"Like I want to go … I want this to finish as soon as possible."

"But you're there. You haven't left. Are you finishing the exam?"

"Yes … but badly … I just want to go," he whined. "I'm looking at the clock all the time … counting the minutes."

"You're doing really well … you're overcoming your nerves. Finish the exam Simon, and when you've finished, stand up and leave the hall calmly, feeling good about yourself and what you've just achieved. Just nod when you're done."

Again there was a pause – this time much longer – as Simon imagined the last few moments of his purgatory in the school hall. Eventually, he nodded as instructed.

"As you leave the hall, in front of you, you see the same stairs that you walked down earlier. Climb those stairs, and each time you take a step, just stop for a moment, breathe in and out deeply to make sure that any remaining black air – the negativity and anxiety – leaves your body for good."

Simon retraced his steps, pausing and breathing deeply as instructed, returning to the forest again. After mirroring the final stages of the first hypnosis, he found himself back in his chair, rubbing his eyes as if waking from a heavy sleep.

"How was that?" Frank asked.

"It … it was, OK. Different."

"How so?"

"At school … during the exam. I, I didn't finish. I mean … I couldn't go on. I had to sit outside the hall on my own to finish."

"OK. Well this time you did. You were capable of regaining confidence in yourself and you were able to continue. Well done."

"But it's not *real*," remonstrated Simon.

"How did it feel to you when you were there, just now?"

Simon played back events in his mind. "I don´t know. I guess … I guess it felt quite, quite similar to when I was there … I suppose. Like I was there again … the same feelings and everything."

"Then this demonstrates that you can overcome these kinds of difficulties. These difficult moments. You have the ability to do this – *you* Simon. I suggested, guided you a little, but you were the one who managed to get back on track and pull through this situation. You should feel very proud of yourself."

"I don´t know." Simon looked uncomfortable with the praise directed at him and confused about the therapeutic methods he was being subjected to.

"I really think we´ve identified one of the moments that is causing you great stress in situations with other people; we´ve found one of the possible roots of your social anxiety, if you like. Knowing this, we can deal with these moments better and use what works for you. You can do this in real life too. Just use the same techniques, and remember how you managed to succeed during this difficult moment, OK?"

Simon breathed in heavily. "OK … I´ll try." He breathed out loudly and looked at the clock, as he had done moments earlier during the re-enactment of the afternoon of the exam.

Smiling, Frank reached down to his right, opened one of the drawers, and took out a leather-bound diary.

"OK …" He pulled on the silky thread protruding from the bottom of the book and opened it up to the place where he had last made an entry. He thumbed through a few more pages and then let it fall open at the start of week number fourteen.

"Just to let you know that I´ll be away for the next couple of weeks." He looked down at the diary and continued speaking. "Next week is Easter, so we´ll see each other again …" he flicked though a few more pages, "on the nineteenth?"

"OK, sure," responded Simon, willing at this moment to accept any suggestion made, without complaint.

Frank placed the diary back in the drawer and closed it noiselessly.

"Are you doing anything nice?"

Frank looked back at Simon, failing to conceal the surprise at hearing the young man in front of him ask such a personal question. "Umm … not especially," he replied. "I´m going to see my sister, up in Wiltshire – take her an egg, hot cross buns, usual things. I can´t stay too long as I have to get back for the cat. And, then probably for the rest of the time, just stay at home. Try to sort the garden out a little bit for summer – if we get one. I´ve got some reading I´d like to get on with too. Nothing so exciting … but thanks for asking."

"That´s OK," Simon said, raising his shoulders a little as he spoke.

"What about you?" Frank dared to ask.

"Umm, not much, I guess. Catch up on some school work … if I can."

"Great, that´s good to hear. Maybe, if you get some time, you could also try to do some of the activities we´ve spoken about doing before? And possibly – you know – get out and about a bit more." Without giving Simon the chance to dismiss the suggestion, Frank continued contentedly, "Anyway, we´ll see each other again in a couple of weeks and you can fill me in on what you´ve been up to. And Simon?"

Frank´s gaze was met by a suspicious look from his patient.

"Keep up the good work."

11.

The door of Frank's consulting room swung inwards as the psychologist breached the threshold of his workplace, arriving with time enough to prepare himself for another day counselling those in need of guidance. Another day in which he would delve into the idiosyncrasies of the behavioural clusters of the various patients he was due to see over the coming hours.

Humming a melody in the key of A minor, Frank unhooked the calendar from the wall, turned it round to reveal a new month and model, before hanging it back up again on the small brass hook that held it in place. He then skirted quickly around the side of his desk into therapist territory, scooped up the small amount of post that had been left for him and placed his rather battered-looking brown leather bag onto the desktop, slipping off the padded strap that was clinging to his shoulder in the process.

With the correspondence tossed to one side, he unfastened each of the metal buckles on the front of the satchel and pulled out a shiny, silver thermos flask. He took off the drinking cup, unscrewed the inner cap, and poured a steaming, light-brown liquid into the vessel in front of him. He then turned on the transistor radio and sat back in his chair to enjoy his hot drink.

A burst of guitar fire and a woman's husky voice met his ears; half-singing, half-screaming, nearly off-key, but with a passion that made Frank glance towards the radio – as if by looking at the small, round holes in the speaker he could imagine who was behind the lyrics.

As she sang, a familiar, gravelly voice could be heard in the background faintly echoing the woman's.

Frank sat there, enjoying the atmosphere of quietude that he had created; this precious time he needed in order to steel himself for what the day ahead could throw at him.

The phone rang, curtailing this moment of reflection and drowning out both guitars and vocalist alike. He turned off the radio and stared at the ringing phone, clearly aware that its tone indicated it was an external call coming in directly to his extension. He picked it up.

"Hello?"

There was no answer. Frank could hear the sound of traffic in the background and the caller´s irregular breathing down the line.

"Simon? Is that you?"

The same hum of traffic, but the breathing could no longer be heard. Frank waited, listening patiently for a few moments, before muffled sounds punctuated the rush hour soundtrack as the caller moved the phone closer to their mouth. Once again, laboured breathing was audible. Frank clumsily stabbed at a few buttons until he found the one that allowed the background noise of the unsolicited call to be heard throughout the room, freeing his hands to grab his notebook and biro.

"Yes … it´s me," Simon eventually said quietly. His voice sounded metallic and distant amplified through the compact, square speaker on the device.

"Are you OK?"

"Not really. Sorry for calling you."

"That´s perfectly alright. I´m glad you did. Where are you?" asked Frank anxiously.

"On the street … near my house."

There was a loud clunking as coins were inserted into the payphone and dropped heavily into the cavity deep inside the machine.

"What are you doing there, Simon?"

There was a long pause before the next words were heard.

"I ... I couldn't be at home. I didn't know what to do ... what I would have done if I'd stayed there."

"Have you hurt yourself? Do you need help?" Frank asked directly.

"No. But ... I nearly ..." his words tapered off.

"I'm here for you if you want to tell me about what happened, OK? You know that, don't you?" added Frank reassuringly.

"Yes," Simon replied after hesitating for some seconds more. "That's why I'm calling ... I, I don't know what else to do ... I—" He was interrupted by a succession of stubbornly repetitive beeps as the phone begged to be fed more money.

"Simon. I want you to come here now, OK? Get in a taxi and come straight here – don't worry about paying, we'll sort that out. Just come straight here and we'll talk these things through, OK?"

There was a long, flat tone as the line went dead. And then ... nothing.

***

Frank waited nervously to see if Simon would arrive, occasionally rising from his seat and pacing around the room, stopping to adjust the angle of the backrest on the couch and moving his patient's chair several times until he found the position that he considered to be just right for him. A white Styrofoam cup was a new addition on his desk, neatly lined up in descending size order next to the shiny thermos flask and Frank's own drinking receptacle. He sat back down and shuffled some papers in an attempt to occupy his hands, which he would otherwise be wringing if they were not tasked with some other duty.

The phone burst into life again; this time with the unmistakeable tone of an internal call from reception.

"Yes ... OK, thank you." He placed the receiver gently back in its cradle, raked his fingers through his thinning hair and put on the most encouraging – yet serious – face he could manage.

A soft knocking on the door followed a few moments later.

"Come in." Frank´s voice sounded hoarse. He cleared his throat as Simon walked into the room.

Frank had never seen his patient look the way he did this morning. The burden of the sleepless nights and perceived guilt that he carried throughout not only his nightmares, but also his waking hours, was there for all to see. His regular scruffy, but predominantly clean appearance, was now superseded by the look of someone who had been sleeping rough for days on end. The knees of his faded jeans were covered with dirt and his fingernails were clogged with something black. There were patches of an anonymous, thick liquid that had solidified into crusty, light-coloured stains splattered all over his sweatshirt and his boots were laden with sandy-coloured mud that matched the colour of the marks on his trousers. The bags under his eyes reached halfway down his cheeks, with the bruising acquired during his recent somnambulism mingling with the consequences of his lack of sleep to form an Arlesian palette of different shades of blues, purples and yellows that dominated the right side of his face.

Frank smiled and poured some of the contents of the thermos into the insulated white cup that had been waiting for Simon´s arrival. "Here, have some tea," he said – as if this cornerstone of the British Empire could somehow alleviate the anguish.

Simon held out his hand and took the drink without thinking. His eyes seemed to be focussed on somewhere else altogether.

"It´s good to see you. Thank you for coming here now." Frank waited, in vain, to see if Simon would bring the cup to his lips. "Can you tell me what happened?" he asked, and then took a sip of his own drink, which somehow seemed to motivate Simon to do the same.

"I didn't know what to do. I was thinking ... thinking the pain of killing myself is nothing in comparison to the pain of living with this ... these feelings. The only urge I had was to end it all ... end all the suffering I'd caused."

"What suffering do you think you've caused, Simon?" Frank asked gently.

"The deaths ... the people dying in my dreams." He winced, a painful expression lingered on his face.

"Do you want to tell me about these dreams again?"

Simon paused, a desperate look in his eyes. "Yes ... please ... I, I need to."

Holding the Styrofoam cup in both hands, with the warmth seeming now to comfort him to some extent, Simon began to recount the horrors of the previous evening.

"I remember it all so clearly ... so raw in my mind. All night I was dreaming and then waking over and over again. Finding myself in different places, flashes of different scenes ... misty hills, warm and humid, and the sounds of insects around me ... birdsong too. But the sounds changed. The birds started, like, shrieking. They were screaming, screaming at something."

Simon was sitting bent forward resting his forearms on his thighs, the tea gripped tightly between his hands, the soft plastic sides of the cup dented inwards from the tension in his fingers.

"The, the vegetation was lush all around ... tropical. The earth, the dirt under my feet, was red. In the sky, columns of storm clouds were forming and the air was like, electric ... I heard what I thought at first was thunder. But as I walked along the dirt road, I realised it was the, the crackle of gunfire in the distance.

"I walked through shanty towns. Along different dirt roads, until I was drawn down one narrow street. I tried to walk in the other direction but it was like my legs had a mind of their own and my body was being controlled by something. Some kind of force. Something powerful I couldn't see. I was ... *pulled* down this track. It was getting narrower and narrower with thick plants on each side ... no escape. I was coming to a dead end, but there was something there ... something at the end getting bigger and bigger as I got nearer. I could see that there was some sort of tree or a bush ... a large bush there, it kind of dominated everything ... but, but there was something strange about it. Something sinister. There were no leaves, but there were small, dark shapes on its branches. As I got closer I saw that they weren't leaves at all, but the bodies of small animals ... mice, tiny birds, lizards ... their tails hanging limply down as they lay there ... impaled on the bush's thorns. What did it mean? Why were they there?" he asked himself gravely, shaking his head.

"The air was misty, or smoky ... or a mix of the two. I don't know. I walked along another road. I could see some things lying all along the sides ... on both sides. They, they were bodies ... corpses ... of black people. They lined the verge, their blood running in rivers into the ditch at the side of the road ... shoes and clothes and other objects were scattered around. I came across a few people here and there moving – still alive – but they were not survivors ... they were dying of their injuries ... unaware of where they were and unaware of my presence as I walked past. I, I heard the sound of approaching vehicles ... a convoy passed, causing red dust to blow all around me and into my face and eyes. But I could see them anyway through my tears. A line of different vehicles ... cars, trucks – most of them white. I could see soldiers in uniform with red berets, pointing their rifles outwards. They looked scared ... scared of something outside. In the cars and the back of the trucks were the passengers ... they were all white, not like the dead and dying people ... everyone was white .... the people and the soldiers with red berets too. As one of the cars passed, I saw a pale, blonde woman looking out of the window. She had a look of shock and sadness – pity maybe – on her face as she stared through the dirty glass. They passed me ... and drove down the road, away from the bodies and the dying. These were the only white people I saw the whole time in this place.

"I walked through village after village, street after street and there were more and more bodies ... broken bodies ... hundreds or maybe even thousands of them. Many had huge cuts and wounds ... some with their heads cut off ... arms or legs missing ... their stomachs open and, and their guts hanging out. Others had been lucky, and had simply been shot.

"I passed burning huts, lines of wooden houses ... shacks mostly. The black, twisted skeletons of what was left of villages ... smoke hanging in the air, slowly drifting around, swirling on the breeze. The charred remains of people ... or what was left of people, lying where they'd been hacked down ... butchered. Their houses, their small huts, burnt around them after they were murdered. Other houses – better houses in more modern neighbourhoods – were destroyed and rubble and broken bricks littered the ground ... many places no more than just piles of debris. Those that were left standing had bullet holes all over the front of them or were empty shells after being burnt down. Many people were lying outside what were once their homes, blood on the dirt around their heads where they had been taken outside and executed. Some with hands tied behind their backs ... others still kneeling where they'd fallen. There were some people around ... in shock, not sure what to do ... silent, open-mouthed ... bewildered.

"One man, lying in the dirt … his head sliced open with four or five hacks of what must've been a large knife or machete … like someone had cut open a melon. The inside of his head visible. No one is alive, only the living ghosts. I walk past these scenes, through more places. Another village devastated, a few people still alive here. I'm not sure if they're from the village … more bodies on the ground. One boy, maybe two years old, naked, standing and crying over what can only be his mother, her clothes ripped from her, blood all over her stomach … terrible … injuries between her legs …"

He broke off at this point, clearly upset about what he was reliving and telling his psychologist. His eyes were full of tears, although none had succumbed to gravity and made its way down his cheeks yet. He sighed a long, sad sigh, and carried on his inexorable journey through the landscape of the slain.

"There was a river … bodies lying on the banks, goats walking among the dead. Pots and pans and other objects dotted around. The wreckage of a wooden bridge could be seen spanning the river. Bodies … people, were trapped under it. A hand bobbed up and down in the water … its owner crushed under the struts of the bridge … invisible somewhere below. Others were floating slowly along with the current … drifting away … their blood mixing with the muddy brown water. Their destination unknown.

"I walked along another road. I got closer and saw that it was impassable. I could see something blocking it ahead … bodies … bodies were blocking the route, piled up like a barricade. I had to … to walk and, and climb over them to continue."

Simon turned paler at this point and stayed quiet.

"Would you like to stop? To talk about something else?" asked Frank softly, kindly.

"No … it's OK. I want to remember this … and tell you."

Frank remained silent, waiting for his patient to continue.

131

"I walked through a grass field with trees around the edge … some, some of the trees had no leaves … just dark shapes, like the other, dead-end bush. But, but these shapes were moving … swinging in the breeze … hanging. People were hanging from the branches. I looked away. I couldn't see these … these strange trees any more. I saw a large red-brick building on the other side of the field. A church … I could see a white cross on the roof. I approached the church … its windows had been broken and its doors were splintered into pieces. One was left hanging by just a single hinge. It … it seemed impossible that it wouldn't break and fall off at any moment … Above the door there was a statue of Christ with his arms stretched out either side of his body, palms up. His clothes … his robes, hanging down from his arms. The statue was brilliant white … this, this image … this image of the white Christ was … was just so surreal above the red earth and the man who was lying, sprawled over the church's steps with a halo of blood around him, while others lay slaughtered nearby. I went inside … I knew what I'd find, but I somehow wanted to see it for myself … to confirm this … this evil."

He sighed again, ridden with grief and shock at the genocide he had been witness to.

"Piles of bodies, shot and … chopped up like meat, or with their heads smashed in. So many stacked onto one another together. Men, women … babies. I walked halfway down the aisle and then turned right through a doorway and along a corridor into a kind of annexe room. Ahead of me was a blackboard … it was a classroom. The blackboard had holes from the bullets that had been fired there … the children were wearing their beige school uniforms. I saw something move … a girl, no more than about twelve years old, shaking, sitting, hugging her knees close to her body, covered in blood but somehow unhurt … she was alive. She had a deep wound on her head and another on one of her hands. Her fingers had been cut off … but she was alive. I left her there alone. I don´t know why, but I knew she´d be fine … in the end. I left the church. Packs of dogs were starting to sniff around the people on the ground … investigating. Drawn by the smell of the blood.

"I found myself on another road. There were lines of people as far as I could see – ten or fifteen-people-wide – snaking across the countryside. Many carrying bundles on their heads, their possessions wrapped in dirty sheets or sacks. Most had nothing … shoeless. Here and there, small groups of people were resting, exhausted from their journey, in kind of makeshift camps, sheltering under the few blankets they had. Scattered among the people, steam from bowls of what little food they had had been able to find being cooked on small fires rose into the air. Babies and small children looked like they were sleeping in their mother´s arms … or maybe they´d died before they could reach their destination. Wherever that was.

"But, but from among all this, this … whatever it was, what I remember most were the eyes … empty … vacant … terrified. The deep, dark eyes of the children. I could see in the way they looked around at everything, and nothing at the same time that they had changed. That they were no longer – and never would be again – children."

12

"Thank you." Simon placed his barely-touched cup of tea on the desk.

"Not at all. I´m always here for you when you need me, Simon," Frank replied, in a tone sounding genuinely like a friend rather than a therapist.

Simon had a frightened, shell-shocked look in his eyes; the memories of the African children in his dream evidently branded freshly into his mind.

"I just needed to talk to someone right away. A person to speak to … as a distraction." Simon´s intonation rose at the end of the phrase like he was questioning himself as he spoke. "Yes … to distract me. Like you said before."

"It´s good that you remembered to do that."

"I, I just didn´t know what to do this morning. The only thing I was thinking about and was going round and round in my head was, was the urge to … to kill myself. This guilt … coping with it is terrible. That´s why … that´s why I feel like I have to end things, to feel relief. To finish with the guilt once and for all."

"Can you tell me what you did after you woke up?"

"I … I went to the bathroom … looked in the cabinet there. I was looking for pills. Something to take … to poison me." He looked angry as he spat out the last three words, the self-hate boiling inside him spilling over into the open.

"But you didn´t, of course. What happened? What did you do to stop yourself?"

"I couldn´t find any … they´d all gone." A dejected look was soon replaced with a wicked grin. "So I went to the kitchen … I normally go there to find something to hurt myself with. There was a knife on the draining board, *that* hadn't been taken away."

Frank's eyes were automatically drawn to Simon's hands and wrists, quickly looking for signs of self-punishment. "But, you didn't cut yourself, did you?" he asked, unsure of the answer he would receive, despite there being no obvious signs of any injuries.

Simon ignored the question. He slapped the inside of his left wrist hard and then held it tightly with his other hand. "I put it here … on its side. I could feel how cold the blade was. I pressed it flat onto my skin … I saw my reflection in it." He uncovered his wrist, the pale skin underneath marked by the imprint of the four fingers responsible for the blow; but otherwise it was unharmed.

"You didn't hurt yourself, Simon. And that's great," a clearly relieved Frank said. "Can I ask you what made you stop?"

A familiar, distant look manifested itself in Simon's eyes. A look that Frank had grown to be uncomfortably accustomed to while his patient told him about the gruesome details of his nightmares.

"The blood. The thought of the blood in the kitchen. I've seen so much recently, staining floors, walls, clothes. I thought, how … how it would make a mess, and someone … someone would maybe have to touch it. Someone would have to clean it up afterwards. Clean it, wipe it away, because I'd made a mess. I didn't want anyone to do that."

Simon fell quiet, staring into nothing; into a void nobody could see. "I can't go on like this," he added in a soft, childlike voice after a brief pause.

"I understand," said Frank, in the most empathetic one he could manage.

Simon suddenly snapped out of his trance.

"How *can* you understand?" he asked incredulously. "How can *you* know what I'm going through?" he hissed in a violent whisper. He challenged Frank's surprised gaze with a defiant one of his own.

It took the psychologist a few dizzy seconds to steady himself after being caught flat-footed by his desperate patient. He sucked in a deep breath, closing his eyes while doing so, and then exhaled slowly. He opened up his eyes again; eyes that suddenly burned with emotion, and said in a slow, firm voice, "I may not be able to judge exactly how you´re feeling ... but I´ve made it my life´s work to try."

Simon continued to look towards Frank, but the confrontational glare had already begun to wane.

"Suicide is a complex emotional landscape, I know ... and something ... something which is a very personal subject to me." He sat back in his chair and folded his arms, concealing the yellow bird sewn onto the breast of his jumper. His pushed his glasses up his nose in his customary manner before speaking.

"Many years ago now, when I was sixteen years old, I was on my way back home from school one afternoon after finishing early for the day. We´d had mock exams and we normally didn´t go back to our other classes after we´d done those – quite a relief for most of us, I have to say. I remember feeling rather pleased with myself as I thought I´d done quite a good job with the exam I´d taken – maths, if I remember correctly. It wasn´t my strongest subject but it´d gone well, so, I remember walking home in pretty good spirits. It was also quite a nice day weather-wise – very sunny and warm for that time of year. I stopped to get a bag of chips to eat on my way home, which had turned into a bit of a habit for me back then actually. I finished the chips just a few houses before mine and stuffed the paper cone – complete with leftover ketchup and little wooden spoon-fork-type-thing and all – into the front hedge of number one hundred and twenty-seven, next door but one from us. I don´t really know why I used to do that. I was a very good kid, a good student overall, very well-behaved. I guess maybe it was my own small way of being

136

some kind of rebel, when really I was a bit of a teacher's pet."

He smiled and chuckled coldly to himself.

"Anyway, I opened the front door with my key and went into the house. I remember thinking that it was unusually quiet for that time of day. Mum normally had the radio on listening to Radio Two and pottering around in the kitchen, or something like that. But that day, it was silent there … I walked down the hall and through into the living room. I noticed that everything had been tidied up and cleaned … more than usual. That's not to say that we lived in a messy house, but with a younger sister and myself – who back then wasn't the most organised of teenagers – keeping the place in order was a bit of a challenge. We didn't normally have people round to visit very often either, so seeing the house like this struck me as … odd."

Frank gazed down at the cracked, green leather of the desk in front of him. His lips twitched as he pulled at the skin on the inside of his mouth with his teeth.

"I walked into the dining room. It was connected to the living room. And then into the kitchen."

He paused for a while, remembering the events of his adolescence; a hint of confusion painted on his face. He sighed profoundly.

"My mother was hanging from the ceiling. From a beam on the ceiling … It was an old house."

He paused again.

"She'd used the rope from the dressing down she'd bought me the previous Christmas. It was good quality, so it must have been the strongest thing she could find at the time. She, she was wearing one of her best dresses and had … had placed a towel under her in case …" He broke his sentence off and his words faded slowly away.

Simon bravely punctuated the silence. "I'm very sorry," he offered.

Frank was forced out of his solemn reverie. "Thank you," he replied warmly. "Thank you. She was a wonderful woman. She looked after my sister and me practically on her own after my father left. I mean, he wasn´t really a bad man. He had his problems with alcohol and drugs, but he was fundamentally a good person. Just not right for my mother ... and not prepared, or capable, of taking care of us. My mother appeared, to my sister and I anyway, to be quite a happy woman. She had a few good friends ... a part-time job. We lived in a nice house ... modest, but nice."

The nostalgia of his distant past dragged Frank away temporarily from the present and left his patient in uncomfortable solitude on the other side of the desk. It was some time until the therapist found sufficient self-control to take up his elegiac narrative again.

"She didn´t leave a note ... I had no idea she was so unhappy. I kept thinking to myself, if only I´d done something. If only I´d spoken to her more ... asked her if she was OK. Not been such a, a moody teenager I guess. But she didn´t look like she had any problems. OK, it´s difficult, of course, to bring up kids as a single mother and hold down a job at the same time, but she really didn´t give the impression of being upset about anything."

Frank looked helpless as he laid his innocent soul bare, sharing just a small fragment of the remorse that had been tearing at his conscience over the last two decades.

"Thinking back over and over again, she even looked a lot happier in the days leading up to her death. More ... energetic. I don´t know if my memory is playing tricks on me now, but I feel like she was acting as if a heavy burden had been lifted off her shoulders."

"You were young. There was probably nothing you could´ve done." Simon´s response surprised the psychologist, who looked both pleased and grateful for his patient´s interjection.

"I don't know … I was determined then that no other people, no other families, would have to go through the pain that my sister and I had to endure. So, I joined the Samaritans as soon as I could. I wanted to save everyone … to try to undo what had been done somehow. I thought that my actions – my interventions – could change things, and if I could just save *one* life, then that one life was worth saving. I wanted to eliminate human misery, loneliness, depression, despair. And I wanted to understand why, *why* my mother did what she did and why people feel so low, so desperate, that they feel like there's no other way out."

Simon leaned forward, clearly interested in hearing about this early phase of Frank's life. "Did you help many people?" he asked.

"Yes and no. I knew I had to respect someone's wishes – their right – to die … and I still do. But back then I was young. I wanted to save everyone. I didn't just want to be another anonymous '*Jo*', like they told us to be in our training. I wanted to get involved and help the individual; I wanted to *be* an individual myself. I began to see that so many people who called up were obviously suffering from things that were out of their control and displayed clear signs of specific mental disorders. These people didn't know what they were doing. These people were not in a position to make rational decisions for themselves; that's when I decided that I wanted to be a psychologist, well, a psychiatrist … but unfortunately I didn't quite make the grade."

He smiled at Simon. Despite the painful memories he had just shared, Frank looked content with how this unplanned session had developed and the opportunity he had been presented with to reveal his rarely talked-about past with the person sitting opposite him and the idea that, in some small way, it may be able to help.

"I thought that my listening and advice would make a difference," he added.

"It does," Simon said immediately.

"But it's complex, Simon. It really is. Understanding one individual won't necessarily help another. Because of this, my work and the work of all psychologists – the study of life – is never-ending." He looked pleadingly at Simon. "So, please forgive me if it looks like I don't understand you or if you think that it's impossible to know how you feel. It's difficult, I know … but I'm trying."

The light above them flickered and hummed and traffic could be heard in the distance as people made their way to work or returned home after dropping their children off at school. Outside, a house martin, with a clump of mud in its beak, flew directly towards the window before changing its trajectory at the last moment as it rose vertically on its way to construct its nest in the angle of the building's cornice. A tiny feather zig-zagged its way down past the window; the only visible evidence of the brief life-cycle that was taking place just feet away from Frank and Simon.

"I think it was Nietzsche who said, *'The thought of suicide is a powerful solace ... by means of it, one gets through many a bad night'*."

Frank left the quote hanging in the air for some time. Simon sat contemplating what the psychologist had just said. The mix of emotions on his twitching face the physical result of the tumult in his mind. Eventually, he broke the silence.

"I think … I think I know what that means and, and how that feels. I …I'm not sure if I could really do it … I mean, kill myself."

His own words seemed to strike Simon like a short, sharp slap in the face. This cold realisation, this admission, almost sounded like a disappointment to him.

"I mean … I've tried … I think. But, in the end I just couldn't do it for one reason or another. The thought of how it would affect my family … the disorder I'd leave behind. You know … if I died in another way it would be OK. Naturally, I mean. I've tried to do it like this even. To stop my heart beating when I've been lying in bed at night and to somehow force a heart attack … stupid, I know. And also wished that I'd catch some illness, or something like that. I've gone out in the middle of winter in just a t-shirt … walking in the freezing cold at night, hoping I'd get hypothermia or something. But always … I always stop. I don't know why … it's like my body goes onto some kind of auto-pilot … some kind of survival instinct kicks in."

"That's right. Our bodies, and our minds, are designed to react to the dangers we find ourselves in. And prevent them."

"Yes … maybe that's what happens." The thought brought an oxymoronic blend of confusion and enlightenment to Simon's face. "I guess … I guess, suicide is like a constant companion to me … because the way I feel – especially after the nightmares – is, is so unimaginably unbearable, and so the idea of doing something to myself feels like a way out … a way to stop the pain and guilt. Thinking about doing something bad, actually kind of … makes me feel better, like when I hurt myself. I guess … I guess it's just more to get rid of the pain, than having a plan to actually kill myself … being suicidal, I mean."

"There is a linguistic problem here too, Simon. The term suicidality – or feeling and being suicidal – may not actually indicate that someone wants to take their own life at all; it's just that this word covers a range of complex emotions, reactions and behaviours that people find very difficult to explain … and to deal with. Saying and even feeling that you're suicidal and thinking about taking your own life can be *very* different from actually going through the process of ending it."

He paused for a moment, a melancholic look cast across his face.

"I've had a lot of clients, people I've worked with for many years, that have almost been in a permanent state of what is commonly, or often mistakenly, referred to as suicide. They use it like a coping tactic – a defence mechanism almost – against the actual act of ending one's own life. Most of them are unable to deal emotionally with a situation, and therefore use these feelings as a way of being, without ever having the intention of doing anything about it. There are other people though, as I mentioned before, who are in no position to control what they're doing; people suffering greater mental problems. That's when, as health professionals, we have to step in and take action. It's not easy, and sometimes we fail … I've failed. Sometimes we don't provide the right treatment in time – medication for example, things like that. But we do our best, and generally reach the most favourable outcome for everyone involved."

Simon was listening intently.

"Look, I was thinking. Maybe it would be good for you to talk to someone else about these feelings? There's, there's a group that a couple of my former clients attend … it could be useful for you to listen and share some experiences with them from time to time."

Simon's usual reaction would have been an acrimonious refusal; but today he was more placid in his rebuttal, not wishing to offend Frank in any way.

"I don't think so. Thank you … just not at the moment … maybe some other time, OK?"

"Sure. The offer's there whenever you're ready." Frank picked up his pen and looked at his notes in an attempt to disguise his disappointment at the rejection of yet another proposal. "So, then I think we need to establish some kind of course of action to make you feel better directly after your dreams; at the times when you're feeling most vulnerable. I know you're starting to use some of the things we've looked at, like distracting yourself and breathing—"

"Oh, I've tried to remember some things from the hypnosis too," Simon interrupted, all of a sudden keen to contribute more to the conversation, as if sensing Frank's prior despondency and trying to make amends. "The black air, you know, breathing out the black, negative air."

"That's great. Has it helped you much?"

"Sometimes ... not really after the dreams, because it's too difficult for me to do anything then, but at other times ... a bit."

Seeing that Simon was taking his time to think about how to articulate his next words, Frank waited patiently for him to continue.

"After the dreams I feel terrible. Like I need to punish myself for what I've done. But later, when I come here and talk to you about them ... when I remember them and describe them to you, I feel and ... I realise that I didn't cause them. That it wasn't me who caused the bad things to happen."

Simon looked tired. Exhausted. But somehow relieved at finally being able to disclose what was happening to him with someone else – someone he could trust.

"I've got an idea. Wait a second." Frank reached into one of the desk drawers as he had done on several other occasions, pulled out three blank TDK cassettes still wrapped in cellophane, and placed them on the desk. "When you wake up, after you've had one of these dreams, why don't you record what you've seen – what you've felt? It may help you to feel better straight afterwards if you can't speak to me in person. I'm always here for you, you know you can call me ... and other people too, but, in theory, we're not going to see each other for another couple of weeks, so maybe this could be like a kind of self-therapy of sorts. What do you think?"

Simon looked at the three tapes stacked on top of each other. He reached out and straightened the pile, adjusting the position of each of them until they were completely aligned with one another.

"I don't know. Writing them down might be a bit easier. You know, it's more private and less embarrassing if someone hears what I'm saying," he replied, his eyes still fixed on the cassettes.

"Whatever works best for you," Frank said in a tired voice without a trace of his usual infectious energy, emotionally drained after what had been one of the hardest sessions of his career. "Whatever works best."

They said their goodbyes until their next programmed appointment after the Easter break, with Frank wishing his patient well and assuring him that he would be readily available should he be needed. Simon responded politely in turn, before disappearing silently through the door, the outline of the corner of one of the cassettes forming a right-angled triangle in his jacket pocket as he left. In his wake, a trail of small Jerusalem crosses of dry mud from the soles of his boots were littered haphazardly towards the exit.

Frank, smiling ruefully to himself, started to prepare for his time with the other patients that had unexpectedly been kept waiting that morning, hastily putting the thermos and cups back into his brown leather satchel and readying files and papers on his desk. He leaned back into his chair, glanced up at the calendar on the wall and contemplated the photograph of the long-haired Maine Coon, perpetually reaching for a small chocolate egg with its paw; a silent witness to events and emotions seldom seen, or even imagined, by most outside the four walls of the secretive world of the psychologist's consulting room.

13.

There was no shy knock to announce Simon´s arrival that mid-April afternoon. He burst into the room, glided through the entrance, and then slammed the door hard behind him. He looked serious; determined. He strode over towards his therapist and slapped the scrunched-up piece of paper that he was carrying in his fist onto the desk.

"I dreamt this," he said sternly.

Frank looked down at the crumpled newspaper clipping that had been torn out of the morning´s edition of one of the national broadsheets. A photo of a man in his mid to late twenties, with blond hair tumbling down across his face as he sang into a microphone, accompanied the text with a bold headline that read:

Grunge rock´s Kurt Cobain dies in apparent suicide.

Frank looked up from the story and back again to Simon, whose close proximity cast a shadow over a large swathe of the desk as he checked that Frank was reading what he had just been handed. The psychologist tried to formulate a suitable response; without success.

"I dreamt this," Simon said again, pointing to the scrap of newspaper that Frank was now holding in his hand.

"When?" was the only word Frank could utter after a lengthy pause. A pause in which he looked unsure of himself and of his own ability to deal with this sudden twist in his patient´s enigmatic case.

"Some time ago … after we last met. After I called you … but, but *before* this happened." Again he gestured to the article, which was now lying back on the desk between them; the vocalist´s closed eyes, open mouth and bulging neck tendons captured for eternity in black and white as he screamed out his silent angst.

Frank had managed to gather himself enough to follow a more logical line of questioning. "OK, Simon. Can you tell me what kind of dream you had?"

Calmer now than he was when he had entered the room and having found his way instinctively into his chair, Simon replied in a steady voice, "It wasn´t like the rest of my dreams with the murders, the blood and the screaming, no. It was almost, I don´t know … pleasant to be there. A nice dream, and so peaceful. It was a whole different thing. Kind of … relaxing. Not really a nightmare, and it didn´t bother me being there. It was like I was in a peaceful place … a peaceful setting, where I was in the presence of someone who´d found … peace, I suppose. I guess that´s why I didn´t call you again. I didn´t feel bad about this dream afterwards. I felt, I don´t know … relieved? Yes, relieved. Relieved to have been part of this. Relieved to feel the end of the pain, not the beginning of it."

"Well, it´s much better that you felt this way about something that you dreamt. Do you think that you´re starting to accept that these are just dreams and that you shouldn´t be feeling guilty about them?"

Simon looked straight at Frank, although he seemed to have paid scant attention to his question.

"I wasn´t sure exactly what I´d dreamt that night, although I´d seen everything so clearly, more or less like I normally do with the other, you know, violent dreams. I saw the house, the trees around … the peace and quiet of the setting … the birds singing. This time they were singing beautifully. I remembered everything. I remember walking up the drive towards the garage, its door open, a car inside … a car with flat tyres, for some reason. I could, I *can* see it all still so clearly. I remember the room above the garage with the windows in the roof. A kind of … greenhouse. I remember going around the garage to the stairs at the back and then walking up to the glass doors – they weren´t locked – going in, and then … then seeing him. At first I thought he was sleeping, just for a split second, until I saw the gun lying across his chest. His blond hair, kind of, kind of falling, flowing, onto the floor behind his head. There was blood … but not like in the other dreams. There was blood coming from his ear. But … little. So little blood … it was strange. The gun … I remember thinking that he must´ve shot himself, it was obvious what with the gun there, but the lack of blood was … well, strange. A relief … but, just …"

He shook his head as the rest of his sentence escaped him, a look of confusion on his face. Frank breathed in, on the point of saying something, but before he could get the words that were forming on his lips out, Simon continued.

"I didn´t know who it was at the time, and I didn´t even think about his identity to be honest … it was just another dream. But, but a few days later, I was out somewhere, driving back from … from buying some … something to smoke. I was driving in the car, but it started to rain really hard. So hard I couldn´t see anything, even though the wipers were at full speed. The windscreen was just … I just couldn´t see anything. It was dark too and the streets were starting to get full of water, starting to flood, overflowing the drains. I pulled over. I´d smoked something and didn´t trust myself too much driving when it was like this. I didn´t want to get stopped by the police either for driving too slowly or something like that. So I sat there, waiting for the rain to stop, listening to the radio. I remember that someone cut into one of the songs, I don´t remember exactly which song, something by Iggy Pop I think, and said that, that Kurt Cobain was dead. That he´d killed himself."

He stared into Frank´s eyes, imploring him to take his story seriously.

"It's not like he was an idol of mine. I mean, I really like Nirvana and am a big fan of his, but I don't believe in having idols. Idols that you don't know who they really are I mean. Maybe the music or the words of songs can have some kind of meaning to you, can help you get through things or something like that. But idolising pop stars or footballers and having posters of them above your bed staring down at you while you're sleeping, it's … it's just weird I guess."

Frank patiently listened, allowing Simon to continue his discourse, waiting for him to untangle his ideas and articulate them in a way that could be analysed professionally.

"But it affected me. It shook me … I, I was kind of paralysed there sitting in the car in the rain as it beat down, drumming above my head. It was like a shockwave crashing through me. I don't know how long I sat there, but it was a long time, I think. I started thinking about the dream. Going over it, and how the person lying there on the floor of the room above the garage must've been him. Must've been Cobain." He paused for a moment, unravelling the various threads of thoughts in his brain. "I don't remember getting back home, but the rest of the night I spent flicking through the radio stations trying to find out more, trying to find similarities between my dream and what had happened." His imploring eyes focussed again on his psychologist. "Over the next few days, I bought all the papers I could find. All the stories I could get my hands on to look for clues to see if I'd dreamt the same things, and … and I *found* them."

Sensing that this was the right moment to enter the conversation, Frank spoke. "Do you think that many of these things could have just been sheer coincidence?"

"No," Simon responded, quickly but softly. "It's impossible. I'd dreamt these things *before* I'd read about them in the papers or seen them on TV. And I was there in these real places. The places in my dream. I'd seen all the things that were reported. The clothes he was wearing, the position he was in, the hospital band on his wrist – all of these things. I saw the note he'd left with the red pen stuck through it left on a pile of earth. I remember thinking at the time about the note, remembering something about time travel or wormholes being explained with a pen making holes in paper … jabbed through them." Simon pierced an imaginary sheet of paper with an index finger in the air in front of his face. "I remember the note. Really. How could I make that up? I saw all the other objects on the floor near him too. A cigar box … other objects. I remember thinking how strange they all were, just next to him … a variety of different things, kind of placed in a, I don't know, like in an artificial way … like, like someone else had put them there on purpose. I know it's weird, but I saw everything *before* it happened … you have to believe me."

"Did you manage to record any of this after you woke up?"

Simon hesitated before answering, looking slightly frustrated with himself and annoyed at the question.

"No, I didn't. But I remember everything. I do." He looked at Frank, pleading with his eyes for the therapist to believe him.

"Don't you think that much of this could be down to simple coincidences? Why don't you just think about that, if you can for a while?" Frank asked, trying again to get his patient to consider this most obvious possibility.

Simon shook his head vigorously from side to side but remained silent, smiling with an air of incredulity at what he was hearing. Frank looked uncomfortable, but stepped into the momentary void in the conversation all the same.

"Simon, the brain, the human memory, has a tendency to selectively recall coincidences and forget about all the other times – the *huge* amount of times – that dreams, or premonitions, simply don't come true. I'm sure you've had many dreams – most of them innocuous – about an infinite amount of events that didn't happen that simply are not as dramatic as the dreams you're experiencing and remembering at the moment. The events in the other dreams don't come true, so there's a strong chance you forget what you dreamt about and you're unable to disconfirm them. Therefore, you don't make the connections between the dreamscape and reality."

Frank passed his eyes over the notes he had to hand while Simon waited patiently, stony-faced, for him to continue.

"Also, if I'm not mistaken, I believe that we dream for several hours per night and have a wide variety of different dreams – five on average, but more in some cases. Over the course of time, that's thousands of hours of images in our heads. Of course there will be some coincidences, especially if we have the tendency to look for them and to try to make connections, but what about all of the other dreams that don't come to pass? What about those?"

Simon had stopped shaking his head now but offered no riposte to his therapist's explanation. Frank struggled on as best he could, not overly confident on a subject he clearly didn't dominate, drawn in by Simon's silence and the pressure of his professional obligations as a psychologist to orchestrate the discussion.

"Or, perhaps you heard something after the dream that you may believe to have actually been dreamt *before* the event? In this case Kurt Cobain's death. You said yourself that you were looking for similarities after what you'd seen in your dream. Maybe you've auto-suggested some things by reading more about what happened and now believe they are part of what you dreamt beforehand?"

Simon was shaking his head again. "I know when I had the dream. It was *before*." He stared ahead into space, visualising something in his mind, before adding, "The other dreams too ... they must've been before things that've happened. The dream in Africa

... the massacres. There *are* things happening in Africa at the moment. I've seen them on the news ... maybe, maybe I dreamt that too? Before."

Frank was visibly debating with himself whether or not to say what he was thinking, aware that the course of the conversation could have potentially serious repercussions on Simon's mental well-being.

"Rwanda," he eventually said, yielding reluctantly to his instincts. "Yes ... I've seen things as well, it's terrible. But we've seen many things like that before. Uganda, Congo, Somalia, the famine in Ethiopia. There have been some quite shocking images over the years that you may have seen from one source or another and then been influenced by. I mean, they may have influenced your dreams; put images into your subconscious."

"But they're so *real*. I can't just imagine – just invent – these things, the specific details and everything. They're coming to me from somewhere. I've got to – *we've* got to – find out why."

Frank's tape recorder, which had been left on the far right side of the desk after presumably having been used earlier with another client, caught Simon's eye. His expression changed as something dawned on him. "The tapes ... yes. I'll use the tapes to record everything, like you said. To have a record of what I dream and *when* I dream it. That'll prove it's real." There was energy in Simon's voice as he spoke and a rare spark in his eyes.

"OK, Simon. It could be a good idea to do that, yes. To record what you've seen and the dates when you dream these things too, just to see if there's some kind of, umm, correlation between them." Frank said, aiming to appease his effusive patient, before adding, "Do you think you could describe how you feel afterwards too? You know, recognise and name the emotions and feelings you're having and rank them in order of intensity."

151

With a distrustful look, Simon answered, "I know what you're trying to do. I know you think it's all in my head, but, but I *know* there's something there. Some truth to this. Some reason why all this is happening." Another realisation seemed to come into his head as he was speaking, leaving an epiphanic expression carved onto his face in the pause in his dialogue. "I didn't realise before. I ... I didn't *cause* these things to happen ... I can *predict* them and ... *prevent* them."

Smiling to himself, Simon stood up and stared out of the window, lost in his own chaotic world. He turned around, ignoring Frank completely, and headed to the door, stopping briefly to scratch his ragged beard as if a memory stirred or another revelation had suddenly struck his consciousness. He opened his mouth like he was about to add something, before changing his mind and silently leaving the consulting room; the day's pre-planned activities uncommenced and the session abandoned long before it had reached its scheduled end.

14

"Here …" Simon placed the cassette on the desk, leaving three of his fingers pressed down hard on its plastic casing as if worried it would escape his grasp or somehow find its way onto the floor. "… more dreams. Now we´ll have *real* proof if something happens."

Glancing down at the transparent, rectangular box and its labelled contents, Frank noticed the yellowish-brown stain of tobacco tattooed between Simon´s index and middle finger; something that was either relatively new or had been unobserved during their previous meetings.

"Thank you. It´s great that you´ve managed to do that. I´ll have a listen to it later, if that´s OK with you?" Frank promised.

Simon finally let go of the cassette box, damaged now by the downward force that had been applied by his rigid fingers. Frank picked it up quickly, moving it out of their field of vision.

"So, how was your week?" he reeled off, aiming to lead Simon into a conversation he would be more adept at dealing with instead of the one that was looming over them like the sharp tip of a precariously hanging blade.

"Sorry. We need to talk about the dreams," Simon replied inevitably. "We need to find a way to tell people that bad things are going to happen." After a few seconds pause he added, "Play the tape, please."

Frank cast his eyes across to the cassette that had been discarded to his right, and then back again to his young patient. "Why don´t you tell me what happened, Simon? I think it would be better if you told me yourself. In your own words."

"OK, OK." Despite having his request for the tape to be played back rebuffed, he was ready to recount the dreams nonetheless; the images still clearly fresh in his mind. Without any hesitation, he began.

"It's night … at night. There are sirens all around me and flashing lights. Red lights, and blue flashing ones all around, everywhere. I'm, I'm disoriented as first by the sirens. They're so loud. They're in my brain, piercing it and making me dizzy. I hold my head and steady myself and focus on what's going on all around me." He held the sides of his head with both hands, mimicking the movements of his dream. "I can see flames and fire – a huge fire – and loads of smaller ones all over the place, and metal everywhere and some other pieces, like, like panels. White panels scattered among the twisted metal. Some with red and blue lines, or patterns or something, like the colour of the sirens … but not a reflection of them. It's hard to see through the smoke and the night, the darkness. My eyes are watering because of the smoke blowing into my face on the breeze. It's an accident, I know it is. Some kind of terrible accident. It looks like the wreckage of something. It must be a plane … or what *was* a plane … an air crash. I'm standing on tarmac – a runway – but I don't remember any more after that." He looked up at Frank. "I *have* to remember more."

"It's OK Simon," Frank said, nodding. "What did you do after the dream? How did you feel?"

"I … I was … alright. I wasn't feeling so guilty, like before, because I knew what I had to do. I had to get back into the dream again. I tried, I did. I imagined myself there again on the runway, and everything else that I'd seen and felt, but I just couldn't do it." He looked angry with himself.

"I think we need to try to put these things into some kind of perspective. Don't you think—"

"There was *another* dream." Simon spoke over his psychologist. "I remember more about that one," he added enthusiastically, his hands now fidgeting in his lap as he failed to hide his agitation.

"OK," Frank said with more than a little trepidation. "Go on."

"I was in Africa, again, I think ... or I thought at first, maybe the Caribbean. I'm not sure. But more likely Africa somewhere," he started, before pausing to focus his mind's eye on the previous night's occurrences. "There was a boat ... on a wide river, but it wasn't so far out from the riverbank. Less than a hundred metres. Maybe fifty or so. It looked like ... like a ferry, full of people – *packed* with people. There were too many of them all squeezed in tightly together on the deck of the boat. I'm, I'm somehow standing on the water. I can feel it under my feet ... I look down, there's muddy water all around me, though in the middle of the river it's more blueish, like it's reflecting the sky. It's quite windy and the water's a bit rough ... kind of, choppy, with small waves that break on the surface ... white horses. The boat has sunk ... it's just sunk in the water. I don't know why. The weather isn't bad enough to have made it sink like that.

"People are screaming, fighting each other to get off, to get out of the boat ... out of the covered deck, half-submerged in the river. They're trying to get out, but there are so many people and bags and bundles of things in the way. People are being squashed against the white metal handrails on the sides. A dark mass of people, some moving and splashing around ... unable to get out. Others are not moving ... although many of these people are *being* moved. Pushed or pulled out of the way by others."

The same hesitation that punctuated the retelling of his other macabre dreams, and the same distant look in his sad eyes, once again came to fore.

"Streams of people are swimming away from the ferry. Another smaller boat approaches and tries to pick some of them up. It's, it's swamped, completely overrun with people trying to get on it. It's

155

leaning over to one side and people are shouting at each other, angry ... desperate. Many people who are swimming away are dragging others with them, using one arm to try to move themselves through the water ... the people they're holding ... they look ... lifeless.

"I can see the name of the boat, half submerged under the water, but, but I can't read it all, just part of it ... if only I could read it, I could, I could find it and save these people, contact someone and warn them not to take the boat." He looked earnestly at Frank as he spoke.

Frank had remained stoical throughout and unsurprisingly chose the path of logic once again in acknowledgement of what he had just heard. "But you would have no idea when these things happen. Even if we had more information, do you really believe that the authorities would take us seriously if we told someone about this?"

In a way that had become increasingly habitual, Simon ignored the question and carried on regardless with his own rationale.

"The other dreams, the ones about Kurt Cobain and about Rwanda, were a few days before those things happened ... so *these* things this time – the plane and the boat – must be going to happen very soon. The crash ... it's far too vague I know, I didn't see much. But the ferry ... I need to remember the name of the ferry!" he shouted excitedly. "How can we do this? Can you hypnotise me again? Can I remember that way?"

"As we said before, Simon. The memory can create falsities and we can't always trust what we think we remember. Even if we do think we have something that might be of use, who's going to believe us? Who's going to physically prevent a ferry sailing, or even check it for technical problems, just because you've seen it in a dream? No one is going to take action. No one is going to believe us." He folded his arms across his chest, momentarily forgetting his empathetic psychologist's bedside manner, with the air of a father putting his foot down to a petulant child.

"But we have to do *something*," insisted Simon. "People are going to die, and, and we´re just going to sit here do nothing to prevent it? *I* can prevent this. If we do nothing, we´ll be stained with the blood of everyone that dies on our hands."

"Hold on. Just a moment," said Frank, seemingly more prepared for the day´s session than he had been a week before. "I´d like you to just stop for a second and think about something." This deliberate pause seemed to break Simon away from his hyperbole for an instant. "If you believe your dreams to be a precursor of events that are going to happen – and I´m not saying that what you believe may or may not be true – but if you really believe that your dreams are precognitive, and they can predict the future, then I´d like you just to consider a couple of things."

"OK," Simon said eagerly, ready for the challenge.

"So, what do you think would happen if we were able to access specific details? In this case the name of the boat. And then, someone actually believed us and we prevented what you saw in the dreams from happening. If by using the specific knowledge from your dream means that the accident – or whatever event we´re talking about – doesn´t even happen, then wouldn´t that mean that you wouldn´t have dreamt of it in the first place? It would never have existed as an event. It would be a kind of, paradox, wouldn´t it?"

Simon was alert today, seemingly sharper than Frank had ever seen him. "No, no." He shook his head. "My dreams would still be there, but, but they would just be dreams about something … and just a possible future that for one reason or another simply didn´t happen. It´s up to *us* to decide the fate of reality." He was smiling at his therapist now. "And I can do it."

Frank sat in silence, taking in the reasoning of Simon´s confident answer; at the same time making an effort to guide the discussion towards what he considered more pressing matters concerning Simon's mental health.

"Have you spoken to anyone else about all of this and how you feel? Your parents? Your mother maybe?"

Annoyed at being distracted from what he considered the importance of the current topic of conversation, Simon snapped. "They've got nothing to do with this. They don't understand me ... they don't understand the things that are going on. No one does ... not even you."

Frank looked taken aback by Simon's quiet aggression. "I'm sure they just want to help you ... as I do," he said encouragingly, using his many years of experience to try to defuse the situation that had started to escalate out of his control. Simon seemed temporarily a little less tense at the sound of Frank's calm voice.

"What we can't forget to do is to try to relax and breathe, so what I sugge—"

"Breathe?" Simon interrupted quietly. "Breathing is the hardest thing to do."

There was a silence as the words lingered in the air, with Frank visibly struck at the desperation in Simon's voice.

"I know what you want to do," Simon continued with hushed ferocity. "You want to nullify me ... to make me some kind of vegetable with medication. To make me catatonic so I don't think about things. You said it yourself, that I shouldn't think more, didn't you?"

"The medicine is simply a harmless way—"

Simon held up his palm and prevented an astonished-looking Frank from completing his sentence. With his open hand raised in the air facing his counsellor, he started to rub his forehead circularly with his other palm in a mix of tiredness and despair.

"The medicine … yes, medicine." He lowered his arm and looked frantically at Frank. "When I first took the pills my dreams were even more clear. I saw more things … more details." His temper had started to abate and now, almost pleadingly, he asked, "I need more medicine. Can you give me more?"

"I´m afraid I can´t prescribe anything." Frank replied, shaking his head as he spoke. "I don´t have the authority to do that. But, I can talk to Doctor Rossouw and see what he thinks about—"

"I´ll go and see him," Simon interrupted again. "I´ll make an appointment, OK?"

"OK," Frank said after a pause. "I think it would do you some good to get another point of view about things anyway."

"Yes, yes. I have to remember the details, the name of the boat … to stop this. To stop all those people from dying. I need to have *more* dreams … I need to sleep."

Buffeted by the shifting tides of Simon´s emotions, a pensive Frank quietly contemplated what to do next with the agitated young man before him. Finally, prior to speaking, he took in a long, large lungful of air.

"Would you like to get up on the couch for a moment?"

Simon pounced on the words. "To help me remember the dream? The name of the boat?" he asked expectantly.

"Let´s just start with a bit of relaxation first and then see where that leads us, OK?" Frank responded, doing his utmost to placate his patient and deflect the last question.

Simon jumped up and took his position on the coach as Frank opened the drawer that contained the cassette player, placing it in the centre of the desk, before making his way to the middle of the room in readiness to give Simon his instructions.

"Would it be OK with you if we recorded this?" Frank asked tentatively.

"Sure." Simon responded calmly, already lying down with his eyes closed and arms stretched out next to him with hands and fingers relaxed, waiting for the voice that would send him into another dimension and towards the words that he believed would save the drowning people.

Frank reached across to the cassette recorder, a blank tape already inside waiting to be filled by their voices, and pressed the red record button. He looked down at Simon and started to give the instructions that would, at first, drain the stress from his patient's body and then subsequently send him into a state of hypnosis. He slowly made his way down Simon's body with his voice and eyes, pausing for a moment to observe the outline of some unidentified, slim, rectangular object in the right-hand pocket of his dark-green combat trousers. Frank shifted his gaze and stared at the floor beneath his brown brogues, acutely aware that to an uninitiated observer his furtive glances stood every chance of being wrongly misinterpreted.

Over the course of the following minutes the stages of the earlier sessions were repeated. Hands were pressed together and then sent tumbling down to rest; parts of a forest were traversed; and again a small flight of stairs was climbed down, with each step sending Simon further into his imagination; until the point where a new instruction was introduced.

"Now, in front of you, at the bottom of the stairs, is a door. There's a key in it ... turn the key and open the door, and then walk through to the other side."

There was a lull in his soft tone, which allowed Simon the time to open the door he had just created in his mind.

"On the other side, you'll find yourself on the bank of a river ... the river from your dream. You can see the boat in the water ... you take a step onto the water ... you can walk on top of it, as you could before. You take another step further out on the river. It's safe, you're not in any danger there. You're just observing. Take another step, and then another towards the boat and look around at what you saw in your dream."

Frank noticed how Simon's brow had started to have a furrowed look to it as he immersed himself into the tragic scene on the muddy river.

"Now, you are in control, Simon. You control your feet, and your actions ... you can go anywhere, and see everything that was happening. When I indicate to you, you can speak to me. You can tell me what you can see all around you, what you're doing and what's happening. It's OK, you're safe and relaxed ... and because you're so relaxed it's easy to see all the things clearly from your dream ... OK. In your own time, explain everything to me, slowly and calmly. Speak to me now."

Simon's voice was broken at first and hard to understand. "I'm ... I'm walking on the water." He cleared his throat with a small cough. "The water is under my feet ... I'm not wearing any shoes and I can feel the water ... it's chilly. I'm starting to hear people ... people screaming, coming from the boat. They're all drowning in the water as the boat has gone down ... it's going down now, sinking. People are trying to get out ... they're holding onto the white bars ... they're rusty."

The two reels of the cassette wound themselves around slowly but incessantly; one, millimetre by millimetre, shrinking in size as the other stole away its virgin silence and filled it instead with the harrowing details of Simon's testament.

"I feel something cold on my hand and look down. It's a young boy ... his eyes are red and swollen ... he takes my hand in his and points to the boat ... to the name of the boat. I can see it ... but the boat's sinking ... people are swimming around the back of it where

161

the name is, trying to scramble up and get out of the water. They cover the writing for a moment … I can't see what's written … they move, swim or, or are dragged away by the current in the water. Now I can see the white letters on the dark blue of the back of the boat. *M* ... *T* ... *O,* but the water's covering the letters fast … the boat's leaning … there's another word below, smaller. I can only see one letter … *M* again, I think. And then … it disappears. The boy's hand slips from mine and he's gone. The people are disappearing under the water or swimming away from me, screams fading. There are no more people moving. No more survivors … just the wind and small waves lapping at my feet."

He stopped speaking and lay in silence. After giving his patient some time to see if there was anything left of the scene to be told, Frank concluded enough had been said and starting to bring Simon out of his trance.

"OK … turn around. You can see the same door you entered on the bank of the river. Walk towards it."

Frank guided Simon through the door and gradually helped him to regain, step by step, his consciousness. Swaying as he got to his feet again, Simon was helped the short distance back to his chair with the aid of his therapist, who was gently holding his right forearm near his elbow for support. After Simon had been seated, Frank quickly positioned himself on his side of the desk.

"How do you feel?"

A lethargic-looking Simon blinked several times before answering in a calm, relaxed manner; worlds apart from the heightened state of anxiety in which he entered the room more than half an hour before.

"OK … more relaxed." He stared at Frank, a determined look had descended onto his otherwise passive face. His hand started to feel around the straight edges of the rectangular object in his trouser pocket, looking for comfort in the knowledge that it was still there. "But, but this is not going to stop. It's not going to stop until I can find a way out of this."

"Don't worry, Simon. We will ... together. If it's the last thing we do."

***

The light was fading outside the clinic and the car park on the west side of the building was now virtually deserted. Inside, behind the grey exterior walls, Frank was sitting at his desk, immersed in the pages of notes and photocopies that were covering the old, green leather; unaware of the clouds of starlings repeatedly sculpting and then destroying, the dark, sinister, yet eerily beautiful shapes they were forming in the twilight as they made their way to nest.

He reached in the direction of the small transistor radio as was customary of him at the end of his shift while he organised his hand-written accounts of the day's appointments. But today the radio was not switched on. No guitar-based music filled the room this late afternoon. Instead, he reached for the tape that Simon had presented to him, which had been sitting on the far side of the desk throughout their time together today. He took it out of its cracked case, ejected the recently recorded material inside, and fed his patient's narrations into the mouth of the machine that he had used earlier in the afternoon. He turned to a new blank page in his notebook, pressed play, and started hastily transcribing the familiar, metallic voice that came into his ears; looking for something – anything – that would help him to shed light on the situation in which he found himself, and make sense of the chaos and confusion that was unfolding all around him.

15.

The air outside the clinic was thick and humid and the sky above ominously leaden as storm clouds began to gather. The warm weather that had been lingering over the country for the last three days was starting to be pushed away eastwards by a cold front gradually rolling in from the South-West. The occasional rumble of thunder could be heard in the distance as dark, impossibly vertical bands of rain showers made their way slowly across the South Downs, randomly soaking their chosen hill, while leaving others nearby unscathed.

A cool wind started to whip around the Brutalist angles of the concrete building that housed Frank Newman's consulting room. Inside, he pulled on a string to raise the blind, its clattering in the breeze having brought the conversation to a temporary standstill, and closed the window.

"Sorry. You were saying."

Simon, who had only been sitting in the room for barely a minute or so, carried on from where he'd left off.

"My week, yes ... it was fine, thank you." He hurriedly rattled the words off, politely dismissing the question so as to move on to more pressing matters. "Look." He reached into the pocket on the front of his sweatshirt and pulled out another newspaper story, which had again been ripped out in great haste; the edges of the clipping rough and unevenly torn. "Tell me *now* if you think I'm imagining things."

Frank took the offering obligingly. "Let's see." He stared at the paper with its uncomplicated, self-explanatory headline.

261 die in Japan air crash horror

Frank hesitated before speaking, seemingly unsure whether to adhere to protocol and his professional duties as a psychologist, or to indulge in the fantasy of his patient. He chewed on his lower lip as he considered his best course of action, not wanting to further exacerbate Simon's anxieties with an inappropriate comment.

"Let's think about this here for a moment," he said pragmatically.

Simon was waiting – with an eagerness incongruous to the majority of the sessions he had so far shared with Frank – to hear what his therapist would say next. He sat on the edge of his chair, unable to keep still, one knee bobbing up and down and his hands fidgeting ceaselessly.

"What about this then? What do you think about that?" He pointed to the clipping.

Frank wrenched his eyes away from the colourless photo of what looked to be rescue workers or crash investigators standing among the blackened wreckage of what was once a passenger airliner.

"Simon. There really must be a large number of aviation accidents every year; most of which we probably never even hear about. This must be purely a coincidence ... you said yourself that you weren't able to find any more details, didn't you? What makes you think that this is the crash you saw in your dream?"

"I know, I know," replied Simon quickly. "It hasn't been one of my clearest dreams, but it *must* have been this one ... this accident. I dreamt it just a day or two before the crash."

Frank looked down again to the story in front of him. His eyes moved sideways and then flicked back centrally again like the cartridge of an old typewriter as he started to read the first paragraph in more detail; although it was not entirely clear whether this was out of interest in the story, or a way to give himself some much-needed breathing space to regroup his thoughts. He took off his glasses and started to clean the greasy finger masks left on the lenses

– the result of the sandwiches he had eaten unenthusiastically at his desk for lunch – with the corrugated-edged cloth that he´d taken quietly out of the top drawer to his right.

Without the thick frames that obscured a large part of it, his naked face appeared much slimmer and had a younger air, leaving him looking more like the age he actually possessed. He squinted, still glancing down at the article as he finished cleaning his glasses, before quickly inspecting them for further fingerprints that he may have missed. Satisfied that they were sufficiently clean he put them back on, and with one small nudge up to the bridge of his nose, they were nestled back in their original position and Frank looked more mature and psychologist-like again.

"OK. I´d like you to imagine that we had more information about the flight that crashed. Imagine that you´d dreamt more details about the plane and could remember things more accurately."

He allowed Simon a second to visualise the scenario. Time enough, if Simon had been looking in Frank´s direction, for his patient to have noticed the look of doubt that plainly contradicted what his psychologist was saying. And time enough, should he have listened more attentively to the conditioned delivery of the words, to realise that the therapist was seemingly unconvinced by the very argument he himself was presenting.

"Do you think that all similar commercial flights would be stopped just because we´ve had a premonition?" Frank continued. "Like the ferry, even if we had the flight number, for example, do you honestly think that someone would listen to us and then act on our warning? We don´t know when these things would happen, and if they´re actually going to happen at all."

Simon was nodding his head in agreement, looking disappointed with himself. "I didn´t have enough information, I know. I needed more … I´ve tried to remember more. The name of the boat. I´ve

166

been trying … but just can't. I've been looking in the papers and watching the news all week but haven't found anything, so far. Maybe … maybe it hasn't happened yet. Maybe I've got more time to try to remember that name and, and stop everything."

Simon's case file was lying next to Frank's left hand, close enough for him to only make the smallest of movements in order to reach it. He glanced down towards the folder and slipped his fingers under the cover until they touched the page that they were searching for, ready to extract it from its place at the top of the pile of papers inside. His hand loitered there for several seconds before returning, empty, to its previous location.

Simon hadn't noticed the psychologist's movements nor the conflict that his therapist was fighting within himself, so wrapped up in his own musings as he was.

"I think that the dreams, they show … pain … lots of pain. Important things that happen that cause vast amounts of people to suffer." Simon shook his head again in disappointment with himself. "I don't why I didn't dream about him then."

"Who exactly?" Frank asked, intrigued.

"Senna." He spoke the word as if it were the answer to the simplest of questions. His eyes bulged in cartoon-like surprise at Frank's innocence.

"The racing driver," Frank replied, his intonation dropping on the last syllable, confirming the information to himself.

"Ayrton Senna. Yes. He … he died at the weekend. He crashed into a wall during a race. Millions of people must've seen it happen … millions of people were shocked, in pain. I *should've* felt it … dreamt it. I don't know why I didn't. Or maybe I did, but I've forgotten. I need to remember things. I've been doing everything to try to think of a way to help me remember."

"What's really important, Simon, is to relax and feel at ease with yourself. If you can stay calm and find a place where you're not troubled by anything – a comfortable place – then you may be able to remember things more easily without so much pressure on yourself. Just don't force these things to come into your head; you're just going to end up getting more frustrated and more anxious." He paused, his demeanour now more reminiscent of the encouraging, empathetic Frank of the first few sessions he shared with Simon. "Have you listened to the relaxation cassette we recorded here or been using some of the techniques from the hypnosis? You told me on another occasion that expelling black air and all your negativity helped you out, didn't you?"

"Yes … no. I don't think I've been doing anything … The hypnosis." Simon frowned as something appeared to have dawned on him. He asked enquiringly, "Is it possible to self-hypnotise?"

Frank smiled as if he'd found the idea amusing, although there was nothing humorous in the delivery of his patient's suggestion.

"I really don't think that's a good idea. These kinds of things need to be done by someone who knows what they're really doing; someone who's trained in these kinds of specific techniques. It could be quite dangerous to attempt something like this as you might not be able to wake up properly and you could put yourself in potentially dangerous situations. Imagine if you were still extremely drowsy and then tried to drive somewhere … things like that."

"If only there was some kind of way," Simon said in quiet desperation to himself.

Deciding that it was time to try to move the discussion on towards a different outcome, as naturally as he could, Frank said, "I see you've had an appointment with Doctor Rossouw, Simon." He looked down at his notes, although he already knew very well the information he was feigning to consult. "Yesterday, in fact."

"Yes."

"And how was it? If you don´t mind me asking." His intonation, once more, already indicated that he knew the result of the meeting.

"OK. I told him what he wanted to hear."

"What do you mean?" asked Frank cautiously, a worried expression flashed across his face at this unexpected response.

"About my thoughts. The negative thoughts about myself. The thoughts of guilt and the self-harming and … sometimes not wanting to carry on living."

Out of Frank´s line of sight beyond the precipice of the edge of the desk between them, Simon pressed his thumb deep into his right thigh. He stared more intently ahead in an attempt to keep an impassive face throughout the shot of pain that he was inflicting upon himself. He sighed deeply, like a drug addict receiving a long overdue hit of their chosen narcotic.

"Are you still hurting yourself, Simon?"

He took his hand quickly away from his leg as if he had been caught red-handed, seemingly surprised and at the same time confused about the verb tense that Frank had just employed.

"No … I mean … yes. But it´s not a problem now … it´s OK," Simon said, appearing convinced about what he was saying.

"How do you mean?"

"I mean. I think I understand why. It´s … it´s my coping mechanism, isn´t it?"

Frank raised one eyebrow, looking surprised but also in a way pleased that Simon had taken on board their discussions from previous sessions and now volunteered this information as if it were his own novel conclusion.

"Like we spoke about with the … the suicidal thoughts. It´s not like I want to do anything to myself really. It´s, it´s a state. A state I live in … a way to cope with the suffering. I self-harm, I guess … to cope."

Frank silently observed Simon – who was clearly trying to gather the strands of his thoughts together – patiently giving him enough time to organise the loose ends in his mind.

"I understand why I … why people do it. I, I'd forgotten about this, but now my mind is much clearer. I'm thinking more … the chaos is quieter now in my head. It's, it's like in Australia, with the aboriginal people. They hurt themselves … cut themselves."

Frank looked a little concerned about where this conversation was leading, but also appeared relieved that the discussion had moved away from the subject of Simon's self-proclaimed prophetic dreams for the time being and was now back on more familiar territory.

"Really? I haven't heard of this. Is it some kind of cultural or spiritual belief they have?" he asked, showing a palpable interest in the topic.

Simon struggled to find an answer to Frank's question, looking disoriented. He carried on determinedly with the line of thought that he was immersed in, appearing fearful that if anything else entered his mind he would lose track of what he was saying.

"I want … wanted, to go to Australia. Maybe after university … so I started looking at things about it. The culture, traditions … and other stuff."

"That great," Frank added enthusiastically. "Great to have some exciting plans for the future." He smiled, content that for once there was – at least it seemed to him at the time – a positive branch of conversation to cling on to instead of the barbs that had been snagging him away from where he believed they should be heading at this stage of their therapy.

Simon looked somewhat angrily at Frank, as if all the effort he had invested in trying to develop the discussion himself was being disturbed by his psychologist's cheerful interventions.

"I, I saw a documentary, and they cut themselves ... they're called sorry cuts, I think. If something bad happens to them, if they lose someone close to them, I think, they do it to release the pain." He started to sound more unsure of himself as he spoke. "Maybe, maybe that's what I'm doing?"

Despite the obvious difficulty he had in holding down what on the surface could be described as a normal conversation, and although he often paused and appeared confused when he spoke, Simon seemed more attentive, approachable and willing to try to understand his condition and look for answers to some of the more worrying questions in his mind. Sensing that the topic of aboriginal Australians had come to an end, Frank stepped in and took control of the conversation.

"I see that you've been prescribed some more medicine. Are you taking it again now?"

Simon broke out of the stupor that he had fallen into. "Yes," he replied with conviction. "Now I've got the drugs to help me sleep ... and remember."

"That's good." Frank didn't sound convinced. "But you need to be *very* careful how you use them. Just take it how the psychiatrist has told you to do so, OK? I'm sure you'll be able to see the benefit of it in a couple of weeks or so. I know I've told you before, but remember, the effects of the medicine take a little time to work properly. We also can't forget our treatment here and what you need to be doing on your own when you're not in session. Remember that real change has to happen outside therapy and comes from within you." He smiled proudly at Simon. "You've made some excellent progress so far, let's keep going."

Frank paused for a moment, looking a little uncomfortable with the way that his young patient was staring back at him with his intense, deep, dark-brown eyes. Eyes, that today, were far removed from being windows into the soul and were more than challenging than ever to read into. Eyes, that at the same time looked both threatening and vulnerable; demonstrating the complex nature of Simon´s personality disorders.

"Of course." Simon broke the deadlock with what sounded like an overly cheery response, as if he had dismissed everything that his psychologist had been saying with a brief smile and these two simple words.

"Umm …" Frank seemed unsure of himself for a moment and looked for refuge in the papers he had prepared before the session began. "Have you been speaking to anyone else over the last few days?"

"Nope."

"Your parents maybe?"

"Nope," again was Simon´s light-hearted response.

"Well, don´t forget that it´s important to co-ordinate your objectives with your family, and, umm, realise that they´re there for you too if you need to share anything with them."

"Sure, I know," Simon chirped, peering closely at a thunder bug that was struggling to make its way through the thicket of hairs on the back of his right hand. Using his opposite thumb nail as a ramp for the tiny insect to ascend, Simon stared at it even more closely as he brought it up level with his eyes, riveted by its jerky movements and the way it contorted its back into impossible arches. He blew gently on the creature and watched it disappear from view before turning his attention back to the person sitting on the other side of the no man´s land of worn leather and antique wood.

Frank was quickly running out of things to say. His experience and talent as a psychologist appeared to be fast abandoning him; his confidence clearly slipping away as his professional exterior was damaged by his own personal misgivings, leaving him as exposed as any one of his patients with their doubts, fears and anxieties. He stroked his chin, thinking hard about what to say next, searching for something other than the typical clichés that would end up having a detrimental effect on the delicate young man sitting and smiling knowingly opposite him.

"Well … you know what to do, don´t you? I mean … try to do some kind of activity, even if you think it´s, you know, trivial … no, not trivial, I mean, something that will make you feel better anyway."

In an almost supportive, kind-hearted tone that Frank had never heard uttered by the bearer of those intense, dark-brown pools that were causing Frank so much insecurity and self-doubt, Simon responded, "OK, I´ll do anything you want me to."

Simon grinned broadly, thanked Frank for the day´s session, and stood up with his hand outstretched, waiting for a reciprocal action from his therapist. Frank sat in his comfortable, old chair, dumbstruck at Simon´s actions and words. Without standing, he automatically reached out to meet Simon´s grasp and they shook hands with over-exaggerated movements, before halting in mid-air. They stared into each other´s eyes. Simon looking down at his psychologist with a look of pity on his face; Frank gazing searchingly up at his patient, a startled expression in his eyes, unable to find the right words to confront this discomforting situation. Simon ultimately loosened his grip and slipped his hand away from Frank´s, their fingers gently brushing together before finally parting.

Simon went to leave the room, smiling to himself happily, shoulders pulled backwards and his chest puffed out, full of the energy and vigour that a healthy eighteen-year-old should possess. There was a sense of self-satisfaction and achievement evident on his face as he opened the door. He turned to give Frank one last confident smile, before closing it firmly behind him.

Frank sat motionless at his desk, his right hand still outstretched but now resting on the leather surface in front of him. He looked around the room, not paying attention to any one particular object, trying to understand what had just happened, but fearful of recognising the truth.

Eventually, he looked down at Simon's file and carefully opened it, exposing the page he had briefly fingered some time ago. He stared down at the article that – unlike the ones Simon had brought him – had been carefully and neatly cut out of a newspaper using what must have been very sharp scissors. He surveyed the photo of the salvaged passenger ferry listing heavily in shallow water close to the muddy banks of a river, and read once again the headline that would not only change the course of the rest of his career; but also his entire life as he knew it.

300 feared drowned in Kenyan ferry sinking, it read.

16

The only light entering the empty consulting room that early in the day was coming from the rectangular halo spilling out from the edges of the drawn blind that Frank had closed before leaving late the previous evening. The transistor radio and the other objects in the room – so familiar during therapy – were now fused into the furniture on which they perched, forming irregular crenellations in the blue half-light. The hulking shadow of the desk flooded across the floor, flowing endlessly in the direction of the closed door; while the thin, dark outline of one of the couch's spindly wooden legs stretched out and then crashed into the nearest skirting board before angling obtusely up the wall and merging into the darkness that awaited above.

In the gloom of one corner, needing no encouragement, a tiny brown spider true to its nature, spun its inevitable web, abseiling down and then climbing back up again as it effortlessly constructed its intricate trap between the leaves of the yucca; safe in the knowledge that it would be unnoticed, undisturbed and accepted in its chosen place.

The room was suddenly filled with light, eliminating all traces of the previous shadows and forming even sharper, newer ones that now reached out towards the wall with the lone window in the middle. Frank stepped inside, unbuckling his satchel as he entered, apparently keen to get started on preparing the day's sessions and sip on the strong, milky tea that was still brewing in his thermos flask. He hit the switch that sparked the ceiling strip light into life. It flickered noisily several times until it reluctantly settled into its steady, bright burn, eradicating the elongated shapes that the surge of illumination from the corridor had just created. But something made him freeze in the process of closing the door behind him; it still a foot or so ajar.

The voice of his receptionist could be heard coming from the end of the corridor, her intonation suggesting that she was asking a question to somebody who had just arrived at the clinic, although the sound travelling via the waiting area was not clear enough to be fully understood. A muted, male voice was heard responding with a low monosyllable and soon afterwards, the door was pushed open with a force that made Frank's arm swing back as if he were about to volley a tennis ball.

Frank and Simon stood face to face, their similar height meaning that barely six inches separated their noses, eyes and lips. Frank took a step backwards.

"Simon?" he said in a voice full of astonishment. "Are you OK?"

"Is it alright if I lie down here for a moment?" Simon replied, wearily pointing to the thin-legged couch opposite the entrance. "I'm very tired."

"Of course, of course, please." Frank, his arm hooked around but not actually touching Simon's back, guided his patient to his requested location. "There," he added as Simon lay down. "Would you like some tea?"

"No, thank you," Simon answered weakly.

Frank stepped back again and had a good look at his most troublesome, yet endearing case, who had already closed his eyes, and started to scan for clues as to why he had unexpectedly turned up in such a state so soon that morning. The psychologist was at first drawn to Simon's hair, which looked longer than on any occasion in the past and was now separated by a crooked centre parting dividing the scruffy curtains that reached down past his temples. Frank noticed for the first time the holes in each of Simon's ear lobes; evidence of the rebellious jewellery that had caused arguments with his father nearly three years before. He saw that he was wearing the same familiar, faded black jeans but instead of his usual boots, he now had on a pair of dirty, black cloth shoes with a white star on the side. The cream-coloured t-shirt he wore had splashes of some unidentified, dark liquid and was almost exaggeratedly creased with one sleeve stretched almost beyond repair, revealing most of his pallid right shoulder and prominent collarbone.

But Frank was now looking no longer at any of Simon´s clothes, nor the state of his hair or the complexion of his skin. His eyes were fixed on the painful-looking red mark, like a bullseye surrounded by a ring of purple bruising, on the vein in the crook of his left arm just inches away from the fresh, pink scars of the cryptic words that had been engraved there just a few months before. The sticky marks that had now accumulated dirt and fluff which extended from either side of the puncture wound a clear indication of the tape that had held a catheter in place.

Frank´s eyes moved across to the opposite arm. Identical to the final, unsolicited jewellery worn in the last days of grunge music´s brightest star, a white plastic band with personal details and other codes printed on it was strapped to the young man´s wrist.

Simon was breathing deeply, as if preparing himself to be hypnotised again.

"If you´re comfortable there, Simon, I just need to pop out for a minute. Is that OK with you? Will you be alright here for a moment?"

"Sure … no problem," was the calm response.

Frank left the room, his diminishing footsteps could be heard making their way along the corridor towards the reception. Simon lay lifeless on the couch. The only perceivable movements his chest heaving up and down and the subtle rocking motion of his locked-together hands, which now rested somewhere near his diaphragm. Very faintly, Frank´s distinctively tender voice could be heard speaking to someone on the phone past the waiting area. After a couple of long minutes, he returned to the consulting room, looking flustered as he grasped the back of the patient´s chair, which now faced where Simon lay, before sitting down as quietly as he could on its comfortable, padded seat.

"Would you like to tell me what happened?" he asked eventually.

There was a long pause, in which Frank waited faithfully for Simon to respond. He crossed his legs and copied the position of his patient´s interwoven fingers, which he placed on the curve of his moderately rounded belly just above the belt of his grey cotton trousers. He glanced towards the satchel that he had put on the floor near the couch, seemingly deciding whether to reach for his notebook, when Simon – who had continued to breathe in and out deeply – began to speak.

"I was in the hospital." He paused, letting the gravity of his words sink in; although the dramatic effect produced by the delay was purely unintentional.

"Please … go on," Frank prompted.

Simon again took in a deep breath. "I spent the night there apparently. I … I was having a dream and, and I nearly saw everything … the sign. I needed to read the sign. I could see the letters but, but I woke up. Too soon. I needed to get back to sleep … to see the sign again so I could try to stop the people being killed."

"What did you do, Simon?"

He answered Frank´s question without a great amount of hesitation, but with a slow, staccato articulation of each word he uttered.

"I took some pills. Sleeping pills, to get back into the dream. I don´t know what happened. They must´ve been strong. Too strong.

I made a mistake."

"Are you taking the medicine that was prescribed to you too?"

"Yes, I am."

Frank´s face was overwhelmed with concern. "What happened to you?"

"My mum. She found me being sick, vomiting in bed … late last night or in the early hours. I don´t know. I, I woke up in the hospital this morning … but I left. I had to leave. I wanted to come here to see you, to *tell* you that … that I think I can do it. I can control what I dream and, and remember things, I mean. I think I know how."

"Simon," Frank said seriously. "Taking drugs – or medicine – is not the way to go about doing this. We can talk together. We can talk about your dreams … I can help you try to remember everything and we can work on this, you and me, OK? Just please don´t try this again." There was exasperation in his voice as he pleaded with Simon. "It´s dangerous and you can hurt yourself. I know you didn´t want to end up like this – in hospital. There are other ways … please trust me."

Even though Simon had his eyes closed and was lying with his face to the ceiling, Frank looked imploringly in his direction, palms pressed together in front of his chest in the form of a prayer.

"Would you like to tell me about this dream?" he asked, at length.

After what must have been somewhere approaching a minute, maybe more, Simon started to speak in the same familiar tone that he had used to describe the atrocities in the other nightmares that had caused so much suffering over the last few months.

"This dream was different … even more vivid. I can remember more details. I was walking down a country road … a lane. It was nearly dark but there was still a little bit of light left in the sky. I was walking along the road … there were these low stone walls on either side of it, and fields … green fields I think, although it was a bit hard to see in that fading light. The air was a little damp … cool but not cold though. I walked further along the road, it had lots of bends, until I came to a white building … there was a sign outside … it was lit up. A large, red letter *T* was illuminated against a white background on the corner of the building. I thought that it must be … must be a pub. I could hear noises coming from inside … some shouting or something like that … crying maybe … and swearing in English. The first time I'd heard it in my dreams."

Simon paused at that moment, as if this information had suddenly unlocked a door to a passage leading to a previously unexplored place in his mind.

"Some people came out of the doors holding onto each other … completely shocked. They had dark stains on their clothes … blood on them. I know it's blood even though it's dusk and the light's going fast … twilight. I walk towards the doors of the pub. There's a man there at the door … he doesn't see me but stops a frantic-looking woman from going inside, hugging her and saying something – whispering something – to her in her ear so no one else can hear … trying to comfort her, I guess. I push open the doors and enter a kind of porch area. I can hear the people more clearly from here. There's mayhem inside … coming from behind the second set of doors. I can smell gunfire. I know it's gunfire now from other dreams … that distinctive smell it has. It's hard to describe if you haven't smelt it before." Simon's nostrils flared as his olfactory memory was stimulated into life.

"I know what I'm going to see there, but I pull the door in front of me open anyway. It's chaos inside … people are lying on the floor all around the small bar … there's blood everywhere … stools have been knocked to the ground and there's smoke still in the air from when the shots were fired. There's broken glass … glasses, everywhere, and I can see people lying on top of one another.

Stacked. There's an old man ... he's smartly dressed, wearing a suit. It's ... it's terrible to see him there. All of these men are innocent victims, but, but this one man with his suit and his ... his age, it, it just left me, I don't know ..."

Simon inhaled deeply again but ended up emitting a sudden choking sound as his breath was cut off by the emotion that had welled up inside his chest. He recovered his composure and carried on with the reconstruction of the bloody scene from his nightmare.

"People are injured ... others I think must be dead. It's carnage. Total carnage. People around are trying to help ... trying to put pressure on wounds to stop them bleeding. A small TV is still on behind the bar in the corner ... it's showing a football match. These men were watching a football match ... the players keep playing, unaware of what's happening here. I just stand there and watch the game for a while and wonder how, how they could carry on when these people are lying here." Simon shook his head. "I can't see who's playing ... can't visualise it. A team in green and a team in white ... and blue maybe. If only I could see ... remember who was playing, then I could know when this happens.

"I go outside again. I can't be there inside with, with everything that's there. I turn left past a garage next to the pub. I see a black and white sign on the wall of the pub, or the garage, but in the near darkness I can't read it ... I can see the letters – old-fashioned letters, kind of old English style – but I couldn't read it all properly. Then I woke up."

Simon had propped himself up on his elbows and had turned his head to look at Frank, who had remained silent during the distressing tale, trying to understand not only what Simon's behaviour meant, but also the significance of his latest dream. Simon sat up completely and swivelled round to face his therapist, legs hanging over the edge of the couch, the white tips of his dirty shoes touching the floor.

"After I woke up I thought I could remember the dream if I got back into it, so I went to the bathroom. I'd already taken some more of what the psychiatrist gave me, but I needed something else. I looked before in the main bathroom but couldn't find anything there … all the medicine had been taken away. But then I went to my parents' bathroom. My mum was asleep … I found all the pills there … I found sleeping pills. Her sleeping pills. I knew what they were from the packet. They weren't like the others … I think, I think you can just buy them anywhere … I don't know. But I took some. I don't know how many, but enough to make me fall asleep again."

Frank was engaged in what Simon was saying, as a child would listen to an enthralling story from a parent or grandparent; an image made even more prominent from the superior angle that Simon was talking from as he looked down upon his listener.

"And, I did it," Simon said grandly.

"Did what?" asked Frank on tenterhooks, still looking like he was enwrapped by what the pale storyteller was saying.

"I got back into the dream." Simon spoke quietly, stretching the last word out like someone gleefully sharing a well-kept secret. "I was back in the pub … it was the same scene. Exactly the same. I looked up at the TV and could see … I could see the score."

The short, sharp sentences of his previous account had been replaced by more excited prose as Simon spoke more fluidly about his experience. "It was one-nil. I could see that one of the teams was winning one-nil. I still don't know who, but I could remember it much more clearly and I could control my movements – where I could walk. So, I went back outside the pub and found the black and white sign on the garage again. I could see this more clearly too. There were three words and I could make out some of the letters there. Not all, but I'm close. If I hadn't woken up again, I would have got it … I just needed to get back into the dream again to

182

complete the words, so I took more pills, all that was left in the packet. But, but I don't know what happened. The next thing I know, I'm waking up in the hospital with some tube in my arm and feeling like shit."

Frank's expression had changed and he looked more like a healthcare professional again than the awestruck child that had been sitting there moments before; his pragmatic side having won the battle for the right to lead the conversation in a more conservative manner.

"Look, the most important thing is that you get some rest – proper rest – and you recover from your ordeal last night. Don't you think it would be a good idea to go home, eat something healthy, have a bath and relax or something like that for some time? You've been through a lot in the last few hours."

"Yes." Simon was nodding his head in agreement with Frank's suggestion. "Yes. I can rest and, and maybe sleep again … *dream* again."

Frank frowned, showing his blatant displeasure and preoccupation at Simon's final words and the distant tone in which they were spoken. "Would you like me to call your parents now?"

This time it was Simon's turn to alter his expression; his tired face clearly showing his own dislike at what he was hearing.

"No … no. I … I'll speak to them later at home. OK?"

"OK," Frank replied doubtfully, stretching the short word out as he spoke. "We'll get you a taxi straight home now. You take all the time you need to feel better … and don't forget, I'm always here for you." He moved around the desk and pulled out his own chair to sit down, the blind still drawn behind him. "Please take a seat here and just rest for a moment."

Simon obediently sat in his usual chair, which was now back to its original position facing the desk, folded his arms and stared down pensively at the white wristband he was wearing; testament to the previous evening's incursion into the accident and emergency department at St Richards's Hospital.

In an efficient, business-like manner, Frank picked up his phone and asked Fiona to arrange for a taxi to take Simon back to his house as soon as was possible.

Several minutes later, the long buzz of the internal line indicated that Simon was to be picked up from outside the building's main entrance. After the now all too familiar sentences from Frank designed at the same time to encourage and calm Simon were delivered, the young patient left the premises and was taken the short distance that separated the clinic from his home.

Frank finally unbuckled the remaining strap on his satchel and pulled out Simon's case file, which in breach of normal protocol he had taken home to study. He located the page with the personal details, pressed nine for an outside line, dialled the number he had found and then waited the few short seconds it took for the phone at the other end to be answered.

"Hello again, Mrs Webb … thank you very much for waiting. We really need to talk about Simon … urgently."

17

Three timid taps, made by scarred knuckles on the medium density fibreboard panel of the consulting room door, announced Simon's arrival for his four o'clock session.

"Come in," Frank replied stiffly, bracing himself for what was to come during the next half hour or so.

In the two days since he last saw his psychologist, Simon's appearance had improved considerably. His normally greasy and unkempt hair – although not particularly tidy today – had a clean shine to it and the evidence of his recent bout of acne was clearing up fast. Under his jacket, which he took off and put carefully on the back of his chair after sitting down, he wore a freshly-ironed, plain black t-shirt; despite having an extremely faded design in the centre of the chest, it showed no traces of the stains that had lately been splashed onto the front of his other clothes. There was also no sign of the trademark mud on his footwear; either a result of the recent dry spell or a change to his usual walking routes. He looked well-rested and on his face he sported what could very well have been a genuine smile.

"Hi, Frank. How are you?"

The psychologist grinned welcomingly back at Simon, although the distinct dilation of his pupils before he spoke betrayed the fact there was something greatly troubling him.

"I'm very well thank you," he answered, in effort to sound upbeat. "And how have you been over the last couple of days? Are you feeling better? You *look* better."

Simon paused for a second or two, seeming to pick up on Frank's vibrations.

"I'm … OK. Good, more or less. I've managed to rest a bit and

… to sleep." Simon smiled a knowing smile to himself this time as his gaze moved away from Frank and over towards the succulent plant in the corner.

The remains of a damaged spider web hung between the branches like the frayed steel cables of a broken suspension bridge; a victim of Frank's satchel as he had swung round the corner of the desk in the dimness of the early morning, eager to drink his tea and pore over his patients' files before his clients started to arrive for their sessions. Simon stopped smiling as he looked at the silky strands hanging limply from the edge of the dark-green leaves, their geometric beauty now reduced to a tangle of intertwined disarray. Traces of an agonising flashback or memory that had been stirred made their presence known on Simon's sharp features, before he managed to bring himself to look back at his therapist again.

"That's great to hear." Frank's forced enthusiasm was more than evident. He hesitated for a moment, biting the end of his biro until the small blue cap on the end broke off in his mouth and rested on the tip of his tongue. He plucked it out with his thumb and forefinger and flicked it onto the floor in a rare display of thoughtlessness, clearly more preoccupied whether he should proceed with the next question he had in mind. He quickly wiped his fingers dry on the thigh of his trousers as he mentally prepared himself for his labours.

"And how are your dreams?" he finally asked.

Simon's eyes narrowed as he himself was plunged deep into thought, an internal debate raging in his head as he decided what to answer in response to Frank's question. His eyes darted back towards the yucca and the detritus it weakly supported. Simon started to shake his head as he made eye contact again, his lips thinning and the corners of his mouth turning downwards as he answered.

"Nothing special really … nothing to talk about." He looked

down at his Converse as if he could find some kind of asylum there in avoiding Frank's stare.

Relative silence was the main protagonist during the next few uncomfortable seconds. The hum of the by-pass, the ticking of the clock and the low buzzing of the light above were all faint background noises as patient and psychologist remained mute. The lull was punctuated by a rustling of papers as Frank organised himself for what was to follow. Their eyes met and the silence between them was broken once and for all by Frank taking in a lungful of static air before he spoke.

"There's nearly always a time during a person's treatment when a psychologist tells a moving story about another client they've had the fortune to come across or been together in treatment with. An account of survival or hope that the listener can connect with and which gives them something to cling on to when they're feeling like they can't go on any longer. Alternatively, maybe they'll retell some old fable, folktale or ancient Chinese story, you know, something with a moral that will make the client feel like they've discovered something enlightening for themselves in the tale; it could be something poetic, something literary, something beautiful to hear perhaps."

Frank stopped speaking and eyed the young man in front of him sympathetically. The old serene look was back on his face but it was mixed with a sadness; an acceptance of how things had developed between the two of them.

"But I'm not going to do that." Frank started to look behind Simon and nod almost imperceptibly as he continued to speak.

"What I'm going to do, is tell you about a young man I read about recently; a sportsman, in fact. You know, I'm not really what you'd call a sports fan. I don't follow any news or support any kind of team or anything like that, but I read about this one individual and ... and think that now would be a good time to share his story with you."

He stared fixedly at Simon, who was waiting patiently for his would-be mentor to begin.

"When he was less than a year old – just a baby – our sportsman´s biological parents put him up for adoption. They were very young – in their teens, I believe. I don´t really know too much about their situation – and of course we shouldn´t judge anyone for what they decide as people do what they have to do for their own reasons – but, they felt like they had to give him up all the same.

"Luckily a family was found for him; a good, middle-class, quite affluent family, so you would´ve thought that he lived quite a comfortable life. However, during his early years it was clear that despite having a doting, loving mother, his father on the other hand – who was a heavy drinker – basically ignored him and let his wife take all responsibility for the child´s upbringing. You could say that it was probably the first form of abuse he experienced in his early life."

Frank, went back to looking past Simon towards somewhere between the door and the corner of the wall that gave on to the corridor, nodding his head again as he paused, seeming to find answers to some of the questions in his own mind.

"Anyway, this abuse from his father was really just the tip of the iceberg. Being half Polynesian and growing up in an all-white neighbourhood while attending a school with the same racial make-up, many of the kids there used to unfortunately bully him due to the colour of his skin. He didn´t just suffer racist abuse though. He was also taunted by the other children who used to pick on him by calling him 'retard' and 'stupid'; things that he went on to falsely believe were true about himself. As a result, he was an extremely sad child, believing that he was worthless and dumb. His academic problems were actually attributed to him having dyslexia, but it wasn´t until his late teens that he found out that this was the case. So, he grew up with several factors making him thoroughly depressed and he continued to beat himself up about how he felt he was – the type of person – and all of his perceived shortcomings. But he did find some escape.

"He was already quite an agile young boy and very good at gymnastics and, little by little, he found himself practising diving into the swimming pool in his back garden, which it turned out, he was quite a natural at. At the age of nine he started diving seriously and despite his incredibly low self-esteem, he´d found something that could give him some kind of goal and bring some of the meaning that was lacking to his life; although overall he was still a very unhappy boy. He felt different from the others, not only because of his skin tone, but somehow, in some way not like the rest of the boys, without really knowing or understanding why at that stage of his life. He also thought a lot about his adoption, believing that if his own natural parents hadn´t loved him enough to keep him, then how could his adoptive parents feel anything for him either?"

Frank started to bite the end of his incomplete biro again in the pause in his story. Through the window, the wail of a siren could be heard in the distance, its destination unknown; the Doppler effect of its alarm the only fading evidence of the incident to which it was rushing. Or fleeing.

"He was excessively depressed and harboured so much sadness inside him that at twelve years old he tried to commit suicide by taking an overdose. This was in fact, the first of three further attempts over the next few years at taking his own life, which all luckily turned out to be in vain. But, he started to think to himself that he was an even greater failure after these unsuccessful attempts as he was convinced he couldn´t do anything right, not even killing himself, and little by little, he turned to the solace of drinking and smoking; even though he still hadn't reached his teens."

Simon was looking at Frank, following his words closely; attentive but unsure as to where this was all leading.

"Nevertheless, he managed to focus on his diving ... it was his salvation, if you like, a respite from the chronic depression he was suffering, and as he moved into his teenage years he started to get noticed as a very talented athlete. He made the Olympic team at sixteen years old but despite winning a medal, was fighting with numerous mental battles; one of which was the dawning realisation that he was homosexual."

At the declaration of the final, hurriedly-delivered word of his sentence, Frank looked awkwardly away from Simon and stared down at his hands, closely inspecting his nails as if checking to see if they were acceptably clean. He raised his head again shortly after and carried on, ignoring the glitch in his otherwise immaculately articulated narrative.

"Although he didn't openly share his feelings with anyone else, people around him suspected him of being gay. What should have been a moment that changed his life for the better, actually got worse as people close to him – including his own teammates – shunned and ignored him. Once again, he faced a whole new form of bullying and abuse from those closest to him."

Frank allowed Simon the time to interiorise his last paragraph.

"But in his sporting life – his diving – he was extremely successful. He went on to win gold medals too, and world championships, and was considered one of the best divers the world had ever seen.

"In his private life he was still sad though, and the abuse didn't stop coming. Even to the extent that he faced physical, sexual and verbal attacks from a so-called partner, but – like many victims in these situations – he thought he deserved it ... deserved to be punished for something … felt he was guilty."

Simon lowered his head as he felt Frank's gaze bore into him, his face flushed as something true to his own story was forced unceremoniously into his mind.

"On the eve of the Olympic Games in Seoul he was diagnosed as being HIV positive. Very little was known about the condition back then, and although he was still a magnificently fit individual, he considered it a death sentence and also believed that if he shared this information publicly, it would lead to him being thrown out of his beloved sport and ostracized from society in general." Frank sighed and shook his head. "Unfortunately, six years on from that, not a great deal has changed."

Frank took off his glasses and reached into one of the desk drawers to retrieve the trusty, square piece of material he used to clean the lenses, despite the fact that today they were remarkably free from finger marks. "Excuse me," he said, as he took a few seconds to meticulously clean the spectacles. Without his glasses it was easy to see that his eyes were watery and he looked close to tears as he appeared to fight back the strong, conflictive emotions running through him.

Simon was watching intently, trying hard to ascertain why his psychologist was so caught up in the story he was telling.

With his glasses now firmly back in place and his composure restored, Frank went on with the tale.

"With the much-needed support and medical advice of his doctor, he faced his fears and went to the Games and competed at the very highest level. During the competition, what happened to him would be remembered for years to come and replayed countless times on video – you've probably seen it yourself, Simon, I'm sure. Anyway, he was about to take a dive and everything seemed more or less normal. He jumped up on the board, bounced again and took off.

"I know that the way I describe it, it doesn't sound at all technical, but he did a couple of somersaults and as he was completing the third one, I think, it was clear that he was going to be pretty close to hitting the board on his way down into the pool; and ended up doing just that. There was an enormous thud as the back of his head crashed into the board and you could hear a gasp as everyone in the crowd held their breath to see if he would be OK."

There was the briefest of intervals in Frank's story as he intentionally gave Simon the opportunity to comment, taking a calculated risk that his patient would have seen the famous footage when he was younger and be willing enough to share this fact.

"Um-hmm, I remember seeing that … yes." Simon dutifully filled the gap left for him.

Frank smiled a satisfied smile and carried on.

"Then I'm sure you know the rest ... but I'll finish if you allow me to."

"Of course," was the polite reply.

"So, as you know, he got gingerly out of the water holding the back of his head, and it turned out that he had quite a nasty gash there. He got stitched up by a doctor at poolside and then remarkably, within around half an hour or so, was up on the board again completing his dives for the day. Well, not just completing, but performing almost perfectly. The next day, he was back at the competition showing no ill-effects and absolutely nailed the dives he had remaining, and as they say, the rest is history. He won two gold medals and went home lauded as a true-blue American hero. Of course, he deserved all the fanfare and accolades that he received from back home and around the world, but he will undoubtedly be remembered – and judged by the vast majority of people – solely on what they saw that afternoon as the world waited for him to surface and then his subsequent triumphant feat. Actions which would define his life forever."

Frank looked serious now, as if the words that were passing his lips aimed at Simon were actually having a more profound effect on himself as he spoke.

"However, there is also another story to tell, something more behind what most people see and what they superficially judge. As he was under the water there, after hitting his head on his third somersault, he was paralysed with the fear that he was bleeding into the pool and would have to reveal his secret. After making his way out of the water, while he was lying down getting stitches in the back of his head, he was fighting a battle in his mind as to whether to tell someone about his condition ... but he didn't tell anyone. He kept the secret to himself. He wanted to succeed so much. He'd gone through enough in his life and had come so far not to back down now.

"But the joy of victory was tainted with guilt and the overriding feeling that he'd been incredibly irresponsible for not sharing with people information that if withheld – at least in his mind – could have potentially put people in danger, above all the doctor who treated the open wound on his head. Although there was no real threat of any kind of transmission, at the time he believed it was very possible."

Yet again, Frank paused, allowing Simon enough time to assimilate the details of the story and try to draw his own conclusions from the unexpected content of the day's session.

"A few years later – just recently in fact – he announced publicly that not only was he homosexual, but that he also had AIDS. Of course, there was quite a backlash and he's come in for a fair amount of strong criticism from some quarters for not revealing he was HIV positive at the Olympics, and of course all the stigma attached to his sexuality, but he carries on ... in therapy ... like us."

He cleared his throat before continuing.

"Simon. If you do nothing else. If there's one thing that, for you, is vitally important to do, is that you figure out who you are and what you believe in. Be that person, put it into practice and don't try to be someone you're not, or someone other people want you to be." Frank drew in a sharp breath through a thin-lipped mouth. "I guess … I guess what I want to say, is that the truth will somehow set you free, all of us … you, and me, alike."

They held each other's gaze for some time, the two trying to make sense of Frank's last words, in synchrony confronting the pain and loneliness they both shared.

Frank's eyes eventually broke free of Simon's dark, hypnotising glare and rested on an official-looking signed document, which had been lying face-up on the desk throughout the session; as of now ignored. Simon's eyes pursued those of his therapist.

"What's that?" he asked suspiciously, recoiling in disgust as he recognised one of the two signatures at the foot of the page.

Frank hung his head and it seemed as if he had slumped down into his chair a little more, clearly ill at ease with the task at hand.

"It's, it's an application signed jointly by your parents – your father, I mean – and Doctor Rossouw. It's requesting that you be sectioned under the Mental Health Act. They believe you're a danger to yourself and to those surrounding you."

The words hung in the air like the acrid smoke from the discharged firearms of Simon's nightmares.

Silent, motionless, Simon stared at his father's upside-down signature at the bottom of the page, the trademark *W* dominating the autograph he had seen on countless cheques and restaurant bills. Eventually, his wide eyes retraced their steps to meet Frank's again.

"I'm very sorry to have to tell you this, Simon," Frank said in a distant voice that was not his own. "It's not what I wanted to happen. My hands are tied, believe me—"

194

"They want to lock me up?" Simon interrupted in a stern, sullen tone.

"Your parents consulted the psychiatrist, and they all believe that it was a real attempt on your own life the other day ... taking the pills."

"And what do *you* think?" asked Simon in a matter-of-fact way that under different circumstances would have sounded like an innocent question.

"I think that you need help," Frank said timidly, seeming to succumb to the pressure he was feeling; powerless to change the course of events. "Help that maybe I´m unable to give you ... I don´t know." He was shaking his head, looking desperate at the situation that was unfolding around him, as if he were the patient and the calm young man in front of him the experienced psychologist. "I think ... I know, that it´s a legal document under the Mental Health Act that allows for you to be detained in order for emergency treatment to be administered." Frank seemed to cringe at every one of the formal utterances he delivered, appearing to realise that this moment – more than ever – called for the compassion and understanding that these cold words lacked.

"And what does that all mean, then?" Simon asked, a mix of sarcasm and anger was starting to rise in his voice.

"It means ... it means that normally there are twenty-four hours between the filing of the application and being admitted to hospital. In that time, you´ll be assessed and a decision made as to whether they keep you in. Look, if they think you´re in danger, they have the power to ... to detain you."

Simon was looking down at the floor under his side of the desk, chewing the nails on his left hand, his thigh nervously moving up and down as he sat lost in the tumult of his mind.

The chaos had returned.

Gazing across at Simon, the weight of responsibility bearing down heavily on him, Frank eventually added in a hushed – almost conspiratorial – tone. "A lot can happen in twenty-four hours, Simon."

In their short time together, Frank had spent a large part of the sessions studying Simon´s alluring features while his patient was either lost in thought or lay supine on his couch. He knew the curve of his prominent cheekbones, the scruffy hair on his chin and jaw, the vertical line that appeared above the centre of his eyebrows when he was in distress. He knew the deep, dark eyes that narrowed when pensive or while challenging his ideas and suggestions, and he knew the full lips that thinned when confronted with something disturbing or arched to form a radiant smile in the few fleeting moments of happiness that he encountered. But there was now a new expression on Simon´s face that Frank hadn´t witnessed before; a look of disappointment – sadness even – but somehow tinged with a burning determination that surprised and intimidated Frank at the same time.

Simon stood up. Frank caught a glimpse of the bruise that was left by the drip that Simon had pulled roughly out of his arm just two days before as he automatically collected his jacket from the back of the chair. He stood there for a few moments seemingly looking into Frank´s eyes, but at the same time all around him. He smiled languidly down at his therapist, who looked penitently back up at him, and uttered from those placid, Adonic lips, the three words that Frank would forever hear echoing in his mind as long as he lived.

"You lied … goodbye."

He turned around, opened the door, and was gone.

18.

Frank watched the second hand tick metronomically towards the top of the clock face, dragging the needle-like minute indicator along with it as it passed the hour mark. He watched as four o´clock passed by; the absence of the notification from reception followed quickly after by muted knocking at his door engulfed him deeper into solitude. With each passing minute the faint desperation that Simon would show up for his usual allotted slot eroded away in the backwash of time.

Unsure what to do with himself inside the unwanted gift of the next thirty minutes, Frank fidgeted around as he sat behind his desk, thumbing through various notes and random pages completed by both Simon and himself over the last few months; although he could practically narrate their entire contents from memory.

Done with his half-hearted perusal of the documents, Frank now turned his attention to the clear plastic freezer bag – complete with small snowflake symbol and blank space for the date and what was frozen inside – that was flimsily paper-clipped onto the inside cover of Simon´s file. He looked at the cracked cassette case that it held, remembering the day that Simon had so excitedly slapped it down on his desk in a fit of eagerness to let the details of his nightmares be heard. He opened the case and held the tape in his hand, looking at it as if he could already hear Simon´s soft voice and imagine the way his mouth moved as he pronounced each word, before inserting it into the gaping hole of the cassette player to his right that was waiting to be fed.

Frank listened to the tape that he had now played back to himself on numerous occasions, again able to recite each of its words by heart should he so be asked. He heard Simon describe in his steady monotone the fires that stretched along the course of the darkened runway that fateful night at – according to his former patient – Tokyo's Nagoya airport. He sat passively listening to the details, recreating once more in his head the events as if they were a scene in a film he had seen a thousand times, closing his eyes to envisage the noise, the breeze and the smell of smoke and burning aviation fuel.

There was a muffled click on the tape as Simon's description came to an end, quickly replaced by various seconds of static as Frank sat in anticipation of the description of the second dream that the tape contained. He waited for Simon to start detailing the events on the African river, paying little attention to the familiar background sounds in the interlude between stories. Suddenly, unexpectedly, his hand shot out quickly and he brought the machine to an abrupt halt, alerted to something that his ears had just picked up.

He rewound the tape ever so slightly, turned up the volume as high as it would go, and then pressed play, immediately hearing the last few phrases of the description of the air crash. Allowing these final sentences to continue until they reached their conclusion, Frank then narrowed his eyes and leant forward, as if he would be able to hear much better the closer he was to the source of the sound.

The piercing hiss of static stung his ears reproduced at such a volume but he carried on listening intently until the underlying sounds he was looking for made their appearance. He could hear various unidentifiable noises as Simon fumbled around with something and then a short metallic snap as some kind of clip or latch was unfastened, soon followed by a louder sound as a metal object was placed down on a hard surface near the machine that he was using to record the account of his nightmare. Despite the electronic interference, Frank heard the swishing of liquid moving quickly in what must have been a bottle or a can and then a recognisable loud gulp as Simon presumably swallowed whatever it was that he had just taken from its metal container and placed into his mouth.

Frank stopped the audio, rewound it again and played it back twice more; each time establishing more clearly to himself that Simon had taken something that was enclosed in some sort of metal box prior to describing the events of the second recorded nightmare. Frank looked confused, a puzzled expression on his face at this new supposition that had just come to light. Without understanding fully what he had just heard and incapable of doing anything about this new finding in any case, he pressed the play button once more and started to listen again as the anguished passengers of the river ferry struggled to escape their destiny on the wide, muddy river they so innocently had tried to cross.

The tape wound its way through Simon's story until it came to its ill-fated conclusion. Frank, who had been listening with eyes closed throughout, let the cassette continue in silence until – deep in thought, or lost in his own contradictory world of theory and counter-theory – he was brought round by a loud click as the player rudely reminded him that there was nothing more left to hear.

He opened up his notebook, which had been lying on the desk next to Simon's case file as he listened to the distant voice of his young patient, and wrote down several quickly scrawled sentences related to the discovery of the previously unheard section of audio between the two dreams.

The internal line buzzed. Frank looked at the phone, appearing surprised that it had suddenly sprung to life. He glanced up at the clock. A quarter past four; too early for his next patient – who was not the most punctual of people – to arrive. He frowned, his forehead creasing in a display of baffled hope.

He pressed the hands-free button on the telephone's console. "Yes?"

Fiona's light West Country accentuated voice was distinctly shaky as she delivered her message. "Mrs Webb is here to see you. Umm, shall I send her in?"

Frank stared at the phone, seeming to instinctively know why his unexpected visitor was here to him.

"Frank?"

"Umm, yes. Please send her through."

Soon after the brief functional exchange with his receptionist, Frank heard two quick knocks on his consulting room door.

"Come in," he replied as he made his torturous way towards the entrance to greet Simon's mother.

The door opened and Veronica Webb entered the room, looking down at the floor as she did so. She shut the door behind her, trying carefully not to make a sound as the latch found its place in the groove of the wooden frame.

As soon as she had stepped foot into the room Frank saw the uncanny resemblance to her son immediately; her dark-brown hair, long – but tied back tightly in a ponytail – was identical in colour to her second-born child's. She had the same high cheek bones and facial structure too, with her masculine nose almost indistinguishable from Simon's, apart from a slight deviation of the bridge where it had previously been broken; and the same mysterious, Persian eyes that had so captivated him from the outset of therapy. She was undeniably attractive in a classic, almost ancient way, although she seemed to be more than a little underweight for a woman of her height; something made more prominent by the tight-fitting jeans and plain white – slightly creased – t-shirt she was wearing. Her thin face and dark bags under her eyes from obvious lack of sleep made her look gaunt; her pale complexion clearly showing her current poor health.

"Hello, Doctor Newman." Her voice was weak. "Nice to see you again," she added without feeling.

"You too, Veronica. Please, call me Frank," he said, braving a smile and stretching out a hand to her, which she shook automatically, using the smallest amount of force possible.

"My husband's unable to come," Veronica said apologetically. "He's in Hong Kong. He's flying back later today," she added as an afterthought.

"No problem. Please have a seat."

The awkward dialogue was mercifully placed on hold as Frank walked slowly around the desk and back to his own chair, staring at the floor himself as he did so, seemingly delaying the inevitable for as long as he could. He sat down and forced another half-smile at Simon's mother, who was sitting down now, dwarfed by the large chair that was used by Frank's patients. She looked down into her lap, avoiding the eyes of the psychologist. It was clear that she had been crying.

They sat in silence for a few vacant moments; Frank too afraid to ask the dreaded question; Veronica too distressed to articulate what she was thinking. Eventually though, she ruptured the silence.

"I'm, I'm really sorry to have to tell this to you." Her voice wavered as she spoke, the emotion threatening to get the better of her. Frank waited patiently, as ever, for her to continue.

"They found the car last night by a bridge in Bristol … They think he jumped." She started to weep silently to herself. "They … they found the, the car with the keys in it," she continued through her sobs, "but they haven't found … found him yet … although they think it's, it's quite clear what happened."

Frank had heard many dramatic and moving sentences in his time as a psychologist – the majority of which within these four walls – but these words unsurprisingly hit him like no others before. He stared ahead, shoved violently into the turmoil of his thoughts and the realisation that his worst fears about Simon, and the doubts about the effectiveness of his own actions and words, had now been well and truly confirmed.

"I´m really very sorry," was all he could muster.

The two sat in silence once more, Veronica´s occasional sniffing the only discernible sound in the room as she dabbed at her eyes with an overused tissue she had taken out of her jeans pocket.

"He was a good boy, he really was," she managed through the tears. "We just wish we could´ve done more to help him. Had more time … Did more things together. Really spoken together about things and tried to understand what he was going through."

She struggled on as Frank listened, giving her as much time and space as she needed, uncertain what to say in order to make an unchangeable situation any better.

"He liked you. He didn´t talk much, but he spoke about his sessions from time to time and he seemed to enjoy coming here, with you."

Frank´s expression was hard to read as he sat facing Veronica Webb. He looked bewildered, as if his whole world had come crashing down all around him, but he was – contrary to previous advice he had given to his patients – making an effort to try to control his emotions and put on a brave face.

"It was a pleasure having him here with me," Frank finally offered. "He really is a special person." He started to pull round as he realised that his own pain paled into comparison with what the bereaved woman in front of him was going through. "If you need anything – anything at all – I´m here for you." Frank´s eyes widened involuntarily as he realised that his words now were an echo of the past.

"Thank you." Veronica saved Frank from his depressive musings. "I just feel so guilty. I just ..." she broke off and began to cry again.

Frank, with no alternative left other than to piece himself together and fulfil his professional duties, ultimately took the initiative and guided the conversation over the next quarter of an hour or so. He extolled the virtues of Veronica's role in Simon's upbringing and the support she had given him throughout the struggles that they had both recently faced. He laid out the foundations of Simon's disorders, explaining the suspected reasons behind his behaviour in an attempt to clarify that she bore no responsibility for things that were beyond her control. He encouraged her to reflect on her guilty feelings and the extent to which these may have been misinterpreted, and cleared a path to embark on the long road to self-forgiveness. He became a psychologist again; for one of the last times.

Veronica absorbed what Frank said, vulnerable as she was, but mature enough not to reject help at such a vital time. In spite of the fact that she looked physically and mentally destroyed by the disappearance and presumed death of her only son, she appeared calmer after having spent this valuable time with Frank. She stuffed her sodden tissue back into one of her pockets and reached down to her left to take the shoulder bag that she had been carrying – unnoticed by Frank up until now – that was now resting on the floor next to her oversized chair. She unclipped the strap to open it and then pulled out a clump of scruffy papers that had been folded carelessly in half. She opened them up and placed them on the desk. Simon's unmistakable handwriting, disrespecting the straight lines on the pages, was clear to see.

"I found these in his room. I think, maybe you ought to have them."

Frank looked down at the pages, but he didn´t read anything that was written upon them; his glazed eyes unfocussed, his brain enveloped in thick fog.

"Thank you," was all the exhausted therapist could manage in way of a response.

"I hate purity, I hate goodness. I don't want virtue to exist anywhere. I want everyone corrupt."

The softly-spoken, Received Pronunciation articulated lead-in was soon followed by an aggressive, choppy guitar riff that paved the way for the singer to release his torrent of seething rage.

Frank allowed the track to play out in its entirety, staring at the small transistor radio throughout the song, immersed in the ferocious intellect of the lyrics. As the machine-gun delivery of the final few words resounded around the room, Frank took a sip of his lukewarm tea and turned off the radio.

He leaned over to his right, opened the bulky filing cabinet, and without the need to search through the names that were inserted into the clear plastic tags attached to the top of the file dividers, directly picked out the desired one towards the back of the rack. He placed the file on the desk, repeating a process that had now become a habit for him both before the start of his morning sessions and at the end of the working day throughout the last six weeks since Simon last set foot in his consulting room.

The file had evolved during this time and now swelled with the extra papers and newspaper cuttings that were neatly inserted inside. Frank opened the cover and sat looking at the clipping from the *Bristol Evening Post* that acted as a sobering forward to the rest of the contents inside, and read the headline as if only seeing it for the first time today.

Teen feared dead after car found near bridge

He continued to look plaintively at the article that accompanied the headline, before finally moistening the end of his index finger with the tip of his tongue in readiness to start flicking through the other pages that followed. He quickly skimmed the rest of the file without stopping too long at any particular place, reaffirming in his mind the schema of Simon's story and preparing himself for the work he was about to undertake.

Reaching across into one of the drawers in his desk, Frank extracted a hand-held electronic device and placed in on the surface in front of him. He then burrowed in again to retrieve various miniature tapes still brand new in their cellophane wrappings. He picked up the small machine and looked at it curiously, tilting it from side to side to examine the lateral buttons; the solitary red one immediately giving away the gadget's recording capabilities. He placed it gently down on the desk and unwrapped one of the mini-cassettes, smiling to himself absently as though amused by its diminutive nature, before opening up the pocket-sized recorder and slipping it inside.

With the Dictaphone placed next to him, Frank turned his attention back to Simon's case file. He interlocked his fingers and stretched his palms away from him, popping two or three knuckles as he did so. A thoughtful expression came across his face at the crack of his joints and he glanced melancholically across at the empty chair opposite him, trying his best to dismiss the intrusive thoughts that had plagued him often in recent weeks. He unlocked his hands, nodded silently to himself, sniffed once, and then pressed the tiny, red record button.

Over the course of the next two and a half hours the sound of Frank speaking softly to himself in his soporific tone filled the room, only pausing now and then to lick his finger and reveal a new page or to eject, turn over or replace the mini-cassettes when they had reached their half-hour capacity per side.

Each sheet of varying contents in Simon's file was read, recorded and then extracted in order to be placed in either one of two piles; the right of which where the numerous, annotated newspaper clippings ended up; and the left, the official-looking documents with the logo of the clinic in the header or footer of the page.

The minutes, and then hours passed by as Frank compiled the story of his most challenging and emotive case yet. Pages and pages were turned, with photos of air crashes, earthquakes, wanton destruction and human suffering passing before his eyes. Diagnostic tests, psychological reports, dramatic headlines, and tables that had been filled in by both patient and therapist alike, were placed in their respective piles. When Frank wasn't reading some newspaper article or other, or one of the many records of test results, he was pacing around the room in the space next to the couch speaking to himself, forming his own conclusions and hypotheses as if addressing an imaginary client.

Frank didn't stop. He carried on relentlessly, seeming to gain energy from his thought process, appearing to find the sought-after answers to the many questions he had in his head as he neared the denouement of his last six months' work. He sat back at his desk, the original bloated file now greatly diminished as the two paper stacks in front of him grew steadily taller.

The afternoon had turned into evening and the sifting of the documents was coming to an end as Frank approached the back of the file; but something made him stop and pause as he turned one of the final pages. A plain, white sheet of paper, slightly crumpled even though it had been sandwiched between others, and with creases dividing it into four sections that indicated that it had been folded into quarters, stopped Frank dead in his tracks. On the page was a forgotten, short list of words that had been written in faint, sloping lines in capital letters; so tightly squeezed together that it made them almost impossible to read.

Pain
Guilt
Anger
Fury
Sadness
Fear
Blood
Death

Frank didn´t dictate these words. Instead, he took the paper in his hand and hesitated, deliberating which pile it should be placed upon, before eventually opting to give it a place on top of the one that was made up mostly of the chronologically-organised newspaper clippings interspersed here and there by occasional pages of the near illegible, dog-eared notes Simon had freshly spewed out as he woke from his nightmares.

Eventually, Frank came to the end of the arduous documentation of the near half-year spent with Simon Webb, and stood there looking at the two mounds of papers and the empty file on the desktop below. He stopped the cassette that was still winding itself around, willingly recording anything that its small microphone could pick up, ejected it and placed it with the others in a small cardboard box also containing several standard-sized tapes. He picked up the pile on the left with the clinic logos and started to collate them again in the file, taking care to leave it as neat and tidy as possible, before placing it again in its original position towards the back of the rack in the filing cabinet; ready for whoever would be the next person to search for it. He then took a new file – which he had prepared earlier – and slotted the newspaper clippings, the scribbled notes that Veronica Webb had so emotionally presented to him, Simon's eight words, and another few pages deemed unnecessary to leave in the filing cabinet inside, and closed the cover.

Frank then started packing away his things as he would have done on any other day at the end of his sessions. He took the new file and placed it in his satchel along with his thermos, Dictaphone and the small box of tapes before turning around to draw the blinds, which he did with a moment's hesitation as he stared out of the window for a few seconds contemplating the view outside.

Turning back around again, he then placed the strap of the bulging satchel over his shoulder and pushed his chair up against his desk. As he passed to the other side of the room he rested his palm momentarily on the cracked green leather that covered his desk before running his fingers along the round heads of the brass tacks along the edge, feeling their bumpy familiarity as he glanced around making sure that he hadn't left anything important behind. He then walked past the site of his countless hypnotic orations and took the tweed jacket with its suede elbow patches from the back of the door, threading it through the strap of his satchel so as not to have to wear it on such a mild evening.

He held the door handle for some seconds and then looked back over his shoulder to survey the room, his eyes moving from corner to corner and from object to object as if trying to remember the exact position of everything there. Facing the door once more, he opened it purposefully and – as his young patient had done six weeks earlier – left the consulting room for the last time, on his way to the now vacant reception area that led to clinic's main entrance.

The elongated shadows of the tops of the tall trees behind the building started to snake their way across the near-empty car park as the Sun made its way slowly down towards the horizon. Although it was nearly three hours after Frank normally finished work, the summer solstice evening still had enough sunlight left in it to leave Frank squinting as he came through the doors leading to the parking area and oblige him to instinctively raise a hand up to block the rays from entering his eyes. He waited for a few moments until he grew accustomed to the brightness, breathed in the fresh, early summer evening air, and started walking in the direction of his car, which was parked in its usual spot as far away from the clinic as possible.

Walking ever faster as he went, with each step that Frank took further away from the plain, grey building behind him, he appeared more energetic – taller even – with a look of defiant excitement on his face, a weight lifting from his shoulders with every stride. He stopped roughly ten metres from his car and spun around to look at the clinic where he had spent the last twelve years of his life.

The window was there, as of course it always had been when he entered or left the building. But this time he paused to really look at it and study the rest of the surrounding façade as if he could see through those grey pebble-dashed exterior walls and spy on himself attending to one of the many clients that trusted in the sanctuary of his consulting room over the years. He remained looking at the window, with its dirty glass and blind drawn down, visible from his vantage point in the middle of the car park. His head angled up to the building's overhanging eave as his attention was drawn to the gravity-defying nest that had been built there only a few weeks before. An excited chirping sound was coming from within, and as one of their parents flew in with a mouthful of insects and perched on the edge of the nest's small hole, three large chicks, on the verge of outgrowing their natal home, could be seen jostling for position for their share of the meal.

Frank showed his back to the building, turning around more

slowly this time, to face the direction of his car, leaving the birds to continue with their delicate survival on the angles of the exterior wall. In the semi-darkness on the other side, an unseen spider was going about the thankless task of setting its geometric traps on the drooping yucca plant, unerringly observed by the wide-eyed silver tabby kitten on the calendar above and to the right of Frank's old desk.

He took the final few paces and reached his car, unfastened the front pocket of his satchel and felt for the keys, which he quickly located by pulling on an old, brown, leather key fob with a faded design of oak leaves and an acorn embossed in gold print. He took a half-step closer, key in hand ready to insert it into the door when he suddenly looked down at the ground in front of him, aware that he had stepped on something that was poking out from under the chassis of the car.

He bent down and picked up the large, yellow, padded envelope that had been placed there, partially in view, for him to find. Frank studied it for no more than a split-second before quickly flipping it over to see if there was any name or address written on the other side. There was. To the left of centre, squeezed tightly together in very small, slanting capital letters was written:

Dr Frank Newman

The psychologist stared at those three small words, seemingly unable to move nor blink for a considerable amount of time.

Eventually, he looked around the car park and at the trees behind, slowly scanning the entire area as if he could feel those intense, dark eyes boring into him. Without averting his suspicious gaze from his surroundings, with a shaking hand he found the car's lock at the second attempt, opened the door and dived into the driver's seat.

Unfazed by the suffocating heat in the interior of the vehicle, Frank sat transfixed at the envelope and the words it carried, which although small, now seemed to be emblazoned onto the package he held in his hands. His licked his lips, gripped by a sudden thirst. A small bead of sweat broke out and ran down his right temple. With heart pounding and with trembling fingers, he ripped open the envelope.

He recognised at once the same, leaning letters that had spelt out his name, although this time they were much more horizontal; the handwritten dates having been crammed into the limited space on the small, white labels stuck to each of the three cassettes which had just tumbled out and now lay – heavy as lead – in the psychologist's lap.

20

09th December 1994

"Hello, good afternoon everyone. Thank you very much for being here and for, umm, being part of this today ... umm, this afternoon. Before I begin, I like to say a big thank you to the university for inviting me here and for their very generous and rather flattering introduction."

Frank gestured with a hand to the four smartly-dressed, smiling individuals who were sitting behind a cloth-covered table to the side of the stage, the empty seat that he had just vacated beside them neatly tucked in at the far end. Frank faced the front of the auditorium again and cleared his throat, clearly nervous about speaking in front of so many people; something he was yet to get used to. He took a sip of water from a glass that had been placed on a stool next to the lectern on which his notes were held and then leaned over to flick on the overhead project to his left, leaving a bright, white rectangle on the screen at the back of the stage.

"I'd just like to apologise for repeating any information to those of you who are already familiar with the case of Simon Webb and also if I use any technicisms or jargon that may not be fully understood by everybody. I'll try to keep it as short and simple as I can as I know that some of you are at the end of a long term, it's late in the afternoon, and I'm sure you're all eager to get to the pub to start celebrating Christmas early."

A polite ripple of laughter came from the audience. Frank took another sip of water, adjusted the badly-tied Windsor knot of his silk tie, looked down at the pile of notes on the stand in front of him, and, inhaling deeply, began his speech.

"Simon first came to see me – at the behest of his parents – on the eighteenth of January this year. I have to say, it was somewhat of a challenge to diagnose him correctly in the relatively short time that we had together. His episodic, sometimes chronic psychotic events, which had been developing since around what I calculate to have been his mid-teens, were of course worrisome but didn´t completely inhibit him from functioning fully at the time I first saw him. That is to say, he was still trying to attend school – albeit with a large amount of missed classes – and he also maintained several social relationships with a small number of friends and family members. However, these aspects of his life did deteriorate considerably in the five months or so we spent in session and had, in fact, already started to become less frequent from approximately the end of last year, the beginning of this."

Frank´s line of vision was drawn high opposite him to one of the only small windows that permitted natural light to enter the large room; through which, light flurries of snow falling diagonally in the wind could be seen, their dark shapes a contradiction of their true appearance silhouetted as they were against the light-grey sky.

"My first diagnosis – based on Simon´s behaviour, diagnostic tests and our conversations while undertaking treatment – led me to lean towards a schizotypal personality disorder as one of my first conclusions. His unusual beliefs and magical thinking – especially that his dreams could influence or predict the future – along with his altered perception of the world, extreme social anxiety and psychosis, all pointed in the schizotypal direction. There was also evidence of some comorbidity with other personality disorders – most notably major depressive disorder and bipolar – which can explain some of Simon´s other symptoms such as his suicidal ideation and self-harm."

Frank flinched at this point; the reason for which lay concealed

214

to those unknown eyes observing him – *burning* into him – from the banked seating of the hall.

"Cranial scans and physical examinations were suggested, but ultimately refused by the patient, who aged eighteen, of course had every right to do so. Thus, we were unable to see if there was any damage to the brain or if normal cerebral function was impaired in any way, or if indeed there was some other physical abnormality contributing to his psychotic episodes. Therefore, we were left with current behaviours, environmental influences, events during childhood, and relationships with family members in order to deduce hypotheses.

"Unfortunately, Simon remained rather a closed book at times and we often didn't have enough quality information about these social or environmental factors and interactions in order to make a clear conclusion pertaining to any one or more specific disorders."

Frank rather inappropriately smiled to himself at this point, the faraway look on his face testimony to the reminiscence that was surging through him, leaving the conference attendees struggling to comprehend why the speaker – that many of them had travelled across the country to see – appeared amused at such a point in his talk. He pushed his glasses up his nose, put on a more serious expression, and carried on.

"According to Simon himself, he admitted to being a frequent drinker of alcohol and a recreational drug user, although testimonies from close family members and friends indicate that he was actually something more of a heavy drinker and quite dependant on the use of marijuana. I also had my own reasons for suspecting that he was taking another form of drug orally; but without firm evidence, this remains pure conjecture." He nodded to himself and a knowing look appeared in his eyes before he realised that his expressions and mannerisms were being more than closely monitored there on the stage in front of so many onlookers. He quickly continued with his speech.

"This substance abuse may have contributed to some of his paranormal beliefs and perceptual abnormalities, such as the visual and – to a lesser extent – the auditory hallucinations that he experienced. It may also have been a factor in the intrusive thoughts he often had about doing harm to members of his own family.

"One thing we do know for sure is that Simon carried ... suffered, a great deal of guilt. Guilt possibly caused – or at least contributed to – by a mix of exposure to some very stressful situations during his childhood or other elements from his actual upbringing itself. This guilt often led directly to him having suicidal thoughts, although I believed from the outset that he had no firm intention of taking his own life and used this behaviour as a fallback and a way of managing the stress and anxiety that certain situations caused. The self-harm too – albeit just as considerably worrying – also indicated to me that such actions were another form of coping strategy that he employed in order to deal with the emotional pain he endured."

There was a pause in Frank's presentation as he took another sip of water. Two drops, unnoticed, escaped the rim of the glass, forming dark stains like teardrops on the breast of his grey shirt. Someone coughed in the audience, followed by several other people using the first exhalation as an excuse to clear their own dry throats. These sounds were accompanied by the hum of the overhead projector's fan attempting to cool itself down as it reflected the bright light of its bulb onto the screen behind the speaker.

Frank looked around at the faces in the audience for the first time, thus far too consumed by nerves and his fear of public speaking to dedicate any attention to his listeners. He blushed, now more than ever acutely aware of the individuals watching him, hanging on his every word.

"In terms of treatment options, SSRIs – namely fluoxetine – were prescribed by Simon's psychiatrist at the time in order to try to counter what was perceived as major depression. This medicine was reluctantly taken at first for a short period but then rejected as Simon claimed that it had an adverse effect on his sleep and accentuated the nightmares that were gradually becoming more and more prevalent. However, at a later stage towards the end of our time together, Simon considered that if he took the medicine again he would be able to remember some of his dreams more easily due to having become convinced that this would be a way to provoke more detail in them. He was prescribed venlafaxine by his psychiatrist – much to my concern – which unfortunately was well-founded when Simon was admitted to hospital after taking an overdose of a combination of the prescribed drug, as well as sleeping tablets found in his parents' bathroom and – although not one hundred percent proven – possibly other unknown substances too."

Frank paused for a moment and breathed in and out deeply several times, trying to reduce his own anxiety levels in the most natural way possible.

"We started off, in principle, with a course of sessions with a Cognitive Behavioural Therapy bias, with the initial time spent on data collection and further evaluation. Time was also afforded to certain principles of Interpersonal Process Therapy as I believed that a blend of these two approaches to treatment were the most suitable options given my initial diagnoses. Nevertheless, the traditional structure of these therapies was hard to follow with Simon as his behaviour was often inconsistent with my constantly shifting hypotheses and he was either reticent or unable to contribute fully during the sessions. He also failed to undertake the additional tasks agreed upon – that is to say the activities outside therapy – or for one reason or another they weren't completed. When something was produced, it was simply a list of negative words relating to how he felt in times of stress."

Frank now pulled out a clear, floppy transparency and placed it on the glowing surface of the overhead projector. The eight hastily-written words that were given in the strictest confidence were now projected onto the screen for all to see. Frank stood looking at the familiar, inclined words, their simple form masking the reality of the moment of despair in which they were first scrawled down onto paper. Turning back to the attentive, silent witnesses to this brief summary of such a complex life, he continued.

"Simon was – in my opinion and that of various people who knew him – a highly intelligent and sometimes very articulate young man. Despite struggling with the order of his thoughts, he was often able to express his feelings and problems relatively coherently, although he did have difficulty in sharing personal information freely and showed little or no interest in undertaking activities that might have been of use in reactivating some kind of much-needed social life. I did, however, have the general impression that he was open to changing his view of his situation for the better and had every intention of receiving ongoing treatment.

"But. And there´s always a but isn´t there?" Frank asked, without any trace of humour in his voice, more to himself than the audience before him. "But. Simon started to be consumed by the dreams he was having and began to believe that, at first, he was responsible for what occurred in them, and then later that they were premonitions of the future to come. That is to say, precognitive dreams. These ... brutal nightmares and the belief that he could prevent them, drove him to the overdose that nearly took his life and led to the attempt to section him against his will under the – much-maligned – nineteen eighty-three Mental Health Act."

Shaking his head to himself at the actions of Simon´s parents and the psychiatrist at his former clinic, Frank looked down at his chestnut-coloured brogues and the drying mud on their tips, absorbed for a moment in the different tones of brown that were highlighted against the light wooden boards of the stage under his feet. He slowly raised his head and looked back up and out at the keen listeners.

"But there was something there in Simon ... something about those vivid dreams and the conviction and detail in which he described them that made me start to question whether there was something else rather than psychosis going on there. We started to see what I believed back then were maybe nothing more than strange coincidences with the dreams he was having. Earthquakes, plane crashes ... massacres and other such events that were happening in real life at the time; all of which had some similarities that corresponded with what Simon had told me, but nothing so concrete that any one dream-event pair in particular could be identified as a genuine and accurate precognition."

His face contorted as he frowned and smiled at the same time.

"That was until the twenty-sixth of April. This was when Simon presented me with a tape recording of two dreams in particular. The first – although containing some quite explicit information – couldn't really give me any insight into the event; in this case what appeared to be a plane crash. But the second did. And with the aid of guided hypnotic recall I was able to glean even more from Simon, who provided me with some quite dramatic mental images – and more significantly – specific, factual details."

Frank signalled to someone at the side of the stage and the auditorium's sound system burst into life with a hiss of white noise before Simon's tired voice filled the room.

"I can see it ... but the boat's sinking ... people are swimming around the back of it where the name is, trying to scramble up and

*get out of the water. They cover the writing for a moment ... I can't
see what's written ... they move, swim or are dragged away by the
current in the water. Now I can see the white letters on the dark blue
of the back of the boat. M ... T ... O, but the water is covering the
letters fast ... the boat's leaning ... there's another word below,
smaller. I can only see one letter ... M again, I think. And then ... it
disappears."*

Frank stared up at the ceiling of the auditorium and the oval,
cloudlike shapes that made the large, echoing room suitable for the
musical events sometimes held there. He drifted away from the
present, lost in thought as Simon's soft voice enticed him away from
where he presently stood, his eyes reddening with the emotion of
hearing his former patient's hoarse words. He signalled for the audio
to be stopped and without speaking, picked up another transparency
and substituted Simon's words, which had been left to burn brightly
on the screen at the back of the stage; a constant reminder of the
adolescent's state of mind several months before.

The article which Frank had so nearly shown to Simon was now
displayed in the middle of the glowing rectangle, allowing those
present the opportunity to take in, without haste, the full meaning of
the headline and the photograph that sat to its right. The image
showed the salvaged passenger ferry, leaning in the shallow water
near the bank of a muddy river. The large, white capital letters that
spelt out MTONGWE sat above the smaller, but equally significant
word MOMBASSA; both names standing out brightly against the
dark-blue background of the hull of the vessel.

The scratching of pens and pencils on paper and the hum of the
overhead projector were the only sounds that ruptured the silence.
A silence in which the realisation of the power of Simon's
precognitive ability was starting to be appreciated.

"This article – found by chance rather than investigation – dated just five or six days after Simon's original dream, kind of jolted something in me and made me start to look at things from a more Jungian way of thinking. Of course, I was still rather sceptical as believing something like this would change my whole perspective of things, but I started to open my mind to possibilities that I'd never really considered before.

"Nevertheless, Simon was suffering greatly. We ... I, felt like I'd let him down ... that I'd failed in his treatment and that I was actually contributing to his fragile state. I didn't show him the support he needed in terms of his belief that he could predict and prevent the future, nor did I act as a metal health professional should have done at the time."

A look of painful regret was evident on Frank's face.

"The last time I saw Simon was on the eleventh of May, after giving him the news of the application to section him. One week later, the car that he used to drive was found near the Clifton Suspension Bridge in Bristol with the keys inside. Despite the fact that a body was never found, it was assumed that Simon had tragically taken his own life."

The look of remorse was replaced by something more confusing, harder to read, on Frank's face. The expected sorrow of recounting the suicide of someone so important to him was strikingly absent. In its place was something else – something strange – an energy in the eyes and a half-smile on his lips.

"Two days before our last session, on the ninth of May, Simon arrived unexpectedly at the clinic after discharging himself from the hospital. He'd spent the night there after the aforementioned overdose. Well, he was in quite a bad state but he managed to tell me about another dream that he'd had and the fact that he'd been able to remember a lot more information from it. He was also convinced that if he managed to get back to sleep, and back into his dream, he would be able to see the images more clearly, remember more information and therefore be in a better position to warn people about the impending danger. That conviction, that attempt to garner more details by taking medicine to get back into his dream, led to the misguided conclusion that he had, in effect, tried to commit suicide. I'd like to share with you some of the details of the dream that he told me that day, if I may."

Frank looked down at his notes and began to read.

"Simon described a white building on a country road. A building with signs on the outside. One of which was a large red letter *T* illuminated on a white background on the corner of the building. He told me that he was sure it was a pub and talked about a football match being shown on the TV inside, describing the detail, even the fact that one team was playing in green and the other in white. He described the bloody aftermath of a shooting; a mass shooting than had taken place inside and the carnage that was left behind. He also described a garage with a white sign on the outside with black letters, right next to the pub."

Frank flicked through his pile of notes, pulled out another transparency and swapped it with the article about the tragic ferry accident. Shining brightly on the screen was a new article and a different picture. This one of a white building. A pub. Next to it was a garage; a white sign with old-fashioned letters could be seen on its side. A uniformed policeman was standing next to an armoured vehicle in the foreground of the black and white picture, slightly obscuring one side of the building, but not enough to block out the rectangular sign with the big letter *T* on it. Next to the photograph was the headline:

Gunmen held outside pub after tip-off

Frank again allowed enough time for those present to absorb the details in the images, the bold words at the top of the article, and the more diminutive – but divisive – sub-headline that followed.

Collusion with RUC and Special Branch under investigation

"On the eighteen of June – as you can see – two men were apprehended, on the basis of an anonymous call, outside a country pub in Northern Ireland. They had assault rifles and ammunition and were very clearly going to use them on the people in the building. Inside at the bar at the time the locals were watching the Republic of Ireland versus Italy in the World Cup. Ireland were of course playing in green ... and Italy – in a change to their usual blue – in white."

There was a murmur as some people in the audience whispered to each other. Frank took a sip of water again, folded his arms, and smiled broadly. His steady voice resonated around the auditorium, its projected clarity free now from the shaking nerves with which he started his speech.

"I can only assume that it was Simon. There is no evidence to confirm this, of course, but for me it´s quite clear that somehow ... somehow he had harnessed the power of his dreams and was ... *is* able to predict, and in this case, alter the course of the future."

21.

The snow continued to fall steadily throughout the afternoon, giving a fresh dusting to the top of the previous days´ inches, hiding the tracks that excited children had furrowed with their sledges on the slopes of the university grounds to leave a uniform blanket of white. From such a high position overlooking the city, the gothic tower of the cathedral could be seen through the tops of the bare trees, dominating the nearby wattle and daub buildings of the medieval centre.

There was no one outside on this bitterly cold winter afternoon and the empty spaces around the campus were quiet. The majority of university students had already started to make their way home for the holidays and the youngsters who had yesterday screamed with excitement as they descended the hill at what to them was breakneck speed, were now sheltering safely under cover as the day drew to a close.

The only sound that could be heard as the snow fell silently all around was coming from the line of tall trees that separated the university from the adjacent farmland. The beeches there were leafless, but there were mysterious, dark shapes positioned on their branches and sporadically dotted in the crook of a random bough; a shadowy reminder of the tribal cleansing that Simon had so vividly foreseen.

Crows. Their cawing carried across the slopes as they came in to roost, fighting raucously for the best position in the nocturnal murder as daylight faded to dusk.

Inside the warmth of the university´s auditorium, Frank Newman, standing and grasping both sides of the lectern – more confident in both mannerism and voice – was arriving to the real purpose of his speech.

"Just two days after hearing the news about the foiled pub shooting, as I was leaving work, I came across a package left for me outside my former clinic. I knew more or less at once who had left it there for me, having suspected over the past forty-eight hours that despite his disappearance, Simon may have had a hand in preventing the attempted attack in the Northern Irish village. And I was proved right. If not about his direct involvement in the call to the police, then about the fact that he was alive. Inside, were several tapes recorded by Simon, in which he explained in great detail about more of the dreams he'd been having. Two more packages arrived, one in August and another towards the end of last month – around two weeks ago in fact. I haven't seen Simon during this time, nor even heard anything else from him apart from the recordings that were sent, each one with the relevant date written on. I set about searching the news, looking at as many sources as possible; newspapers, T.V, the radio; and ended up finding some quite remarkable results."

Simon's voice came drifting through the packed auditorium's sound system several more times over the course of the next twenty minutes or so as Frank let the carefully selected sections of his patient's prophesies echo around the room and fall on the ears of the astonished listeners. They heard descriptions of buildings with their façades ripped off and reduced to rubble; burnt-out farmhouses with horrific scenes of mass human sacrifice inside; and the collapse of a bridge with smashed vehicles and broken bodies scattered on the wrecked section far below. People in the audience fought back tears as they followed Simon as he painfully and meticulously told of his passage through the dark-skinned corpses of dozens of women and children; the victims of a combination of police brutality and the ensuing stampede as panicking hordes searched in vain for an inch of space that would allow them to survive the crush.

Someone sobbed loudly as Simon stuttered his way through his account of witnessing a large group of men in suits escape what seemed to be a burning Chinese theatre; while scores of schoolchildren were killed by the flames and smoke inside.

Each tragic tale was followed by a different article or copy of a photograph placed upon the projector. The striking similarities were evident for all to see.

Frank stood silently behind the lectern, the brief interlude allowing enough time for the attendees present to make notes, search for a tissue, or simply sit quietly and let the potential enormity of what they had just been shown be absorbed. The four representatives of the university sitting on the side of the stage exchanged whispered comments and disbelieving looks with each other.

"There were patterns as you can see," continued Frank, "maybe the dreams were coming true, or maybe I was looking desperately for links that simply weren´t there. It is, after all, part of human nature to try to make connections between events; to find meaning where maybe there isn´t any. But whatever was going on, it was clear that the Mtongwe ferry dream-event pair was not a one-off and there were undoubtedly other occurrences that had too many similarities to be ignored.

"But what could we do? Many of these tragedies that were described were impossible to prevent. How can we stop earthquakes, mudslides, hurricanes, and other unexpected natural disasters and accidents? Then of course there´s the ambiguous time delay between the dreams and the possible events, which ranged anywhere between one day and a month and a half in some cases. This would of course be an obvious stumbling block to any possible warning – even if we found someone willing enough to listen. If only we had some kind of clear, detailed information, maybe we could warn people about the possible hazards … But, most of the time we didn't have enough to deduce accurately where or when these things would be likely to happen. Not enough to convince what is – understandably so – a very sceptical society.

"However, one of Simon's dreams really stood out. It was different, as he seemed to have dreamt the same dream on numerous occasions. This became a realisation to me after I had come into possession of a number of pages that Simon had written down after some of his nightmares, many of which contained fragments that described – from various perspectives – a large passenger ship sinking during the middle of the night, resulting in the death of a considerable amount of people. It was as if this dream, unlike the others, had somehow started to repeat itself – or be provoked even – over and over again.

"I searched for clues to try to identify something in the muddled notes, but couldn't. That was, not until the details of a dream that contained clear similarities to Simon's notes appeared on one of the tapes I was sent. There was something in it, something concrete, even more so than what he had described on the muddy river in Kenya. Three clear words … Estline, Estonia, Tallinn. He described a large ferry in his dream, listing heavily in the water at night, as you can hear from this."

Frank gestured again for the extract to be played and once more, for the last time that afternoon, Simon's voice filtered through the speakers installed around the auditorium, explaining in further depth this time, the contents of his most graphic precognitive experience.

"I contacted the authorities and the ferry company and asked them – pleaded with them – if additional safety checks could be carried out in the weeks after the dream. But, of course, to no avail." He snorted through his nose and smiled sadly. "Eight hundred and fifty-two deaths later, and one of the world's worst peacetime navel tragedies, not a single person has admitted to having received any kind of communication from me.

"I suppose they can´t be blamed though. What do you think they would do with information like this? These kinds of things are simply not accepted in our culture and are viewed as some kind of mindless divination. People are stigmatised by society or their crazy thoughts are eliminated by drugs and cured by healthcare professionals; as I myself used to try to do. But why are these warnings not heeded? Maybe we´re ignoring some vital clues ... some important information. OK, I´m not saying that if a client comes to you and tells you that he´s had a device planted in his brain and that aliens are communicating with him daily and the world is going to be invaded within a fortnight that we should ready our nukes and dust off the Star Wars program, no. But some ideas, some mental images ... and some dreams need to be investigated further. We can´t inhibit them all. We need to sift through them with an open mind in order to find the useful ones ... the ones that can save lives."

Frank moved away from the security of the lectern and his notes and paced across the stage, his body language mimicking his stance during his past hypnotherapy sessions.

"Without doubt, this topic is not a new one. The Society for Psychical Research was founded in 1882 here in the UK to investigate the paranormal. And of course, there is the widely documented work of the psychiatrist John Barker and his investigations into the premonitions that apparently foretold the Aberfan disaster in 1966, which then led to the establishment of the British Premonitions Bureau and thrust this issue into the mainstream. As many of you may know, the Bureau was designed to finally give people the means to communicate to the proper authorities their premonitions, feelings or dreams; and people did, with some relative success. In fact, there were two regular contributors to the Bureau, Lorna Middleton and Alan Hencher, with the latter predicting that there would be an air crash and a hundred and twenty-three or a hundred and twenty-four people would die. A month later, a plane plunged into hills in Cyprus, killing one hundred and twenty-four people."

Frank stopped pacing around the stage and licked his lips, seemingly enjoying for once his time in the spotlight, finding pleasure in the liberation of his inhibitions and the removal of the mental and physical barriers he was used to hiding behind.

"Of course, a dream is only a precognitive dream if we come across the events in real life that can be paired with it and prove it to be so. Otherwise, it's just a dream. Hencher's premonitions could, after all, be down to the law of large numbers. How many times in the thirty days between his dream and the plane crash were there flights with a hundred and twenty-threeish people on board? And of course, aviation safety thirty years ago was not what it is today either."

The former clinical psychologist was revelling in the role of devil's advocate as he spoke to his rapt followers.

"I do understand that there is scepticism about the ability to tell the future, of course I do. And why not? I understand that in our culture there is a great deal of rejection and fear of the idea. We feel threatened by what we don't understand. It's like Pandora's box. Once we open it, we won't be able to handle the consequences; it's beyond our comprehension."

Frank found himself on the far left side of the stage. He swivelled on his right heel and started to pace slowly back towards the lectern.

"And yet. Everybody relates to this. Everybody wants to and often tries to predict what is to come. We look at clues to our own future and imagine ourselves twenty years from now, for instance. We bet on things. How many people wouldn't like to be able to effortlessly pick the winner of the Grand National?"

Frank paused in mid-stride. A number of people laughed quietly at his last comment, happy to find some temporary light-relief to ease the pain caused by the descriptions of Simon′s shocking dreams that still hung heavily in their hearts.

"One quarter of the world′s population believes in the ability to foretell the future and I′m sure that practically everyone has experienced some kind of premonition or paranormal experience themselves that they can recall. I know it′s a typical example, but think about how many times you′ve thought about a person and then they call you up or you bump into them on the street. What about déjà vu?"

Again Frank paused as the audience accessed their own personal experiences in their memory banks, becoming more immersed in the speech as they did so.

"And still, this subject is not taken seriously by the authorities; when, and if, proper investigation and funding is provided, this innate human ability really does have the potential to save lives."

Frank stopped speaking and looked around the room, trying now to make eye contact with as many of the people watching him as he could.

"Undoubtable evidence exists to support the presumption that precognitive dreams are, in fact, a reality and should be viewed not as a threat, but rather a precious gift. Therefore, I′d like to undertake a campaign to gather support, and lobby for the reestablishment of official departments such as the Premonitions Bureau here in the U.K and the Central Premonitions Registry, set up back in the seventies over in the U.S.A."

The sound of pages turning in notebooks and the scribbling of pens and pencils on paper again could be heard throughout the audience.

"Somehow Simon has found a way to bridge the gap between the future and the present; to reverse the normal, one-directional flow of time and to challenge the accepted wisdom that cause precedes effect. The future already exists. Simon has just found a way to arrive there before the rest of us."

Frank now found himself standing behind his pile of notes, although this time he didn't need them. He knew exactly what he was going to say.

"Precognition is a natural human skill – a psychic skill – that undeniably does exist and can, and should, be developed." Frank's eyes narrowed and he nodded his head as he spoke. "And I know that Simon is not alone. I know there are more people like him out there. We need to find them, these special people like Simon Webb. People that believe in other things that are not normally considered possible; the supernatural, the paranormal, and who have the ability to predict important emotional events and mass pain … and in consequence change and shape the future."

There was a loud, sharp snap as Frank finished his sentence. He jumped in surprise at the noise and looked down at the empty water glass resting on the stool beside him which had split in two and fallen apart. He stared at the two large shards before his attention was drawn to the sound of a door closing loudly at the back of the auditorium as someone left the room in great haste. He looked thoughtfully towards the exit that had just slammed shut and then glanced back down at the broken glass. He took a deep breath, smiled to himself, pushed his glasses up his nose one last time, and came to the end of his discourse.

"What would happen if we started to believe these people? To remove the illusions and biases that shackle us. To seriously investigate their predictions. What would happen if we discovered that there was truth behind their, and even *our* visions of the future? And what would happen if we allowed what was to come … this so-called retro-causality that is warning us about the future, to influence our lives today?"

There was complete silence as Frank let his rhetorical questions resonate around the large room.

"I think all of us here would agree on one thing. That it would not only change us as people and how we think; but also world around us as we know it."

22

The snow had finally stopped and settled even more thickly than before on the grass areas in the grounds of the university and the slopes leading down to the city centre. A pristine half-moon shone above, with only the brightest stars in the night sky visible as they competed against the westerly afterglow of the freezing December day and the light of Earth´s only truly faithful satellite.

Frank strode along the corridor that led from the auditorium to the entrance of the building, a satisfied but somewhat sad look on his face. Carrying his old leather satchel over his shoulder, he fumbled for his car keys in the pocket of his jacket as he made his way towards the exit.

"Doctor Newman?"

A soft, female voice stopped him in his tracks. He turned around to see a young, blonde woman in her early twenties; a flash of blue dye in her fringe, the rest of her hair mostly hidden by the hood of the black jacket she was wearing.

She bowed her head and stared down at the ground in front of her, but their eyes had met long enough for Frank to recognise that familiar look of tired desperation in her gaze before he heard the halting delivery of her words.

"Can I ... can I talk to you for a moment, please? There´s something that I think you should hear."

A NOTE FROM THE AUTHOR

This book is a work of fiction. However, much of the content is based on fact; sad, tragic facts in most cases.

The dreams that Simon suffers throughout the book are loosely-based on a number of real-life events that occurred during the year 1994. I would like to make it very clear that no offense or disrespect was meant towards those that lost loved ones or were affected by these terrible occurrences and should you be personally involved in or upset by any of my descriptions, I sincerely apologise.

By mentioning or alluding to these incidents in my work I wish to bring to light the fate of those who lost their lives at the hands of injustice, and ensure the impact they had so many years ago is not lost with the passing of time.

The topic of suicide that runs throughout this book is also a delicate subject, I know. I hope that by bringing my own personal experiences with these thoughts and feelings out into the open by means of the conversations between Simon and Frank – characters with real people behind them – will be of benefit to those suffering their own personal struggles.

The work of healthcare professionals and organisations dedicated to this field is vital for many people around the world and they really do wonderful, unseen work that is appreciated immeasurably.

So, with this in mind, please never forget what Frank once told Simon in one of his darkest moments;

You're not alone.

Steven Richard Harris

REFERENCES

Although no lyrics were reprinted in *The Butcherbird Tree*, the following songs were either mentioned by title or artist or described by the author:

p. 12   *No Rain,* from the album *No Rain* (1992) by Blind Melon

p. 36   *Rape Me,* from the album *In Utero* (1993) by Nirvana

p. 48   *Don't Follow,* from the album *Jar of Flies* (1994) by Alice in Chains

p. 72   *Black Hole Sun,* from the album *Superunknown* (1994) by Soundgarden

p. 124 *Asking For It,* from the album *Live Through This* (1994) by Hole

p. 205 *Faster,* from the album *The Holy Bible* (1994) by The Manic Street Preachers

STEVEN RICHARD HARRIS grew up in the United Kingdom, and has spent time living and working in Australia, New Zealand and more recently Spain. Along with his wife, Natalia, he now divides most of his time between Europe and Asia, being inspired by the people, places and stories he comes across on the way.

Steven is co-author of the collection of short, but true, stories *Covidiots – Idiotic acts and bizarre behaviour*, published in the spring of 2020.

The first part of a two-book series, *The Butcherbird Tree* is his debut full-length novel. Part two is due for release early in 2022.

For more about Steven, go to:
stevenrichardharris.com
twitter.com/srharrisauthor
amazon.com/author/stevenrichardharris
facebook.com/SRHauthor

If you would like to help the author reach a wider audience, please leave a review of *The Butcherbird Tree* using the links below:

For **amazon.com** readers:
amazon.com/review/create-review?&B09DDZ8C39=

For **amazon.co.uk** readers:
amazon.co.uk/review/create-review/listing?&B09DDZ8C39=

For any other comments please contact Steven Richard Harris via the website and social media links given on the previous page. He will do his best to get back to you as quickly as possible.

Thank you.

Printed in Great Britain
by Amazon

67807834R00144